LOBO 3

JOHN DEACON

Lobo 3 is a work of fiction. Characters, names, places, and events are either the product of the author's imagination or used fictitiously. Any similarity to real persons, living or dead, is purely coincidental.

Cover design by Angie on Fiverr

Edited by Karen Bennett

Special thanks to advance readers Chris Gibson, Jeff Benham, Max Thompson, and Cindy Koda.

Want to know when my next book is released? SIGN UP HERE.

❀ Created with Vellum

PROLOGUE

As its title suggests, *Lobo 3* is book three in the *Lobo* Trilogy. I recommend reading the books in order, as they tell a continuing story. If you would like a refresher, here's the story so far, along with a list of characters.

Lobo

Lobo, a gunslinger with a savage past, reluctantly teams up with a young orphan girl, **Tilly**, to avenge the murder of **the Padre** who saved them both.

Before heading into the rough town of **Jasper Flats** to hunt the Padre's seven killers, Lobo meets **Hannah Miles**, a young woman struggling to singlehandedly run a failing ranch. Lobo defends Hannah against the aggressive rancher next door, then leaves Tilly in her care as he goes to town, seeking vengeance.

With the help of **Marshal Tubbs** and his deputy, **Shaw**, Lobo tracks down the killers and slowly sets things right. Meanwhile, he and Hannah develop feelings for each other, but neither feels comfortable sharing this truth.

Hannah considers herself plain and can't fathom any man having interest in her. Lobo, having been raised by wolves, struggles to fit in, thinks Hannah deserves better, and fears he might be cursed, since his loved ones always seem to die.

When the final and worst villain, **The Maestro**, captures Lobo, brave Tilly comes to the rescue and frees Lobo, who then takes out the last of the bad men. Meanwhile, Hannah kills her wicked brother in self-defense.

Lobo, Tilly, and Hannah are reunited. Tilly is like a daughter to Hannah now. Lobo loves them both but plans to set out after the man who killed his wolf pack, imprisoned him as the main attraction in a brutal sideshow, and caused the death of the Padre.

Lobo 2

After hiring two men, **Junius Tuttle** and **Plug**, to work the ranch and protect **Hannah** and **Tilly**, **Lobo** sets out to find the **sideshow man**—a daunting task because he doesn't know the man's name or location.

On the trail, Lobo learns of **Ernest "Hat" Hatley**, a notorious outlaw with a high-dollar bounty. Hunting Hatley as he scours the West for any sign of the sideshow man, Lobo finds himself helping people along the way, sometimes at great risk or expense. This, in turn, makes him question why he is becoming more compassionate and more human.

Meanwhile, cattle baron **Brock Boone** moves in next to Hannah and Tilly. He presents himself as the ultimate neighbor, but Tilly doesn't trust him, understanding he wants to marry Hannah.

Boone makes Hannah an enormously generous business deal, hoping to entwine their lives and futures, but Hannah refuses. Undaunted, the powerful cattleman vows to win her over no matter what it takes.

Helping an outgunned marshal, Lobo takes out Hatley and his gang and wires Hannah enough money for her to expand her cattle operation.

A clue leads him at last to the sideshow man—or at least to the spot where the man had been. Here, Lobo meets **Paul Smoger**, the man who helped the Padre set him free from the sideshow. Smoger gives him the sideshow man's name and location, then stuns him with shocking news: Lobo has family, and they've been looking for him.

Before Lobo can get on with his life, however, before he can track down his family then head back to Hannah and Tilly, he must head to **Slagville** and kill his old tormentor, **Ahab Jackson**.

Lobo 3 picks up shortly after the events of *Lobo 2,* when Lobo travels to Slagville to kill Ahab Jackson.

Cast of Characters:

Lobo Guerrero: around 20, a gunslinger raised by wolves, tough yet increasingly compassionate after his time with Hannah and Tilly.

Hannah Miles: 24, kind, humble, God-fearing, an overwhelmed ranch owner, who loves Lobo but is afraid to tell him. Despite her fear, she is determined to confess her love when he finally comes home.

Matilda Kershaw Frampton, "Tilly": 10, an impulsive, courageous orphan girl full of laughter and love and a bit of mischief.

Marshal Everett Tubbs: Jasper Flats lawman, friend to Lobo.

Shaw: Tubbs's deputy, friend to Lobo.

The Padre: Now deceased, the Padre rescued Lobo from a brutal sideshow and did his best to teach him the ways of human civilization. Also raised Tilly after she was orphaned.

Brock Boone: early 30s, Hannah's new neighbor, a handsome, strong, wealthy, generous, well-educated cattleman from

Texas. He is infatuated with Hannah and vows to win her hand, no matter the cost.

Junius Tuttle: older ranch hand now working for Hannah, very dependable, father figure to Plug.

Plug: 15, a hulking young ranch hand with knockout power in his fists. Loyal and hardworking, Plug adores Tilly and does best when he avoids alcohol.

The sideshow man / Ahab Jackson: killed Lobo's wolfpack, caged him, beat him, used him as a sideshow attraction. Hired the Maestro to capture Lobo, leading to the death of the Padre. Having struck it rich, Jackson now runs saloons in Slagville.

The One-Eyed Man: A sinister figure in Lobo's nightmares. Is he real or imaginary?

CHAPTER 1

As the late afternoon sunlight slanted hard across the rutted Slagville streets, a stagecoach pulled into town. The driver and the man riding shotgun climbed down from their elevated perch.

The driver opened the coach door and stood ready as the passengers emerged. He helped the ladies and nodded at the men, then hurried around back and retrieved everyone's luggage.

The man who'd ridden beside him remained at the front of the coach, stretching his wiry muscles and sweeping his gaze up and down Slagville's main thoroughfare.

Passengers glanced at this man and quickly looked away, not wanting to anger him.

The man stood alone, apart from the others. He was a frightening vision with his scarred face, tied-down pistols, stubby coach gun, and blazing eyes. He was dusty and drawn and had a restless, hungry, dangerous look, like a man starving not for food but for violence.

And in this estimation, they were correct.

Because Lobo Guerrero had come to Slagville with one purpose: to kill Ahab Jackson.

"Sure do appreciate you riding shotgun, mister," the driver said as the last of the passengers tottered off.

Lobo nodded. "Had this new scattergun," he said, indicating the sawed-off, double-barreled 12-gauge. "Figured I might as well ride shotgun."

The man lifted a hand as if to pat Lobo's shoulder, hesitated, then let the hand drop again, seeming to think better of it. "Well, I appreciate it. Let me buy you a cup of coffee?"

Lobo shook his head. "You know this town?"

The driver shrugged. "Not too well. Stayed here a few times."

"Know a man named Ahab Jackson?"

The driver shook his head. "Can't say as I do. He a friend of yours?"

"No," Lobo said, and walked away.

He swept his gaze from side to side as he strode up the rutted street. Slagville was a filthy, rough-hewn town that had started as a mining community and bloated into a festering abscess upon the decimated land.

He passed a livery, a hardware store, several shops selling mining equipment, three assayers' offices, and what looked like a dilapidated private residence, save for barred windows, a high fence in the back, and a sign over the door reading "Jail and Constable."

He saw a dozen men for every woman. These men favored

mustaches but not beards, and most of them wore suspenders and small hats.

They looked at Lobo, saw his scarred face and guns, and looked away again.

At last, he came to the Mountaintop Saloon and went inside. Piano music and raucous cheering filled the air, along with the smells of stale beer, stale cigars, and stale bodies.

Men filled the bar and crowded together at the far end of the seedy establishment, cheering for a woman dancing awkwardly on stage.

What, precisely, they were cheering, Lobo could not say.

She danced listlessly in a formless dress, looking tired and bored as she shuffled back and forth across the stage, seeming not even to notice the men calling out to her and slapping the stage boards.

Lobo scanned the whole room, looking for Jackson.

Seeing no sign of the man who'd tortured him, killed his pack, and caused the death of the Padre, Lobo went to the bar.

The bartender came over. "What can I get for you, mister?"

"Is Ahab Jackson around?"

The bartender's eyes grew suspicious. "Who wants to know?"

"An old acquaintance. He's been looking for me."

The bartender shook his head. "I haven't seen Mr. Jackson."

"He owns this saloon?"

The bartender nodded. "Mr. Jackson owns a lot of things. But like I said, I haven't seen him. Might be out of town. You leave your name, I'll make sure he—"

But Lobo had already turned and walked away.

He visited two more saloons, a bordello, and a gambling

hall, and received similar receptions every time he asked for Jackson.

Which meant Jackson was expecting him. Or had at least prepared in case Lobo showed up.

That was unfortunate but unsurprising.

After all, Jackson had hired the Maestro, hadn't he? It was only logical that he would have checked on the killer's progress —and learned that someone named Lobo had killed the Maestro.

Of course, Jackson hadn't known Lobo by that name. He'd called him the Wolf Boy and used him as a big sideshow attraction.

But it wouldn't be hard to make the connection.

And then, recently, Jackson probably would have heard about Lobo killing Ernest "Hat" Hatley and his gang not far from here.

So yes, the man was apparently expecting him.

Lobo had hoped to walk up to the man, state his case, and put a bullet through Jackson's brain. But now things would be more difficult, more involved.

If he kept poking around Slagville, Jackson might even get spooked and run.

And Lobo did not want that to happen.

He wanted to take care of this now. Because only by reckoning with the past would he be free to pursue the future he craved.

So rather than searching the rest of Slagville, Lobo went straight to the Jackson Hotel, where he asked for a room with no windows.

"No windows, sir?"

"That's right. I don't want the morning light waking me."

"Yes, sir, but our curtains—"

"No windows."

"Yes, sir. Not a problem. We have a room with no windows. I just wanted you to understand your options."

"I don't want options. I want a room with no windows."

"Yes, sir."

"Where's Jackson?"

The man's eyes swelled. Like the others, he took a moment, studying Lobo's face. He licked his lips and leaned back slightly. "Mr. Jackson, sir?"

"That's right. I'm looking for Ahab Jackson. He owns this hotel, doesn't he?"

"Yes, sir. It's just, well, I haven't seen him. If you give me your name, sir—"

"It's Lobo. But he didn't know me by that name. Tell him the Wolf Boy was asking for him."

All the color drained from the man's face. He steadied himself against the counter. "Yes, sir."

A short time later, Lobo was alone in his windowless room.

He was playing a dangerous but not entirely reckless game, locking himself in this box of death. After all, he was determined to find Jackson, even if the only way to find him was to trick Jackson into finding him first.

Won't be long now, Lobo thought, stuffing pillows and a bedroll under the bed covers and laying his hat on the pillow.

He snuffed the lamp and crawled under the bed and set his Colts close at hand and shouldered the coach gun.

Then, with all the deadly patience of an old wolf, he waited, watching the strip of light beneath the door.

CHAPTER 2

An hour later, he heard them coming up the stairs. They came down the hall, talking quietly in muffled tones.

Four dark shapes appeared, blocking most of the light at the base of the door.

He heard the key they must have gotten from the desk man. Then, the doorknob gave a grinding whisper, turning slowly.

The door swung open, revealing two pairs of boots side by side in the doorway.

Lobo adjusted his aim.

There was a bright flash and the loud bark of a revolver firing over and over as one of the men shot the bed.

When it was over, a man's voice said, "We was supposed to take him alive."

"And face the wolf man? You're dumber than a fence post. We'll tell Jackson he drew on us."

"Is he dead?"

"I emptied my gun into his head. Can't imagine it did him much good."

They stepped closer, and Lobo, who'd been waiting to make sure there weren't other thugs in the hall behind them, pulled both triggers.

The men screamed and fell hard to the ground. At that range—not even ten feet—the big-bore coach gun had pretty near blown their feet off, and they were down hard.

Grabbing his Colts, Lobo finished the one on the left. He was the one who'd shot the bed.

Then he crawled out, keeping one Colt on the screaming man, who had dropped his gun and made no move to recover it now. He was holding onto his mangled legs and staring at Lobo with terror.

"You're gonna tell me what I want to know," Lobo said.

"Okay," the wounded man blubbered. "Just don't shoot me no more."

"Where's Jackson?"

"At his house."

"Where's that?"

"North Poplar Street. Last house on the left."

A face appeared in the doorway.

Lobo pointed his revolver at it.

The woman gave a yelp and held up her hands.

"Who are you?" Lobo demanded.

"The m-m-maid," she said. "I was s-s-sleeping… down the hall."

"These men broke in here and tried to kill me," Lobo said. "Fetch the constable and a doctor. First, the constable."

The frightened woman nodded. "Yes, sir."

"Go," Lobo said. "You don't hurry, this man'll bleed out."

"Yes, sir," the maid said again and hurried off down the hall.

"Look at my face," Lobo said.

The man looked at him, whimpered, and looked away.

"Look at it. Look at my eyes."

"I don't want to."

"Look me in the eyes, or I pull the trigger."

With great effort, the man forced his eyes to face Lobo's. He gave a low whimper.

"What do you see?"

"You."

"Who am I?"

"The Wolf Man."

"Lobo."

Instead of responding, the man looked away again.

"Look at me, friend. Three… two…"

The man jerked his eyes back in Lobo's direction.

"If you lie to me, I will hunt you down and kill you slowly," Lobo said. "Do you understand?"

The whimpering man nodded emphatically.

"Say it."

"I understand what you'll do."

"Which is?"

"Kill me if I lie."

"Slowly."

"Yes, sir."

"So tell me."

"Sir?"

"Where is Jackson?"

"In his house. I mean, I reckon that's where he is. I can't say for sure. But that's where he was tonight. In his house on North Poplar."

Lobo believed him. Which meant he had to get to North Poplar before Jackson heard about this and ran. "Where's Poplar Street?"

The man told him then set to moaning.

"Take off your belt and make a tourniquet halfway to the knee if you don't want to bleed to death," Lobo said. "No, not that leg. The other one first. It's bleeding faster."

The man set to work.

Lobo holstered one weapon and watched the bleeding man closely, ready to pull the trigger if he went for a gun.

Once the man had applied the makeshift tourniquet, Lobo told him to strip off his buddy's belt and use that on the other leg.

"And don't let your hands get close to his gun. Tourniquets don't work on bellies."

Careful to avoid the dead man's holster, the injured man stripped the belt and set to cinching it around his other leg. He would never walk again. Not without crutches. Served him right, going out on a job like this.

But Lobo didn't reckon he deserved to die, not when he hadn't done any shooting himself, so he was pleased when the man slowed the bleeding to a trickle. At least he would live.

There was a commotion in the stairwell, and a short time later, a lean, gray-haired man with a long mustache appeared in the doorway, revolver in hand.

Seeing the badge on the man's chest, Lobo lowered his own weapon. The maid had done his bidding. Hopefully, a doctor would show up soon, too.

The constable understandably proceeded with caution, training his weapon on Lobo. "Put that shooting iron away," he demanded.

"Yes, sir," Lobo said, and slid the Colt back into its holster.

"Put your hands on top of your head until I get this figured out," the constable said.

Lobo did as he was told. "Thanks for coming, Constable. These men broke in here and tried to kill me."

The lawman glanced at the wounded man. "That right, Dave?"

"No, sir," the wounded man said. "We broke in, but we weren't supposed to kill him. Mr. Jackson wanted him alive. Ben did all the shooting."

"Would you swear to that in a court of law, Dave?" the constable asked.

"Yes, sir. I sure would."

The constable shot Dave in the back of the head then turned his weapon onto Lobo again. "You're under arrest," he said, "for the murder of these two men."

CHAPTER 3

A round the time Lobo was checking saloons, Hannah and Tilly were cleaning up supper dishes.

Once they finished, they sat at the table and started reading *Heidi* again.

They took turns reading aloud, Tilly reading almost as well as Hannah now. The young orphan was very smart. Everything Hannah taught her, from long division to darning socks, she picked up in a flash.

Hannah was enjoying the many voices Tilly used for different characters when a knock at the door startled them both.

Hannah's hand automatically dipped into her dress pocket and closed around the derringer as she stood and went to the door.

Would it be an angry Brock Boone?

She hadn't heard from the cattleman since sending him a letter refusing the proposed right-of-way.

But when she opened the door, it wasn't Brock Boone standing there but old Junius Tuttle, one of the two ranch hands Lobo had hired before hitting the trail.

Which showed just how frayed her nerves had grown, waiting for Mr. Boone's response.

Because just this morning, she had sent word for Mr. Tuttle to stop by after supper.

Mr. Tuttle held his hat in his hands. "Evening, ma'am. Tilly. Plug said you wanted to see me?"

"Hi, Mr. Tuttle!" Tilly said. "Come on in. We're reading *Heidi.*"

"Yes, please do come in, Mr. Tuttle," Hannah said. "Tilly, be a good girl and pour Mr. Tuttle a cup of coffee."

"Yes, ma'am," Tilly said and set in motion.

"Come on inside and have a seat, Mr. Tuttle," Hannah said, gesturing toward the table. "Did you have enough supper?"

"Oh yes, ma'am. Thank you. There's no danger of your men going hungry. Me and Plug sure did like the chicken and dumplings tonight. And the apple pie was a nice surprise."

Hannah smiled, genuinely pleased. She had grown up cooking for her father and brothers and always loved it when a man appreciated the food she made. "Care for another slice?"

Mr. Tuttle went to the table and waited for her to sit. "No, ma'am. I had plenty, thank you."

"There you are, Mr. Tuttle," Tilly said, setting a mug of coffee at his place.

"Thank you, darling. You're a good girl."

"Thanks, Mr. Tuttle," Tilly said and went back around the table, where she picked up Faith, the simple doll Lobo had bought her, and sat down beside Hannah.

Once the females were seated, Mr. Tuttle sat down across from Hannah. His hat disappeared under the table.

"Mr. Tuttle," Hannah said, "I've been making some ambitious plans, and I'm hoping you'll tell me what you think of them."

"All right, ma'am."

"The beef market is booming."

"Yes, ma'am."

"I'd like to build up the herd and get in on the boom before it busts."

Mr. Tuttle nodded, a thoughtful expression coming onto his face. "How many head you looking to add, ma'am?"

"Fifty."

Mr. Tuttle frowned. "You could expand the herd a bit, ma'am. But if you add too many cows, you're gonna cut into your profits, buying grain. This is good ground, but if you add more than a dozen cows or so, you're gonna run out of forage."

"Yes, I understand," she said, "which is why I'm hoping to buy some land off my neighbor to the west, Mr. Baldwin."

"Oh," Mr. Tuttle said, nodding. "I see. You know Mr. Baldwin?"

"We've met." In truth, she hadn't even seen the tough old rancher since she was around Tilly's age and had ridden over with Pa and sat in the wagon while the men talked business of some sort.

"I worked for him a time or two back when he was younger and still sending big herds up the trail."

"Which is what I'm hoping to do next spring."

"Next spring? With all due respect, ma'am, you pick up some

heifers and bulls, their calves will need at least a couple of years before they're ready for market."

"Yes, Mr. Tuttle, I'm aware of how that works."

"I didn't mean no offense, ma'am."

Hannah smiled. "None taken, of course. But I believe I have a way to buy healthy steers at a fair price."

"From Mr. Boone?" Mr. Tuttle guessed.

"Yes."

Mr. Tuttle squinted at her as he sipped his hot coffee. "So he wasn't mad about you turning down his right-of-way?"

Hannah spread her hands. "I haven't spoken with Mr. Boone since then."

"Oh," Mr. Tuttle said.

She could tell he was harboring concerns similar to those gnawing at her.

Mr. Boone represented the simplest, safest, and most affordable way to procure cattle and deliver them to market next season.

But if she had offended Mr. Boone, he might refuse to help her expand the herd.

She hoped that wasn't the case; even if it was, it wouldn't stop her. She was determined to succeed.

"I'll bet if you ask him nice, he'll still sell you cows," Tilly said. "He's richer than old King Nebuchadnezzar."

Hannah chuckled at that. She knew it wasn't really appropriate for a child to speak up during a conversation between adults, but she wasn't going to muzzle Tilly.

Yes, it was best for a young lady to be pretty and soft and quiet, but Tilly would never fit that description. She was pretty enough with her quick smile and golden hair, but she would never be soft or quiet, so Hannah refused to discourage the girl's intelligence or toughness. On this rough frontier, Tilly would need both to get ahead.

Which was one reason Hannah was so determined to succeed at this venture. She had no interest in being rich, but she wanted to be self-sufficient. And she wanted Tilly to live in safe and stable circumstances.

She also thought, perhaps nonsensically, of how proud it would have made Pa if she were to expand the ranch and herd and capitalize on the beef market.

And she would love to set those things in motion before Lobo came home, both to impress him and to show him that she was interested in him, not his money.

But the beef market could go belly up anytime, so she had to act now, and she hoped dearly that Mr. Boone would still honor his offer to sell healthy steers for eight dollars a head.

"I do expect you are right, Tilly," Hannah said. "Mr. Boone is a gentleman, after all. I think he will honor his original proposition."

"You gonna ask Mr. Boone before you talk to Baldwin?"

"No," Hannah said. "It's a risk I'm prepared to take, Mr. Tuttle. If Mr. Boone changes his price or refuses to sell altogether, I still want the ground. It's good grazing land."

"Yes, ma'am, it is. And old Baldwin is getting up there. He never married, never did have any kids, and he's quit the trail. Last I heard, he was running a small herd on that big old ranch."

"I've heard the same thing, Mr. Tuttle, which is exactly why I'm hoping he'll sell a chunk of ground."

"How many acres you hoping to get?"

"That's where I need your help. I'm guessing he'll want a fair amount. Fifteen or twenty dollars an acre."

Mr. Tuttle nodded. "That much or more. Curtis Baldwin's a good enough old fella. He gives you his word, you can ride it all the way home. He's tough and fair and decent. But he's a businessman, too, and I reckon he'll be looking to haggle on his death bed. You go over there, asking to buy land, there's no telling what he'll ask per acre."

Hannah nodded thoughtfully. "I'm hoping to purchase a hundred acres and then buy fifty head of cattle."

"Like we were saying, that's good ground over yonder. You could run more than fifty head on land like that. You could run probably eighty, maybe even ninety since you never pushed this ranch."

"Perhaps," Hannah said. "In the end, much of what I do will come down to money."

"That's the way of the world," Mr. Tuttle said. "Need money to make money."

"If I am successful, how many additional hands will I need to hire?"

"Me and Plug could handle the herd. Might wear us a little thin, though, and sooner or later, you're gonna want to put up a fence, probably."

Inwardly, Hannah winced at his words. She hadn't even considered the fence. How much would that cost?

As long as the cattle were branded and the men weren't overworked, the herd should be fine without a fence until spring. But if she was going to buy more bulls and heifers, too, she would sooner or later need that fence.

Why hadn't she thought of it in the first place?

Because you don't know what you're doing, she told herself. *You're biting off way more than you can chew here... perhaps foolishly.*

But she had committed to this course of action and would not turn back now. She would learn by doing and by asking questions of people like Mr. Tuttle.

"What if I hired one more hand and then hired more men, on a temporary basis, to help with a fence down the road?"

Mr. Tuttle nodded. "That ought to do just fine, ma'am, especially if you hire the right men. Though that might be tough right now. There aren't a lot of good men available, what with Mr. Boone hiring so many. But I'd be happy to help if you like."

"Thank you, Mr. Tuttle. I would very much appreciate that," Hannah said. She understood she had to be mindful of her strengths and weaknesses. She knew nothing about hiring hands and would indeed lean heavily on Mr. Tuttle's knowledge and judgment.

Part of being successful is knowing when to step aside and trust someone else to take the lead. Another part of being successful, of course, is trusting the right people to do that.

And she trusted Mr. Tuttle.

"All right, then. I'll be happy to help you hire the right man if one is available."

"I appreciate that, Mr. Tuttle," Hannah said. "First, we will visit Mr. Baldwin and see about the land."

"Yes, ma'am," Mr. Tuttle said. "You were right when you said you had an ambitious plan."

"Do you think I'm being overly ambitious?"

He thought about that for a moment then shook his head. "No, ma'am, I reckon not. But I don't know how things are gonna go. Curtis Baldwin is part of the old breed, if you know what I mean."

"Meaning he won't take me seriously."

"I don't reckon he will, ma'am. Maybe I'm wrong, maybe I'm not. I just don't want you riding in there with unrealistic expectations."

"I appreciate the warning, Mr. Tuttle."

"Man drives a hard bargain. Takes pride in it. You want, ma'am, I'll do the talking for you."

Hannah shook her head and sat up a little straighter. "I appreciate the offer, Mr. Tuttle, and I would appreciate you riding along, but I will do the talking. If Mr. Baldwin does not respect me, I will make him respect me."

Mr. Tuttle nodded.

"Miss Hannah can be tough when she has to be," Tilly said, pointing to the rug Lobo had used to cover the bloodstain where Jeb fell. "If you don't believe me, Mr. Tuttle, just look under that mat."

CHAPTER 4

"Put his hat on his head," the constable told the hotel clerk.

"All right, Orville," the rattled clerk said and stepped gingerly over the dead men. "This is a mess. Who's gonna clean it up?"

The constable chuckled. "I guess that'd be you. The maid told me she quit."

The clerk shook his head woefully and picked up Lobo's hat and poked a finger through the new hole in its crown. "How did this all play out?"

"He lured Dave and Gus in here and murdered them," the constable said.

"That's a lie," Lobo said. "I didn't murder anybody."

"Yes, you did," the constable said, his eyes full of malice. "I have witnesses."

"Witnesses?" Lobo said incredulously. "Who?"

"Don't you worry about it. I will produce them in good time."

"I'll bet. What are you, in Jackson's pocket?"

"You have a smart mouth, stranger. You keep talking that way, I might have an accident and pull this trigger."

The clerk set Lobo's hat on his head and skittered out of the way, telling Lobo the constable's threat might just be valid.

Lobo judged the situation, looking for a way out, but found none.

The constable was cagey. Lobo had to give him that. The constable stayed in the doorway, five feet away, and never looked away or let the weapon's barrel drop.

"Turn out his pockets and confiscate everything," he told the clerk. "That's it. Stuff that wallet in my pocket. Lift his shirt up. Heh, look at that. A nice money belt. Bring that over here, too."

"You want me to open it up and see what's inside?" the clerk asked, sounding intrigued.

"No. Just fasten it around my waist. That's it. Now, pat him down. Make sure he isn't hiding anything. Pull off his boots and check inside."

The clerk did as he was told. "He's clear."

"All right. Now gather up the guns. His and theirs. I'll be back for them in the morning. Now, I gotta take this murderer down to the jail and lock him up."

"Sure thing, Orville. Be careful. What about the bodies?"

"Fetch the undertaker. He's probably over at the Mountaintop."

"All right. But who's gonna pay?"

"Don't worry about it. Mr. Jackson will take care of everything."

The constable stepped into the hall and ordered Lobo out of the room.

Lobo hoped the man would slip up and give him a chance, but the constable tended a gap and kept his eyes and weapon trained on him.

Which was bad. Because he knew he'd never get a fair shake in Slagville, not when Jackson clearly controlled the constable.

Walking with his hands on top of his damaged hat, Lobo went down the street, followed by the gun-toting lawman, who told him to turn down the path to the jail he'd noticed earlier.

Through the barred windows, a light burned on the main floor. The second story was dark beneath its sagging roof.

The constable ushered him inside, grabbed a lamp from the desk, and ushered Lobo upstairs, where he led him to a makeshift cell in the back corner of the house.

The cell had apparently once been a bedroom, but they had taken three walls down to the studs and added bars. Bars also ran in front of the intact back wall, which featured a window that overlooked the fenced backyard.

Lobo's heart sped up. He hadn't been behind bars since Jackson had kept him locked in a cage all those years before.

He stared at the tiny space within, taking in the rumbled blankets likely crawling with lice, the filthy cot, and the waste bucket. The floor was covered with stains, and the patched and mildew-spotted ceiling bowed mightily, sagging like it might collapse any minute.

A breeze blew through the barred window, stirring unpleasant smells.

He did not want to go in there.

As if reading his mind, the constable gestured toward the open cell with his six-shooter. "Go on, boy. Get in there."

Suddenly, Lobo felt something he hadn't experienced in a long, long time: fear.

"Hold on," he said. "I didn't murder those men, and you know it."

"What I know and don't know is no concern of yours," the constable said. "And what I think doesn't matter. I am the law. That's it. You were involved in a shooting. It's my job to put you in that cage and let you back out tomorrow, when you'll stand in front of the justice of the peace. You can tell him whatever you want, and he'll pass judgment, not me. Now, get in there, or I'll shoot you for resisting arrest."

Lobo stared for a second, reading the man's expression. In the flickering light of the lamp, the constable's angular face caught shadows, looking primal and brutal, like a graven image hacked by crude tools into a semblance of life.

What Lobo didn't see was any bluff. The man meant what he said.

Lobo entered the cell, heart hammering in his chest.

The constable shut and locked the barred door.

Lobo broke out in a sweat and had to fight the urge to start shouting or reasoning or throwing his shoulder into the bars.

The constable grinned. "The infamous Lobo. I've heard of you. Gotta say, you ain't half what you're chalked up to be."

Lobo, feeling like a wolf with his leg in a trap, snarled, "Tell that to the men back in the hotel."

The constable chuckled. "You can tell them yourself after we hang you."

CHAPTER 5

The constable lit another lamp then left the jail, promising to return shortly.

Lobo, who'd been pacing back and forth in the cell, seized the bars in his iron grip and shook for all he was worth.

It was no good. The bars didn't budge.

He threw his shoulder into the door. No good. Kicked it. Still nothing.

He realized he was breathing rapidly and shallowly.

Being in this cell had hurled him back in time and space, returning him to a place he had never expected to experience again, a place of fear and impotence and despair.

Suddenly, he was just a boy again, a boy with no words, a boy bleeding from terrible wounds given to him by the man with the whip, a boy who had just watched the same man murder his pack, using the boy as bait.

I'm panicking, Lobo thought, and slammed his eyes shut so as not to see the bars surrounding him.

Get control, he told himself. *Whatever this is, wherever you are, whatever happens, you're not in the cage. You're here. You're not that boy anymore. You're a man now. A man called Lobo. Lobo Guerrero. The wolf warrior. And when you get out of this cell, you are going to set things right.*

He focused on his breath, drawing in slow, deep breaths through his nose. The terrible smells nearly made him gag, but he continued to focus on his breathing. He drew his lungs full, held the air, and released it just as slowly, telling himself with every breath to calm down, get control, and prepare himself for what was to come.

When he heard footsteps coming up the stairs, he opened his eyes, having moved through the panic into a calm state of confidence.

He was ready for whatever happened next.

Or so he thought, until the constable walked through the door, bringing with him a grinning Ahab Jackson.

"Well, well, well," Jackson said with a smile Lobo knew and hated. "At last, we meet again."

He was older than Lobo remembered and not quite so large, and he had shaved his beard, but otherwise, he looked much the same. The broad shoulders, stiff walk, and crumpled nose were all there, and his dark eyes still twinkled with cruelty that combined triumph and amusement.

Realizing he was growling, Lobo silenced his throat. He wouldn't give Jackson the satisfaction of knowing he was getting to him.

"What do you say, Wolf Boy? Huh? You can talk now, can't you? I hope that thieving priest taught you that much, anyway."

Lobo just looked at him.

"You've been a busy boy," Jackson said. "I heard about the Maestro and those men he hired. Didn't know you had it in you. Oh, you were scrappy enough as a boy. But once the whip came out, you were just a frightened little pup. Just a whimpering little puppy."

Lobo burned with rage. Suddenly, he wanted an answer to an old question he'd never bothered to ponder. "Why?"

"Oh, you can speak," Jackson laughed. "Why what?"

"Why did you do it?"

"Do what?"

"Why did you put me in the cage and whip me? I needed help, but you hurt me instead."

"Aw, you're breaking my heart, kid. You know, you used to be tough. That thieving priest must have softened you up. Probably filled your head with a bunch of nonsense about God. Well, let me set you straight. There is no higher power."

Lobo stared, hating him, and prayed, *Lord, please don't let this wicked man get away with this. Don't let him mock you.*

"You're born, you live, you die. And that's it. Show's over. No life after death, no starting over. You're just dead. And while you're here, you're either strong or weak. You should know that, growing up with wolves."

How Lobo wished he was on the other side of the bars. He would rip Jackson's throat out for even speaking of the wolves.

"The strong do what they want to the weak," Jackson said. "That's why I did what I did. Because I could. Because I was strong, and you were weak. And because I wanted to."

Lobo stared, wanting to kill him. The bitterness was overwhelming. After all these years, he had finally caught up to Jackson, but here he was in a cage again, powerless before the man who had killed his pack and the Padre and beaten Lobo half to death time and time again.

"You still do that, huh? Growl at folks?" Jackson chuckled.

"Laugh all you want," Lobo said, half-growling the words, "but remember one thing."

"What's that?"

"Remember you could have helped me."

Jackson looked confused. "What are you jabbering about, boy?"

"When I was a kid, you could have helped me. But instead you killed my pack and beat me and made me fight grown men. You turned me into what I am. And that's what I want you to remember just before I kill you."

Jackson threw back his head and filled the stinking room with laughter.

When he finally stopped, he wiped theatrically at the corners of his eyes and glared murderously at Lobo. "You never should've come back, Wolf Boy. Tomorrow, you're going up before old Noose Newsom. Just as sure as my name's Ahab Jackson, you're gonna hang. But I'm gonna bring my whip, and before we string you up, you and me are gonna have a little fun for old time's sake."

CHAPTER 6

B rock Boone paced beneath a gibbous moon, striding back and forth across the long balcony outside his bedchamber, alone and restless and filled with regret.

He should never have made the right-of-way offer to Miss Miles.

It hadn't occurred to him that she might not trust his word, but in hindsight, the offer had been so magnanimous, it must have put her on edge.

Is that why she hadn't delivered her refusal in person? Had he somehow frightened her?

Whatever the case, he'd botched his attempt at charity, and now, with the party at the Masterson estate rapidly approaching, it looked like he would be attending alone.

He could go to Jasper Flats and invite an eligible woman, of course, or show up at the party alone and concentrate on meeting one of the well-bred, young women who always attended such parties, but he wanted nothing to do with either of those things.

His mind—and, more importantly, his heart—were set on Hannah Miles.

The best thing to do would be to make a new offer, something equally magnanimous but with fewer moving parts and potential risks.

Looking back, his original offer had been quite foolish. Miss Miles could have had no idea that he had no plans of actually using the right-of-way. She might have considered all the potential risks and consequences of his taking a large herd back and forth across her land and wondered if he was trying to ruin her.

So yes, this new offer needed to be just as generous with none of the risk, nothing for her to misinterpret, especially since she would likely be extra leery of him now.

The simplest thing to offer was money, but she'd never take it. Nor would she accept any of the cattle he would happily give her. She would insist on paying for them.

He smiled at the thought of her. She had pride, that was for sure. And morals. She detested the idea of handouts. He liked that about her, even though it made things difficult for him.

Well, he would offer to sell her cattle at a cheap rate, then keep and care for the cattle and transport them to market free of charge. Which would amount to offering her an investment opportunity. She could profit fifty to sixty dollars per steer with no risk to herself.

She couldn't refuse such an offer, could she?

It wouldn't seem so, but he couldn't say for sure. Miss

Hannah Miles had proven herself capable of surprising him, after all.

But he suspected she would agree. He certainly hoped so. Because that would put them in business together, and once she relaxed enough to understand what he had done for her, surely she would warm to him.

Perhaps, she would even warm to him considerably—and romantically.

That was what he wanted. He wanted Hannah Miles as his wife.

The idea of her appealed to him. The notion of moving into this ranch, only to discover an eligible bachelorette living next door and struggling to stay afloat had interested him and enflamed his sense of chivalry.

Then, meeting her, he'd been struck by her beauty and charm. It had seemed too good to be true, moving in next to a lovely, unmarried, young woman, as if God Himself had smiled on Brock, placing him in a perfect position.

Her proximity would make courting her terribly convenient. But she remained a challenge because she had not responded to him the way women usually do.

At first, he wondered if she was engaged to another, but he'd seen no men on the ranch at all, save for the two hands, one too old and one too young, and, of course, Lobo, the gunman with the dusty clothes and horribly scarred face.

Surely, she couldn't be interested in such a man.

So she was alone and available. She just didn't act that way.

But Brock Boone was a man who had built his life by accepting challenges, overcoming obstacles, and beating the odds by whatever means necessary, and he was determined to have Hannah Miles's hand in marriage no matter what it cost him.

Tilly was another consideration. The child did not seem to like him very much, but she'd liked him well enough when he'd brought her the doll.

Before visiting again, he would have to buy her something else at the mercantile. Another doll perhaps, or a pretty dress, along with some candy. Children loved sweets.

Then, after striking a deal with Hannah, he would try to ease into courting her. He wished now that he had been straight with her all along and simply stated his romantic intentions, but he hadn't believed she was available.

And now, after the right-of-way fiasco, he couldn't risk being too straightforward. She might misconstrue his interest as an attempt to manipulate her into granting him a right-of-way or something else... when all he really wanted was Hannah Miles herself.

Well, he couldn't just ride over and propose this. He might scare her again.

But when he next saw her, he would offer the cattle. She would have to accept.

First, she would accept the cattle. Then she would accept him.

CHAPTER 7

As Lobo completed his inspection of the iron bars, he growled with frustration. There were no loose bars, no weak points.

Only a shaft of pale moonlight, shadow-striped by the barred window through which it fell, illuminated the gloomy cell.

He had to get out of here. Had to get his revenge. Had to go find his long-lost family, then make good on his promise to return to Hannah and Tilly.

That more than anything.

He needed to get home.

But how?

He had no idea. He was just as clueless, just as powerless, as he had been all those years ago as the boy in the cage.

But no.

He would not let himself slide into those dark memories. There was no time to wallow in self-pity.

He had to think.

He was out of ideas. He couldn't see a way to escape on his own.

He knelt and prayed, asking the Lord for help.

He knelt there on the hard floor for a long time, hoping God would speak or stir a new line of thinking, but nothing happened.

Frustrated, he hammered a fist against the stained floorboards.

And then an idea occurred to him. The floor was old and worn. Were any of the floorboards weak?

Could he pry some up, break through the ceiling beneath, and lower himself to the first floor?

He moved across the floor quickly but carefully, scuttling from board to board, searching for any weakness, but found nothing.

Which left only one possibility.

He studied the bowed, water-damaged ceiling, remembering a story he'd heard about a lawman named Wyatt Earp, who'd gotten famous a couple of years earlier by winning a gunfight at the O.K. Corral.

Like many lawmen, Wyatt Earp had a shady past. When, long before the O.K. Corral, Earp landed in an Arkansas jail, he and his fellow prisoners busted through the ceiling of their cell and escaped.

Climbing onto the cot, Lobo placed his palms against the old ceiling and smoothed them along, pleased by the weakness he felt. Reaching the water-stained back corner, he gave a push.

Plaster rained down like mana from heaven.

Uttering a prayer of thanks, Lobo started smashing the spot

with palm strikes, squinting as chunks of weak plaster fell away, filling the air with dust.

The more progress he made, the more furiously he pounded at the ceiling. It fell away more easily with every blow, and soon, he had cleared a hole large enough to crawl through.

Lean as he was, he thought he could make it between the joists. Of course, he would still need to get through the attic floor.

The boards up there were narrow and splintery from age and water damage. Lobo knew a lot of early frontiersmen had cut corners with construction, making temporary floors out of split softwood until they had everything established. Lower floors were replaced with hardwood planks. Oftentimes, however, men never got around to rebuilding attic floors, needing only an upper crawlspace for a light storage.

Hoping this was one of those cases, Lobo drilled the overhead floor with his palm and heard an encouraging crack.

He looked around for something—anything to use as a tool now—but saw nothing. The only thing in the room was the waste bucket, and it was too big to fit between the joists.

He delivered a few more palm strikes, driven on by the cracking sounds, but it was awkward, delivering palm strikes straight overhead. He could deliver much more powerful blows with a clenched fist, but that would rip his hands to shreds.

Then he had it. Removing his shirt, he wrapped it tightly around his hand, cushioning his knuckles. Then he started punching the boards for all he was worth.

Every punch cracked a board. This stoked the fire within him, making him punch harder still.

A board snapped away.

He growled with triumph and kept punching.

Another board snapped. And another.

Breathing hard and sweating profusely, Lobo hammered the attic floor, punching again and again, giving it all the force in his powerful body, smashing through board after board until he'd broken away a hole large enough for him to fit through.

He rested for a minute, coughing from the dust, then put his shirt back on and buttoned it most of the way up.

He examined the hole he'd made, making sure it was relatively clean, and reached up and grabbed the attic floor and pulled himself up.

His first attempt, he managed only to get his head into the space above.

The attic was empty, save for a profusion of spiderwebs, which glowed like spun silver in the moonlight falling through windows at either end of the dusty room and a small hole in the back slope of the roof.

He was disappointed to see that someone had barred these windows as well, but his eyes lingered on the hole in the roof.

He lowered himself onto the bed again, thinking.

The damaged roof faced the back of the house. If he could somehow enlarge the hole and drop to the ground, he would be in the fenced backyard, which probably served as an exercise area for long-term prisoners.

That would be a long drop.

Gathering the filthy sheets and blankets, he tied them together, end to end. Securing one end of this makeshift rope to his belt, he once more climbed on top of the bed and reached up through the hole to grip the attic floor.

This time, however, he placed the stinking waste bucket

upside down on the cot and stood on it and spread his hands farther apart and in this way was able to bring his chest even with the joists.

For a second, it felt like he might be wedged there, so tight was the fit, but with great effort, he shot out one elbow, braced it on the attic floor, pushed up, planted the other elbow, and lifted himself out of the cell and into the cobwebby attic.

Batting away the spiderwebs and brushing his arms and neck when he felt things crawling there, Lobo crouched and moved along the floor, which creaked and groaned beneath his weight.

"Don't break," he growled at the floor beneath him and moved slowly forward, trying to guess where the joists were.

A moment later, he reached the small hole in the roof and peered out through it at the gorgeous night sky and freedom.

He pushed at the roof and snarled with appreciation when it moved easily. Whoever had made this house had done a poor job of it, and Lobo loved them for it.

He once more removed his shirt, wrapped his fist, and set to work, gripping the rafter to one side of the hole as he pounded at the roof, which snapped and fell away, as brittle as old cornhusks.

A short time later, he was peering down into the fenced backyard and beyond, where the world opened with the limitless possibilities of freedom.

It was about eighteen feet to the ground, he judged. The drop wouldn't kill him, but it might break a leg if he landed wrong or hit something hard, so he broke away a bit more of the roof, exposing the bottom of one rafter, then rechecked his makeshift rope of sheets and blankets, lashed one end securely to the exposed rafter, and tossed the free end out the hole, where it dropped to within five feet of the ground.

He tested the rope and rafter one last time, then went out through the hole he'd made, and a moment later, he dropped from the end of the last sheet and landed softly on the ground, wild with triumph.

LOBO SPRINTED ACROSS THE YARD, JUMPED, GRABBED HOLD OF the top of the fence, and hauled himself over.

A second later, he dropped down on the other side and ran into the night, eager as a wolf scenting fresh blood.

CHAPTER 8

L obo hurried across town, slipping from shadow to shadow, avoiding contact, circled behind the Jackson Hotel, and went in the back.

He waited in the hall just out of sight of the clerk's counter and listened for a while. Hearing only the creak of a chair and the riffling of paper, he walked around the front and vaulted over the counter.

Before the clerk knew what was happening, he was on his back, pinned to the floor, his scream muffled by Lobo's hand. The clerk's eyes bulged with terror.

"I'm here for my guns," Lobo said.

The terrified man pointed across his station to where the shotgun leaned against the wall. On the floor beside it sat Lobo's gun belt, complete with both Colts and his Bowie.

"Good," Lobo said. "But you and I have a problem."

The man shook his head.

"Yes, we do. You told Jackson I checked in here."

The man shook his head again.

"You sure you want to deny that? If there's one thing I hate, it's a liar."

The man just stared at him.

"Now, let's try that again," Lobo said. "You told Jackson when I checked in." He moved his hand so the clerk could speak.

"Yes, sir, I did. But don't be mad. It was my job. Everybody in town, we were all on the lookout for you. A gunfighter with a..."

"Scarred-up face?"

"Yes, sir. No offense, sir."

"What's your name?"

"Marcus, sir."

"I don't trust you, Marcus."

"I'm sorry, sir."

"But I won't kill you for what you did."

Marcus's eyes fluttered with relief. "Thank you, sir."

"I am going to tie you up and gag you, though. That's for your good, not mine. Because if you sound any alarms, I will come back and kill you." Lobo stared directly into the man's eyes. "Do you understand?"

Marcus looked away. "Yes, sir. I understand."

The clerk didn't make a peep when Lobo let him up and put on his gun belt and checked and reloaded his weapons.

He slung the dead men's gun belts over his shoulder and took a key from the rack and prodded the clerk down the hall, where he tied him up and gagged him inside a vacant unit.

Then he went back out.

Sticking to an alley that ran parallel to the main street, Lobo slipped through the night, crossing town until he came to North Poplar.

It was a short street. The houses were dark. Except one.

At the back of the last house on the left, lights burned.

Lobo went around the back. Through the windows, he saw a well-lit kitchen.

And there stood Jackson, gripping a tumbler of whiskey and talking to someone Lobo couldn't see.

Probably the constable, Lobo thought. *They're probably sitting there, gloating.*

He approached the side of the house and slid along it to the door at the edge of the bright room. Peering through the window from this angle, he could see that his suspicions had been correct. The constable sat at the table, sipping from his own tumbler and listening to Jackson.

Good, Lobo thought, hearing the drone of Jackson's voice through the door. *Keep talking.*

He reached down, gripped the doorknob, and tried to turn it slightly.

It moved easily.

He turned it slowly, listening, pleased that Jackson's voice droned on without a hiccup.

When he'd turned the knob to its limit, he positioned his body and coach gun and threw open the door and strode inside, leveling his weapon, ready to fire.

"Hands up," he said.

Jackson dropped his whiskey with a startled cry then shot his hands into the air.

The constable lifted his hands and stared at Lobo with narrowed eyes.

"Don't even think about it," Lobo told the constable, "or I'll paint that wall red."

"I don't understand," Jackson said. "You're supposed to be locked up."

"I was," Lobo said, "and now I'm not."

"You're making a big mistake, coming in here, threatening us," the constable said. His voice was calm, almost amused. He'd lowered his hands to ear level. "You know what's good for you, you'll clear out of here, pronto. Mr. Jackson runs this town, and I am an officer of the law."

"An officer of the law?" Lobo said. "You killed that man and said I murdered him. You were going to hang me in the morning."

"We weren't gonna hang you," Jackson said. "We were just having a little fun with you. We were gonna let you go in the morning, isn't that right, Orville?"

The constable grinned. Whatever else he was, he was a hard-case. He ignored Jackson, focusing on Lobo.

This was between them now. And Lobo knew what was coming, knew it by the man's grin and the twinkle in his eye and the fact that he'd lowered his hands to his jawline.

"Dave would have talked," the constable said, "muddied the waters. I had to put him down."

"There's nothing worse in this world than a bad man with a badge," Lobo said.

The constable shrugged. "Man's gotta make a living. Seems kind of odd, a man like you, a man with a reputation for—"

And he went for it, pushing back from the table and going for his gun just as Lobo had known he would.

The constable was fast. That's probably why Jackson had hired him.

But nobody's faster than buckshot.

Lobo let him have one barrel, painting the wall red as promised, then turned the other barrel on Jackson.

"No!" Jackson said. "Wait!"

The man's fear was delicious, stirring feelings of justice in Lobo. But as Jackson hunched and started to weep, begging for mercy, it stirred something else in Lobo, something dark and dangerous, bringing to life a part of him that wanted to match cruelty with cruelty.

"You killed my pack," Lobo said.

"They were wolves. I didn't know."

"You knew. You knew they'd raised me. Then you used me as bait. And killed them right in front of me."

"I'm sorry."

"It's too late for sorry."

"No, it's not. Look. That priest, he must've taught you about forgiveness, right?"

"You killed him, too."

"No, I didn't."

"The Maestro did. And you sent him."

"I'm sorry. I didn't know he was going to do that."

"You sent him. If you hadn't sent him, the Padre would still be alive."

Jackson clasped his hands in front of his face as if praying and knelt before Lobo. "Have mercy. The Padre would want you to forgive me. God wants you to forgive me."

"You don't believe in God."

"I do. I was just kidding before. That's all this was. A big joke."

Lobo's eyes swept across a side table and found Jackson's whip curled there like a serpent.

The dark thing in him cried out for suffering.

"You whipped me so many times," he growled.

Jackson's eyes flicked toward the whip, then flicked away quickly as if they'd been burned by the image. "I'm sorry. I'm so sorry."

"The wolves scarred my face when we ate together because it was their nature to fight over a kill. They didn't know any better. But you knew better. You hurt me because you like to hurt people. And I was just a child."

"That was a long time ago," Jackson blubbered. His tears stoked Lobo's anger, increased that dark thing in him demanding blood and screams. "I wouldn't do that now. Honest. I'm sorry."

"How could you be sorry if you don't know how it felt?" Lobo said, picking up the whip with one hand and still gripping the shotgun with the other.

The darkness in him, the desire to repay cruelty for cruelty, burned higher, making terrible demands.

"I should whip you to death," he said.

"No," Jackson wept. "Don't. I'll pay you. I have lots of money."

"I don't want money."

"I'll give you anything you want. Land, buildings, women."

"I don't want any of those things."

"What do you want? Whatever it is, I'll give it to you. What do you want?"

The darkness in Lobo answered, *I want you to suffer like I suffered.*

But those thoughts did not become words.

Lobo didn't allow it. Because he knew he was standing at the very edge of something that would determine not only what he did to Jackson but also the fate of Lobo's soul.

And he would not give in to that darkness. Yes, he had come here to avenge unforgivable wrongs, but he refused to let revenge corrupt him.

"I won't torture you," Lobo said, tossing the whip aside.

"Oh, thank you," Jackson said, sobbing with relief. "Thank you, thank you, thank you."

"Because I didn't come here to become you. I came here to set things right."

Jackson smiled briefly then saw the barrel coming up and understood.

"Wolf Boy, wait!" he shouted. "You dirty little—"

Whatever he'd been going to say whipped away with the rest of him in the blast of the shotgun.

CHAPTER 9

L obo took Jackson's big gelding and rode through the night, his pockets and money belt stuffed with Jackson's cash.

There was a lot of it. He reckoned it was a few thousand dollars, maybe more.

There hadn't been time to count. He'd gotten out of Jackson's house as quick as he could then ridden straight out of town.

Come morning, someone would find the clerk.

Smartest thing to do would've been to shoot him, too, but Lobo refused to commit cold-blooded murder.

So he rode, not slowing to eat or sleep, let alone count money. He had to get back to Granville before word spread about what he'd done.

And with their telegraph stations likely opening at eight in the morning, he was running short on time indeed.

He reached the livery as the first light of day was splintering through the wooded ridge east of town, hitched Jackson's horse, and pounded on the door of the hostler's house.

He heard footsteps and the door opened. Just a crack.

"What do you want?" the hostler demanded.

"My horse."

"Come back at nine. That's when I open." The man started to shut the door.

Lobo stopped it with his hand. "I need my horse. Now."

"I told you, mister. We're closed."

"See that buckskin yonder?"

"What about him?"

"He's yours if you just unlock the livery and let me get my horse."

"Mine? Look, buddy, I don't want to get into any trouble. Why don't you just come back later and—"

"You're not hearing me," Lobo said, and he drilled his gaze into the hostler's eyes. "I'm taking my horse now. I'm just trying to be polite is all. If polite doesn't work, I have another side."

"Fine. But you take that buckskin with you. Whatever kind of trouble you got yourself into, I want no part of it."

Ten minutes later, Lobo rode off there atop Paddy.

Half a mile outside of town, he stopped and spoke with a farmer starting to load a wagon with pumpkins.

"My horse is played out," Lobo said, indicating the buckskin. "You want him?"

"How much?"

"Free."

"Free? That's a nice horse, mister."

"Yes, he is. So treat him right."

"You're serious?"

51

"I am. But I gotta be on my way. Take good care of that horse."

"Hey, mister!" the farmer called after him. "What about the saddle?"

"Keep it," Lobo called back, and disappeared around a stand of trees.

He was tired, but that didn't matter. He had to keep riding, had to put some miles between him and anyone who might try coming after him.

He was glad to be on a fresh horse—especially Paddy. The blood bay had a lot of go in him and had never let Lobo down.

"Paddy," Lobo said, "we gotta get on down the road, old boy."

They rode through the morning, pausing every hour so Paddy could rest and drink. Lobo did not push it. He knew he had a pretty good lead on anyone who might follow, and they'd passed several crossroads, so he was probably safe.

Probably.

But when your life is on the line, *probably* isn't much of a comfort.

So he kept on riding until late that afternoon, when they arrived at yet another crossroads.

This one he knew.

If he turned right and headed north, the road would lead him back to Hannah and Tilly.

If he went straight, continuing west, he would eventually come to Green Valley, where his long-lost family reportedly lived.

He paused there, having never felt so free—or so conflicted.

He wanted badly to turn north and ride straight home, to

hug Tilly and tell Hannah the truth: he loved her and wanted to marry her.

His one fear, that he might arrive too late and find that Hannah had already accepted a proposal from Brock Boone, made him want to clap Paddy's sides and race home as fast as the powerful stallion could carry him.

But despite the freedom he felt from killing Jackson and uncoupling himself from that responsibility, he wouldn't truly free himself from the past until he had reunited with the family who probably thought he was long dead.

He had to ride on, had to visit Green Valley, had to meet his family and answer the many questions whirling in his mind.

He urged Paddy forward, heading west, hoping beyond hope that Hannah would wait for him.

CHAPTER 10

Wearing a modest yet well-made dress, Hannah rode on the buckboard between Mr. Tuttle and Tilly.

She was, of course, completely capable of driving the wagon herself, and truth be told, riding when she might drive was mildly annoying, but today, everything was about appearances.

Dogs barked as the wagon rounded a bend and the ranch of Curtis Baldwin came into view.

Hannah adjusted her smile, changing its width and brightness and making little adjustments with her eyes and the tilt of her chin, trying to imagine what sort of impression she would make with each change.

But it was no good. She had no experience with affectation.

"Just smile," Tilly said, watching her and understanding, as always. "Don't think about it."

And then Hannah did smile, appreciating the girl's intelligent awareness. "You know me better than I know myself, Tilly."

Several dogs with wagging tails surrounded them as they pulled to a stop outside the house.

A few seconds later, Mr. Baldwin came through the door and stood on the porch. He looked older than Hannah remembered. Of course, it had been a while. He had to be fifty. Maybe even sixty, older than Pa would have been.

Baldwin hooked his thumbs in his suspenders and eyed them with suspicion for a moment.

Hannah waved.

Baldwin ignored her. Then, recognizing the driver, he said, "Junius Tuttle. What brings you around, old timer?"

"Well, if that ain't the pot calling the kettle black, I don't know what is," Mr. Tuttle laughed. "You look like you're ready to be put out to pasture."

"Pshaw! That'll be the day. You gonna sit there in your wagon or come over? Or do you need me to fetch you a cane, old man?"

Laughing, Mr. Tuttle climbed down then offered his hand to Hannah, who, feeling Mr. Baldwin's eyes upon her, did her best to descend gracefully.

"Tilly," she said, "please hand me the basket before joining us."

"Yes, Miss Hannah," Tilly said, and fetched the basket.

"Hannah?" Mr. Baldwin said with mock confusion. "Wasn't that the name of Ed Miles's little girl?"

Hannah smiled up at him. "Yes, sir, Mr. Baldwin. It's been a long time."

"You've grown up," Mr. Baldwin said, shaking his head. "I suppose that's how it goes, but the older I get, I am constantly bewildered by the rate of change around me. Why, it seems like it was only a year or two ago that you came over here with your pa."

"That was closer to fifteen years ago, sir."

"Fifteen years?" Mr. Baldwin shook his head. "Doesn't seem possible. Well, it's good to see you again, young lady. And you, too, Junius. But who's that little blond-haired girl holding a doll behind you?"

"I'm Matilda Kershaw Frampton, sir," Tilly said with a curtsy and a bright smile. "But everybody calls me Tilly. It's very nice to meet you."

"Very nice to meet you, too, Tilly," Mr. Baldwin said warmly. "But what did you say your last name was, Frampton?"

"Yes, sir."

"There's a name I've never heard before. Not around these parts, anyhow."

"I'm not from around here, Mr. Baldwin. But I live here now. I'm an orphan. Miss Hannah takes care of me."

"Is that right? Well, that's very kind of her, isn't it?"

"Oh, yes, sir. I'm the luckiest girl in the world," Tilly said then blurted, "She baked you a pie."

"A pie? Well, then, I guess that makes me the luckiest man in the world. Why don't you folks come on inside, and we'll take a look inside that basket."

Mr. Baldwin held the door for them, and they filed indoors.

The place was spotless and smelled pleasantly of bacon grease and old applewood fires, the good aromas seeming to have seasoned the hardwood floors and raw beams and heavy furniture.

Mr. Baldwin set the basket on the counter and opened the

lid and peered inside and smiled. "Well, doesn't that look nice? Thank you very much, Miss Miles."

"You're very welcome, Mr. Baldwin," Hannah said. "I hope you like apple?"

"Like it? Apple pie is my favorite. And I suppose apple season has arrived yet again. Doesn't even seem possible. Wasn't it just strawberry season?"

"I love strawberries," Tilly volunteered.

"So do I," Baldwin said. He invited them to have a seat at the dinner table.

Mr. Tuttle pulled out a chair for Hannah, and she thanked him and lowered herself into it. Mr. Tuttle sat to her right. Tilly sat to her left, clutching Faith and smiling at Mr. Baldwin, who asked if they would like some coffee.

Hannah didn't really need any coffee, but she didn't want to start their talk with a refusal. "That would be lovely, Mr. Baldwin, if it isn't too much trouble."

"No trouble at all, Miss Miles, no trouble at all. And how about you, little Tilly? Would you care for a molasses cookie?"

"I'd love one, thank you!" Tilly chimed.

This clearly pleased Mr. Baldwin, who opened a cupboard full of plates. "Anyone else want a cookie? Miss Miles?"

"No thank you, sir."

"How about you, Junius. You still got any teeth left to chew a cookie with?"

"I got plenty of teeth, you old coot. And sure, I'll have a cookie with my coffee."

"All right, then," Mr. Baldwin said, pulling down three small plates. He set them on the counter and went to a ceramic jar and lifted the lid and pulled out three, large, molasses cookies and set one on each plate and replaced the cookie jar lid and carried over the plates, setting them before Tilly and Mr. Tuttle and placing one at the head of the table, where he would apparently be sitting.

But first he went to work on the coffee, saying, "I've become quite domesticated in my retirement. My cook's mother had a stroke two years ago, so my cook moved out, and I've been fending for myself since then. I've gotten to be quite a good cook and an even better baker, if you want to know the truth of it. Gave me something to do now that I'm not taking herds up the trail anymore."

"Wow," Tilly said, swallowing a bite of the cookie, "you weren't kidding. This is wonderful. You're a great baker, Mr. Baldwin!"

He smiled, clearly pleased. "Don't you go telling that around. My reputation among the cattlemen would suffer greatly if they knew I was wearing an apron and baking cookies."

Tilly laughed. "Well, if they have any trouble with that, you can just give them a cookie, and that'll fix everything."

Baldwin laughed. "You are a smart young lady, Tilly."

Hannah was pleased that Mr. Baldwin was being so warm and welcoming and that everyone was getting along so well. In her memory, he had been a tough man who'd barely glanced in her direction.

So yes, this was a much nicer reception than she'd been expecting, but it was mildly troubling, too.

After all, she had come here to make a business proposition, so she needed Mr. Baldwin to take her seriously.

"Mr. Baldwin," she said, meaning to explain her reason for visiting.

But he interrupted, saying, "No, no, you sit right there, Miss Miles. I'm perfectly capable of making coffee."

"All right," she said. "We came here today, because I wanted to talk to you about—"

"Hold that thought," Mr. Baldwin interrupted again. "Patience, young lady. You were doing so well. Here we are, old neighbors, reunited after what was it? Twelve years? Let's just have our coffee and cookies and talk after that, okay?"

"Yes, sir," Hannah said, feeling stupid.

Mr. Baldwin made the coffee then asked Tilly if she'd like another cookie.

She said yes, please, if it wasn't too much trouble, and he said it was nice to have an appreciative guest and fetched her another cookie before sitting down to his own cookie and coffee.

He talked mostly to Mr. Tuttle, the two men sharing gossip about folks they knew in common, men who'd struck it rich or fallen into ruin or gotten killed or scalped or robbed at gunpoint.

Between these anecdotes, he asked Tilly questions. How old was she? Where was she born? Did she remember her parents?

And Tilly, being Tilly, answered everything with chirpy candor, delighting the old bachelor.

Just when Hannah was starting to feel ignored, Mr. Baldwin said, "Now, Miss Miles, apparently, you have some business you'd like to discuss."

CHAPTER 11

L obo tossed and turned on his bedroll, growling softly, locked in the jaws of another nightmare.

This time, he dreamed not of the past but the future.

The dream started pleasantly. He was in a dream version of Green Valley, standing alone beside a field of tall, bright green corn that stretched away as far as he could see in both directions.

A warm breeze sighed across the valley, filling his nostrils with the good smell of the corn and his ears with the happy whispering of papery leaves as the stalks swayed.

He felt incredibly happy and welcome. This was home. This was where he belonged.

But then, the breeze strengthened, turning cold, and as he squinted and shivered, he saw the corn changing. Its ears fell away as the stalks withered, turning brown, and the sound of its leaves became dry and foreboding, the whispering of dead oracles bearing word of the coming apocalypse.

Terror rippled through Lobo as the sky darkened to a deep purple.

He stared, waiting, his apprehension growing with every beat of his panicked heart. He didn't know what he was waiting for, but he feared it more than he had ever feared anything before. And yet the dream would not allow him to look away.

The world grew cold as ice.

A great eye opened in the sky overhead and blinked down at him, full of wisdom and malice.

Lobo whimpered.

For this giant, all-seeing eye could belong to only one person: the one-eyed man.

Frozen before the gigantic eye like a rabbit paralyzed by the cry of a diving hawk, Lobo stared in horror as the one-eyed man said, "Come to me now, Lobo. Come back to where it all began and to where it all will end. In the land of the blind, the one-eyed man is king. Come to me now, and the king will finally have his kingdom."

Lobo came awake with a scream that startled Paddy, who was cropping grass in the midmorning sun a short distance away.

Panting for breath, Lobo sat up, his hand going automatically to the scattergun beside his bedroll.

The cold of the dream yet clung to him, despite the mild morning into which he'd awakened and the bullets of perspiration streaming down his body.

"Just a dream," he muttered then stood and stretched, looking around.

All was well. He'd slept late. The day was crisp and bright, a perfect harvest day if ever there was one.

He gave one final shake like a wolf shedding water then set to gathering his things.

Why had he dreamed of the one-eyed man?

He had hoped the nightmares would end with the death of Ahab Jackson.

But here he was, still struggling to catch his breath in the wake of another nightmare featuring the man who earlier declared himself the alpha and the omega, claiming to have created Lobo and promising to finish him.

What did it all mean?

Why hadn't Jackson's death, which righted the wrongs of his childhood, finally put this past—whether real or imagined—to rest?

Did that mean there was still something out of his past, something he couldn't remember, that demanded reckoning?

Would he escape these nightmares simply by reuniting with his family? Or was there some trouble awaiting him there, some problem he needed to eliminate in order to sleep peacefully again?

Was it possible that the one-eyed man was more than a ghost haunting his dreams? Was it possible that he was a real person out of Lobo's past, not a ghost at all but a man of flesh and blood whom Lobo had known before whatever tragedy had left him in the care of wolves?

Saddling Paddy, he shook his head.

The human mind was a wild and untamable thing. Who knew where dreams came from or what they meant?

One thing was for certain: whether the one-eyed man proved to be real or imagined, it changed nothing. Lobo was heading home after all these years, home to meet his long-lost family.

He wouldn't allow some dreamed-up boogeyman to change that. And, if against all odds, the one-eyed man did end up being real, Lobo would deal with him here, in the waking world, preferably by putting a bullet through his single eye.

CHAPTER 12

"Yes, sir," Hannah said, looking Mr. Baldwin in the eyes. "I do wish to discuss business with you."

"Is it about that new neighbor, Mr. Boone?" Mr. Baldwin asked. "Is he giving you trouble?"

"No, sir. Mr. Boone has been a perfect gentleman."

"Ah, good. So he's not like Hutchins, huh? That man was a snake."

"Yes, sir. What I wanted to ask you, sir, was if you would consider selling me some land."

"Land? What do you want land for?"

"I'm looking to expand my herd, Mr. Baldwin."

"What for?"

"For profit."

He smiled and sipped his coffee. "Profit is good. Did you marry a cattleman?"

"No, sir. I am running the ranch myself. With the help of my hired hands, of course."

"That would be you, Junius?"

"Yup," Mr. Tuttle said. "Me and another fella."

"Who's that?"

"Name's Plug."

"Plug? Never heard of him."

"He's young, but he's strong as an ox and learning fast. Good hand."

"How young?"

"Fifteen."

Mr. Baldwin smiled and folded his hands over his flat stomach and leaned back on the back legs of his chair. "How many head are you running these days, Miss Miles?"

Hannah felt her face grow warm with embarrassment. This wasn't going as planned. "Not many, sir."

"How many is not many, if you don't mind my asking? I'm just trying to figure out your situation is all."

"Thirty-some."

"Thirty-some."

"Yes, sir. For now. But what I'm planning—"

"You raise longhorns like your Pa did?"

"Yes, sir. Though, what I'm thinking—"

"Good animals, longhorns. Tough. They thrive on forage that'd starve other breeds. Smart, too. Wily, even. I've heard some folks say they're gentle. Heh. A man who says that hasn't spent much time with longhorns. You get one with a mean streak, don't go following him into the brush."

"No, sir," Hannah said, wanting to present her case.

But Baldwin said, "You have what, four hundred acres over there?"

"Yes, sir. Four hundred, give or take."

"And unless something has changed, that's good land. Good grass, plenty of water."

"Yes, sir. We couldn't ask for better land."

"Why don't you just run more head on the land you got? Land like that, you could double your herd. Triple it, even. No problem."

"Yes, sir, but—"

"But you've been hearing about all the millionaires up in Cheyenne."

"Sir?"

"What did I hear it was now? One out of every three hundred and fifty Cheyenne residents is a millionaire now?"

"I hadn't heard that, sir."

"Cattle money. Every last dime of it. So that's what you're chasing, cattle money?"

"Yes, sir."

"How you gonna get them to market? Lot of things can go wrong between here and there. Floods, lightning, stampedes, blizzards, bandits, Indians…"

"Yes, sir. I have everything lined up, though."

"With that new neighbor of yours?"

"Yes, sir."

"And is he the one selling you the cows?"

"Yes, sir. I think so."

"Hmm. You think so, huh? And just how many head were you looking to buy?"

"That depends on you, sir. On how many acres, if any, that you'll sell me."

Mr. Baldwin leaned forward. "I suppose you're wanting the land across the river from your place."

"Yes, sir."

"That's prime ground. Top grazing land. And the way the foothill wraps around from the northwest, it cuts the wind some. Then you got the groves. You see the groves driving in here?"

"Yes, sir. I did."

"I planted those groves thirty-five years ago. Now look at them. They bust up the wind, too, and give good shade in the summer. Your cattle, they could shelter there during bad weather."

Hannah nodded. "It's good land, sir."

"And you were thinking since I'm not running much of a herd anymore that I'll sell it to you for a song, huh? Or maybe for a fresh-baked apple pie?" Mr. Baldwin smiled at this, but his eyes shone with irritation.

"I brought the pie to be neighborly," Hannah said, feeling her own irritation rise. "And yes, I thought maybe you would consider selling me some land since you clearly aren't using it anymore."

"This season. What if I want to build my herd back up? What if I want to be a millionaire, too?"

"Then I suppose you shouldn't sell me any land. Which is fine by me. I just thought—"

"Thirty dollars an acre," Mr. Baldwin said abruptly.

Everyone looked to Hannah, who picked up her coffee and took a measured sip, doing her best to disguise the fact that she was reeling inside.

Thirty dollars an acre? That was ridiculous.

Thanks to Lobo, she had thirty-nine hundred dollars. Mentally, she had earmarked half of that for acquiring land, which would leave enough to buy cattle and retain several hundred dollars for expenses and savings.

Thirty dollars an acre was far too expensive. She would be a fool to spend that much, and doing so would leave her with diminished prospects and security.

She set her mug on its saucer with an audible clink.

"Mr. Baldwin, no one would pay thirty dollars an acre for this land."

"Fine by me. I didn't come to you, Miss Miles, you came to me. What would you pay?"

She hesitated, measuring her response. Come in too low, and she might offend Mr. Baldwin and squander the opportunity. Come in too high, and she would regret it if he accepted.

"Eighteen dollars an acre."

Mr. Baldwin made a face. "Eighteen an acre? Did you come here for business or charity?"

"Eighteen dollars an acre is hardly charity, Mr. Baldwin."

"Twenty-seven."

"Twenty. I'll go no higher."

"Twenty-five," Mr. Baldwin said, eyes blazing now. The haggling seemed to have ignited a territorial fire within him. "And I'll go no lower."

"In that case, I'm sorry to have wasted your time," Hannah said, rising from her chair. "Thank you for the coffee."

Mr. Baldwin crossed his arms over his chest and nodded. "You're welcome. And thank you for the pie, Miss Miles. Contrary to what you might think, I am pleased to see you again."

"In that case," Hannah said, shaking with emotion, "I am glad we visited. Mr. Tuttle, Tilly, come along. Let's be going."

Tilly stood and frowned across the table at Mr. Baldwin. "I don't get it, Mr. Baldwin. You seemed nice. How come you don't want to sell Miss Hannah any land? You aren't even using it anymore, and we're trying to get a start. Why not help us?"

Hannah was mortified. She grabbed Tilly's hand and gave a squeeze. "That is highly inappropriate, Tilly. Apologize to Mr. Baldwin."

"That's all right," Mr. Baldwin said. "I like the girl's fire. And yours, too, Miss Miles, if you don't mind my saying so. You might be thinking I'm more likely to sell my land since I don't need to graze it anymore. But you'd be wrong. With no cattle to mention, the land itself has become more important to me. I love it, you see. When I walk out there among the groves, I remember planting them. I remember hot summers and hard winters. I remember how I worked, keeping the cattle alive and driving them to market and then coming back and starting all over again."

Hannah looked at him, taken by the transformation in his demeanor, certain that for the first time, they were seeing the real Mr. Baldwin.

"Do I need all the land?" he asked. "No, I do not. But like I said, I love it. It has become my life, this ranch. And it's worth more than money to me now."

"Again, I am very sorry to have wasted your time, Mr. Baldwin," Hannah said. "I certainly never meant to offend you."

"You didn't," Mr. Baldwin said. "I just want you—and more importantly, Tilly—to understand why I seem so unreasonable. And there's more to it. I think you're getting in over your head."

Hannah straightened at that. "I can assure you, Mr. Baldwin, you don't need to worry about me. I am quite capable of handling my affairs."

"No offense, Miss Miles, but you are not. If I gave in to your final offer, selling you ground for twenty dollars an acre, you'd be in trouble. How many acres were you wanting?"

"I was hoping for a hundred acres."

"So two thousand dollars for the land. And how many head of cattle would you buy?"

"A hundred, since I'm only running such a small herd currently."

"So there's another two thousand dollars for a mixed lot."

He has no idea that Mr. Boone offered me prime steers for eight dollars a head, she thought.

But of course, she had no idea if that offer still stood…

Mr. Baldwin asked, "How many of them would be ready for market next year? Half? And what if we get a bad winter? What if we have a drought? We're overdue. How much money do you have?"

"I'm afraid that's none of your business, Mr. Baldwin."

"Fair enough. I'm only trying to help you see the situation. But I can't imagine you have much money. Your Pa never did."

Hannah said nothing to that.

"I don't mean to give you trouble, Miss Miles. I'm trying to save you trouble. It costs money to drive cattle."

"I know that, sir."

"All right. So you know it, then. But it still costs money. And more than money. It takes people. You gotta know people. You have a good trail boss lined up? Dependable drovers? A cook and a chuckwagon?"

Hannah did not want to confess how heavily she was

leaning on Brock Boone's generosity—a thing she was realizing more and more as Mr. Baldwin interrogated her—so she merely nodded.

"Well, then, you're further along than I figured," Mr. Baldwin said, but neither his tone nor his facial expression lightened. "You will lose cattle on the drive. It's unavoidable. But let's be optimistic. Let's say you manage to deliver fifty head to market. What then? Miss Miles, Texans are bringing in herds like we've never seen. Ten thousand head or more. You get your tiny herd to market, those buyers will eat you alive. To put it bluntly, Miss, they don't need your cattle, not with those big herds coming in all the time. You will not get top dollar. You'll get whatever they feel like offering."

She just stared at him. Again, his scathing commentary, which felt very much like wisdom, underscored just how much she needed the help of Mr. Boone.

But she would not mention Mr. Boone, not now, not when she needed to make Mr. Baldwin understand that she was a capable woman.

"Mr. Baldwin," she said, "while I appreciate your warnings, I want you to understand my position. I am well aware of the costs and risks involved in this undertaking. But I have the money now. The money and the means. And the determination. Meanwhile, the beef market is booming. Like you said, that could change at any moment. If I wait two or three years to build up a larger herd, I might miss the opportunity."

He nodded, studying her.

She stared back at him. "I have grit, Mr. Baldwin. Let me prove that to you. All I lack is grass. Sell me the land for a fair price. Give me a chance to prove myself and build something."

For a moment, Mr. Baldwin said nothing. He leaned back, then smiled. "I like your style, Miss Miles, but you're taking a big risk here. If I help you with this, and you go bust, I don't want you to come crying to me."

Hannah felt a surge of hope. She didn't let it show. She stared straight into his eyes. "I wouldn't, sir."

Mr. Baldwin nodded, looking thoughtful. "I won't sell you the land."

All that hope came crashing down inside her. Again, she tried not to let her emotions show.

"But I will lease it to you," Mr. Baldwin said.

His words flooded her once more with hope. "Under what terms, sir?"

"I'm interested to see how this venture pans out, so I'll cut you a break. I'll lease you more than you're wanting to buy for twenty-five cents an acre."

Her hope grew less cautious. "For a year, sir?"

"That's right. Let's call it a thousand acres. We can ride it later and set out markers. I'll charge you for a thousand, but it won't be less ground than that. Then, you can take some of the money you were planning to invest in land and build up a bigger herd. And with all that ground, you can push them around. It'll be better for the cattle and the land."

"Yes, sir," Hannah said, and finally, a smile broke through on her face. She stood and stuck out her hand. "You have a deal, sir, and thank you for this opportunity."

Mr. Baldwin shook her hand. "Don't go thanking me just yet, Miss Miles. Your so-called opportunity just might end up being the worst mistake of your life."

CHAPTER 13

L obo doubted anyone was on his trail, but in case they were, he used a pine branch to brush away obvious signs of his campsite.

He rode for a couple of miles before topping a ridge and spying a town in the foothills below. The town, which he suspected to be Redville, was neither big nor small.

He hoped the town had a telegraph station. After killing Jackson, he hadn't slowed down long enough to send Hannah and Tilly the news. Before going on to Green Valley, however, he would stop in Redville and send them an update.

Halfway down the long slope, he came to an overgrown farm disappearing back into the great, green embrace of the wilderness. But a thin tendril of smoke rose from a cabin near the road, and Lobo saw a lone figure hard at work a short distance from the home.

An old woman was out there, sawing logs from a dried-up, beaver-dropped tree her mule had dragged close to the cabin.

Lobo rode up.

The mule noticed him before the woman, who, despite her age and small stature, was working hard with the saw.

The mule gave a bray, and the woman looked up, one gnarled hand going to the old flintlock pistol shoved through her belt.

Lobo touched the brim of his hat. "Ma'am."

She eyed him with suspicion. "Who are you?"

"Name's Lobo," he said, and for the first time, added, "Lobo Guerrero."

The fact that he now had a last name did not seem to impress the old woman.

"Never heard of you. Horse trough's over there. Help yourself. I got hay if you need some, too. If you've come to rob me, I got nothing worth taking, and if you've come to romance me, you're fifty years too late."

She gave a great, wheezing laugh that pinched her eyes shut and opened a mouth missing a good number of teeth.

Lobo liked her instantly.

"I could use water and hay," Lobo said. "You have any food to share?"

"I might scare up some ham and beans, maybe even a tater or two. What do you offer in trade?"

"Well, I could take care of that firewood for starters. Saw it, split it, stack it."

"Now, that's what I call getting off on the right foot," the old woman said. She spat a long stream of dark juice and grinned, her remaining teeth stained brown with chewing tobacco. "Name's Mary McGee, but folks around here just call me Crazy Mary."

"Why do they call you that?"

"On account of my good looks," Crazy Mary McGee said and let go with another explosion of laughter. When she'd finished, she dabbed at the corners of her twinkling eyes with one sleeve. "And I reckon on account of an old woman like me's got to be crazy to buy a mountain farm and move all the way up here by herself."

"Doesn't seem crazy to me," Lobo said. "I'd sooner be snakebit than live in town, Miss McGee."

"Well, you've stopped at the right farm, then. But if you call me Miss McGee again, I'll blast you right out of your saddle. Let's leave the formalities to all those townsfolk we both loathe. Call me Mary or Crazy Mary, your choice."

"All right, Mary. Call me Lobo."

"That works. Tell you what, Lobo. If you've got a strong back and an appetite, why don't you hang around for a few days? I got more work than I can handle, and I'm not getting any younger. You give me a hand, I'll put you up and feed you real good."

Lobo hesitated only briefly. He wanted to get on down the trail and meet his family. For that matter, he wanted to put that happy reunion behind him and get back to Hannah and Tilly and what he hoped would become his real home.

But he liked this strange woman, and she needed his help, so he put his own desires on the back burner for the moment.

"Sounds good to me, Mary. Tell me where to start."

CHAPTER 14

S eventy miles to the east, a pair of riders dismounted in front of a marshal's office.

A dead man was lashed to the back of one of the horses.

The man riding that horse had long hair and wore two, tied-down Colts, their pearl handles crosshatched with hash marks; a long, dark range jacket; and a crumpled top hat. Despite his dusty, darkly stained clothes, he also wore rumpled and filthy cravat like some Eastern gentleman who'd fallen upon hard times.

He had a long face bristling with black stubble. To either side of his long, crooked nose, ice-blue eyes gleamed with quiet menace. Beneath his drooping mustache jutted the long, curving stem of a slender pipe, from which issued clouds of sickly-sweet smoke. The off-white pipe had been carved from some kind of bone. Etched into its bowl was the ghastly image of a grinning skull.

The other man wore the full beard, fur cap, and fringed

buckskins of a buffalo hunter, an impression which was rein-
forced by his stench and the .50 caliber 1874 Sharps rifle that
rode in his saddle scabbard.

Despite the man's beard and buckskins, he was clearly kin to
the man with the pipe.

They were, in fact, the Chantilly brothers, Laverne and
Chester, the two most feared bounty hunters in the territory.
They hitched their horses to the rack and unfastened the dead
man and let him drop to the ground then each took an end and
pushed through the door and carried him inside the marshal's
office.

They dropped him just inside the door.

"Mr. Chantilly," the marshal said, coming to his feet and
nodding to Laverne, who still smoked his pipe, filling the office
with cloying smoke. Nodding then to Chester, the brother in
buckskins, he said, "Mr. Chantilly."

"Fresh meat, Marshal," Laverne Chantilly said.

The marshal blinked at the dead man. "You boys sure did
put a lot of holes in him."

"We didn't put none in his face, so you can see who he is and
give us our money," Chester said.

"He looks familiar."

"It's Gunther Freitas," Laverne said, "the mad
saloonkeeper."

The marshal raised his brows. "Good work. He was
supposed to be a dangerous man."

Chester grinned. "Weren't no danger to it. Caught him
coming out of the privy and shot him all to pieces."

"I see," the marshal said. "Well, I'll write out the affidavit. I
believe his bounty was—"

"Two-hundred and fifty dollars," Laverne said. "You got any fresh paper?"

The marshal rustled through the mess atop his desk. "As a matter of fact, I do have something new for you. Not sure you'll want it, though."

"We'll take any paper you got," Laverne said, "unless it's our dear old Ma… and she's been dead twenty years."

"Man's a bounty hunter, like you," the marshal said. "They say he's a cold-blooded killer and faster than lightning. He's wanted for killing two men in Slagville. One was an important, well-to-do citizen. The other was a constable."

The marshal held up the wanted poster. Beneath the scarred face, a one-word caption stood out in bold print: *LOBO*.

Laverne snatched the paper from the lawman, a terrible grin stretching across his face. "He's the one that stole the Hatley bounty."

His bearded brother nodded. "Twenty-five hundred dollars. That's what we'd make shooting ten renegade saloonkeepers. Wonder if he still has it on him."

Laverne puffed at his bone pipe. "We're fixing to find out, brother."

CHAPTER 15

As the Boone ranch came into view, Hannah took a deep breath and prayed for strength.

Her only passenger, the ever-observant Tilly, asked, "Are you nervous, Miss Hannah?"

Hannah smiled but nodded. She wouldn't lie to the girl. "Yes, Tilly. If you must know the truth, I am nervous."

"Don't be, Miss Hannah. You did a great job with Mr. Baldwin. I know you'll do a great job today, too."

"I hope you are right. There's so much on the line, especially since we've already paid Mr. Baldwin to lease the acreage. If Mr. Boone refuses to sell us cattle…"

"Mr. Boone won't do that," Tilly said. "He's fond of you."

"He *was* fond of me. But we haven't spoken since I refused his right-of-way offer. His silence makes me wonder if we're even welcome here."

"He'll welcome us," Tilly said with comforting confidence.

Hannah loved that about the girl. "He's a gentleman. Even if he's upset, he'll welcome us. He cares about his reputation."

"Sometimes, Tilly, you amaze me."

Tilly beamed at that. "And don't worry, Miss Hannah," the girl said, clutching the plain little doll to her chest. "I'll be on my best behavior today." No sooner had the words left her mouth than her smile faltered a little. "At least, I'll try to be on my best behavior."

"That's all I can ask of you, Tilly. But please do try your hardest. This is a very important day for our future."

"Well, I'll be polite, ma'am, but I won't lie."

Hannah smiled at that. "Neither will I, dear."

As usual, Mr. Boone's estate bustled with activity. People came and went, and the pasture beyond the sprawling mansion teemed with cattle and cowboys.

As they pulled up to the house, they were greeted by a tough-looking yet not unfriendly horseman with graying hair.

"Afternoon, ladies," the man said. "Would you be Miss Miles?"

"Yes, sir," she said, feeling a wave of fresh apprehension. "I am Hannah Miles."

"I'll let Mr. Boone know you're here."

But before the man could even turn in the direction of the mansion, Mr. Boone came striding out of its wide doors, wearing a bright smile and a suit the color of muddled raspberries.

"Miss Miles and young Tilly," he said, hurrying down the stairs with seeming excitement. "What a wonderful surprise. It's so nice to see you both."

"It's nice to see you, too," Hannah said, and glanced at Tilly, who was grinning like a monkey in a blond wig. The sight almost made Hannah laugh, it was so unnatural.

Oh well, she thought. *At least she isn't scowling.*

Mr. Boone spoke to a servant coming down the steps behind him, telling him to secure the horse and carriage. Then he came to Hannah's side and held out his hand and helped her down.

"Thank you, sir."

"My pleasure. And Tilly?"

Still grinning, the girl came to the driver's side and allowed Mr. Boone to lift her from the carriage and place her on the ground beside Hannah.

"Thank you, Mr. Boone," Tilly said with a curtsy.

"My pleasure again. I am so very pleased to see you ladies. Will you join me for lunch?"

"Thank you for the offer, Mr. Boone, but we do have to get back to the ranch."

"My loss, but I understand. We ranchers do live busy lives. Speaking of which, I must apologize, Miss Miles, for not contacting you sooner. I want to thank you for considering my offer, and I do hope it didn't offend you in any way."

The apology seemed sincere. Instantly, Hannah filled with relief. Strengthened by it, she said, "Not at all, Mr. Boone. In fact, one reason for this visit was to thank you again for your generous offer."

"Well, that is the best news I have had in quite a spell," Mr. Boone said. "Will you come inside?"

"I don't want to interrupt anything."

Mr. Boone smiled, staring directly into her eyes for a heartbeat before saying, "Miss Miles, you couldn't possibly interrupt anything. I welcome you anytime for any reason and will always remain your faithful servant."

Hannah smiled uncertainly at his grand promise, remembering Tilly's insistence that Mr. Boone had designs on her. It didn't seem possible, but of course, there weren't many women out here on the range. Perhaps he was under some kind of temporary delusion.

"Thank you, Mr. Boone," she said. "In that case, we would love to come inside for a short visit."

He led them inside and seated them in a newly furnished parlor that, with all its mahogany and lace, looked to have been shipped here from the home of some Eastern socialite.

For an awkward moment, they sat in pretty chairs opposite each other and smiled with a sense of waiting.

Then, Mr. Boone said, "This certainly is a wonderful surprise, and I do hope you will change your mind about lunch."

"No thank you, Mr. Boone," Hannah said. "We were busy in the kitchen this morning, and... oh my goodness, Tilly. We've forgotten Mr. Boone's basket. Will you be a dear and go out to the carriage and fetch it, please?"

"Sure, Miss Hannah," the little orphan girl said, hopping up at once.

"A delightful child," Mr. Boone said as Tilly left.

"She is, indeed, Mr. Boone. She is my heart. But I must apologize for her behavior the last time we visited."

"Please don't apologize," he said, staring at her strangely again. "Not for that. Not for anything. Ever."

And now, even his voice was strange. Thick with intensity.

"Miss Miles," he said after a brief hesitation, "I'm so glad to have a moment alone with you."

Panicked by what he might say next, Hannah pounced. "As am I, Mr. Boone. I've been hoping we might still talk business."

For a split second, disappointment showed on his face. A broad smile wiped it away almost instantly. "Of course, Miss Miles. I am always happy to talk business with you."

"I've leased a thousand acres from my neighbor to the west, Mr. Baldwin." She knew it was dangerous, starting this way because the confession empowered Mr. Boone. With her having already leased the ground, she needed cattle, so Mr. Boone could easily up the price.

But she was counting on his goodwill.

His smile widened. "That's a fair piece of ground, Miss Miles. I'm happy to hear you've secured it... and hopeful that you'll allow me to sell you some cattle."

"Thank you, Mr. Boone. I've been afraid that my refusal of your right-of-way might have offended you."

He leaned back and shook his head. "Not at all, Miss Miles, not at all. Again, I must apologize for not saying something sooner. I could kick myself."

"No need to apologize, Mr. Boone. I'm just pleased that I didn't offend you."

"Of course not," he said and glanced to the side as a man in tails rolled a tea cart into the room. "Ah, our tea service has arrived. Thank you, Mr. Williams."

"Of course, sir."

As the man was serving them tea, Tilly returned with the basket Hannah had forgotten in her nervousness.

She presented it to Mr. Boone, who opened the lid with

great ceremony and exclaimed at the sight of a fresh-baked apple pie.

His enthusiasm made Hannah very happy.

Mr. Boone sent the pie away with Mr. Williams, and the three of them settled down to their tea.

Hannah was trying to think of the best way to say what she needed to say, when Mr. Boone surprised her.

"You need cattle to fill those acres, correct?" he said.

"Yes, sir."

"Then you have come to the right place."

"I'm very pleased to hear that, Mr. Boone."

"And I'm very pleased to find myself sitting across from you again." During the awkward pause that followed, he gave her another strange smile.

Tilly slurped her tea loudly.

Hannah glanced in her direction, saw the child grinning like a monkey again, and realized Tilly had meant to break the awkward moment.

"Excuse me," Tilly said.

"Nonsense," Mr. Boone laughed. "It does my heart good to hear a young lady enjoying her tea. Do try the biscuits, Miss Tilly. They are quite delicious."

"Thank you very much, Mr. Boone," the girl said, lifting the tiny plate of biscuits from her setting. "I will."

"Now, Miss Miles," Mr. Boone said, turning to Hannah again, "the last time you were here, I believe I offered you steers for eight dollars a head."

"Yes, Mr. Boone. It was very generous of you."

"Nonsense, Miss Miles. I am happy to sell cattle to you. I might make more money by waiting and selling them in

Cheyenne but selling you cattle won't cost me a thing. In fact, I'll still make money. And as I've said, I have plenty of money. At this point in my life, I am more concerned with other things, things money can't buy, things like family."

"And friends?" Tilly asked.

He smiled at the orphan girl. "Yes, Miss Tilly. And friends."

"You're very kind, Mr. Boone, and very wise," Hannah said.

"I could say the same of you, Miss Miles. As I said last time you visited, I hope we can do business together and marry our fates and fortunes."

Inwardly, she flinched at his phrasing. She did remember his saying something similar that night at supper. It rattled her.

Was Tilly right? Was he trying to ensnare her romantically?

Her response was cautious. "Well, I certainly would like to buy some cattle from you, at least."

"Excellent," Mr. Boone said. "How many head?"

"That will depend upon the price, of course," Hannah said. "Likely somewhere between two hundred and four hundred."

A huge smile lit Mr. Boone's face. "Outstanding. That's a much larger number than you had previously considered."

"Yes, the acquisition of grazing land allows me to make such a consideration."

"Well, I applaud you. I really do. It takes courage to consider such a business move."

"Thank you, Mr. Boone."

"I believe in rewarding courage," he said. "Here is my proposition. I will sell you as many steers or whatever cattle you prefer for six dollars a head."

"Six dollars a head?" she asked, shocked to her core. "I could never accept that rate, sir. It's far too low. I would feel forever indebted to you."

And that I do not want, she thought.

Mr. Boone's talk of being neighborly and not needing the money had convinced her to accept an offer at eight dollars per head, but anything below that would indeed leave her feeling a great debt toward him, a debt, she was beginning to fear, that he would expect to be paid not in dollars but affection.

"Not at all, not at all," Mr. Boone said. "I merely want—"

"No, Mr. Boone," she said, putting a little more iron in her voice than she had intended. "I refuse to pay any less than eight dollars per head."

Mr. Boone's smile flattened for a moment. For whatever reason, he was clearly hoping she would allow his generosity. But then his smile returned, albeit slightly less enthusiastic. "I understand, Miss Miles, and I respect your stand. It is a rare person, indeed, who would insist on paying more."

"Thank you for understanding, Mr. Boone. Will you sell me cattle at eight dollars a head?"

"Yes, I will… with one caveat," he said, and stared at her again.

Oh no, she thought, suddenly certain that Tilly had been right all along. *Here it comes.*

"I insist on paying all delivery costs come spring."

She filled with relief. He hadn't proposed romance. "You mustn't," she said. "I am prepared to pay one dollar and fifty cents per head if you will be so kind as to drive my cattle to market next spring."

Mr. Boone shook his head. "I refuse to sell you so much as a single steer unless you submit to my wishes on this matter,

Miss Miles. I am already sending nine thousand head north come spring. And the cattle I'm selling you are already accounted for. I've already hired the drovers."

"But the money—"

"Means nothing to me," he interrupted. "You make it very difficult for a man to be kind, Miss Miles. Besides, you will recall my concern about water."

"Yes," she said, feeling bad now for having turned down his right-of-way request. It seemed foolish now, having thought he might consider ruining her by driving his herd back and forth over her property.

"Well, by cutting out a few hundred head, you will be alleviating my water requirement. The wells are coming along, but it will put my mind at ease, knowing that I have fewer cattle to water." He stuck out his big hand. "Do we have a deal, Miss Hannah?"

She hesitated only briefly, not because she was uncertain about the deal but because she was doing new calculations in her head.

"Yes, Mr. Boone," she said, shaking his hand. "We do."

"And how many head would you care to purchase?"

"Four hundred head," she said, and her stomach twisted within her.

She was gambling everything on this deal. After leasing ground and buying cattle, she would have fewer than five hundred dollars remaining.

That was a lot of money, of course, but she still needed to hire additional hands to oversee the new cattle. Besides, having grown up on the ranch, she knew the truth that all ranchers learned sooner or later: what seemed like a lot of money never ended up being a lot of money once it came time to spend it.

Unless, of course, this cattle deal worked out the way Mr. Boone said it would.

Because if she sent four hundred head of cattle to the market, she stood to make over twenty-two thousand dollars... and over nineteen thousand dollars of pure profit after recuperating her costs.

That wouldn't make her rich, but she had no interest in being rich, just as she had no interest in buying fine things like Mr. Boone's estate. What she was interested in were more fundamental things: stability, independence, and never, ever having to worry again.

"Wonderful," Mr. Boone said, his brightest smile returning again. "Very courageous, indeed. I salute you, Miss Miles."

"Thank you," she said, suddenly awash in happiness. She'd done it. She'd secured the ground and the cattle, and even if this deal didn't make her the unfathomable profits it promised, she definitely stood to earn a tremendous amount of money.

So she was very content as they ironed out the details and continued their pleasant tea... until the end, when Mr. Boone smiled again with strange intensity and said, "Please excuse me for being so forward, Miss Miles, but I've been wanting to talk to you about another matter. You see, I've been invited by Mr. J.W. Masterson, one of Jasper Flats' leading citizens, to attend a party soon, and I was wondering if—"

"Oh, I'm certain you will have a good time there, Mr. Boone," a panicked Hannah said, trying to stop him before he could ask the question that she knew was coming her way. "I do so wish I could appreciate parties the way you do. But I would die. I could never stand around, talking to strangers like that. But I am so happy to hear that you have been invited. Do have a wonderful time, sir."

His face fell at her preemptive refusal, which made her feel bad, but her tactic worked, and she was glad for that despite the fact that once more, she saw something hard and dark flash in his eyes.

Was Mr. Boone merely disappointed, or was he cross with her?

CHAPTER 16

"You're a hard worker, Lobo," Crazy Mary said at the end of Lobo's third and final day with her, "and you sure did put your back into that plate of ham and beans."

He stood at the pump, rinsing off his plate after yet another delicious meal taken outside and alone, as was his custom.

Mary ribbed him about that. She seemed to rib him about everything but also respected his wishes.

In their short time together, Lobo had grown fond of the old woman. She was a little on the crazy side, and he was certain she'd make quite a stir in most towns with her wild sense of humor and constant tobacco spitting, but she was an open book, and he found her big spirit and lack of guile refreshing.

"You do any thinking on what I told you?" Mary asked.

"Which part?" Lobo said. "You never stop talking."

Her irreverent nature had loosened something in Lobo, too, freeing him to joke with her as she did with him.

She grinned. "Well, if you weren't so pigheaded, maybe I wouldn't have to give you so much advice, whippersnapper."

"Maybe you're right," Lobo said, "but I am stubborn, so you might as well save your breath. I never did listen well."

"You'd best start. Especially where love is concerned. Seems to old Crazy Mary that if you mess up things with Hannah and Tilly, you'll ruin your whole life."

He hadn't meant to tell the old woman or anyone else about his hopes and dreams concerning Hannah and Tilly, but Mary had somehow wormed her way into his confidence. Or rather, she'd barged into it after constant attacks on his silent nature. Once he'd started talking, he didn't stop. He told her everything, not seeing any sense in holding back.

"Forget Green Valley. Head home. If you're right about this dandy boy who moved in next to Hannah, you don't want to wait a minute longer. A young woman gets lonely, there's no telling what she might do, especially because you, my pigheaded friend, have apparently neglected to tell her that you're in love."

Lobo's face grew hot at Mary's blunt attack.

He hoped she wasn't right. He hoped Hannah wouldn't fall for Brock Boone before Lobo could get back and at least tell her how he felt.

"I can't go back yet," he told her. "I won't be any good to Hannah or anybody else until I set things right with my past."

Mary spat a line of brown juice that kicked up dust near Lobo's boot. "That's a cockamamie excuse if I ever heard one. Folks are always saying they gotta fix something from the past before seeing to the future. Nonsense! Whatever you gotta do, do it when you should, regardless of the past. Get back there and tell this young lady how you feel before it's too late. These other folks, you don't even know them."

"They're kin," Lobo said, but couldn't bring himself to tell even Mary what that meant to him.

"Blood is strong, but love is stronger. Go tell this woman you love her. Then, after she tells you that she loves you, too, come on back and see your kin. Bring your woman with you and stop in to see me. Maybe I'll be able to talk some sense into her before she goes and marries a pigheaded fella like you."

Lobo laughed.

"And bring that Tilly, too," Mary said. "She sounds like a pistol."

"She is that. Come to think of it, you two are birds of a feather."

"Well, then you'd better adopt her before that cattleman does, or you'll spend the rest of your life regretting it," Crazy Mary said, sounding far from crazy.

"As soon as I finish up in Green Valley, I'll head back to Hannah and tell her how I feel."

"And what if she's already signed on the dotted line with the cattleman?"

Lobo frowned at that. "Not long ago, I would've just respected her decision and ridden on. But I couldn't do that now. Not unless they were already married. I'd have to tell her how I feel."

Mary grinned. "Sounds like a good way to get shot."

Lobo shrugged. "I never have developed a proper fear of bullets. And I sure would hate to let Hannah go without telling her the truth."

"Good man. You do that. And if she says yes, you come on back and tell me sometime."

"All right."

"But if she says no, keep away. I can't stomach whiners."

Lobo laughed. No one had ever made him laugh like Mary. Except maybe for Tilly. "I'll come back. Unless you just save me the trouble and come with me when I pass back through here."

Mary shook her head. "I can't go living among other people."

"You say that, but you seem to be doing all right, having me around."

"That doesn't count. You're weirder than I am."

"Heh. I beg to differ."

"We'll agree to disagree, O strange one. Besides, what would I do with all my stuff?"

Lobo panned his gaze back and forth across the dilapidated homestead. He had, indeed, worked from dawn to dusk for the last three days, fixing everything he could for the old woman, but the place still looked one stiff wind from falling in on itself. "I'd suggest burning it."

Mary threw back her head with a wild cackle. "That's what I like about you, Lobo. You have no class whatsoever yet still manage to speak the truth. I hate this place almost as much as I love it. And if that doesn't make any sense to you, well, I'm sorry you ain't brighter."

Lobo chuckled at her strange insult, but then he looked her in the eyes. "I'm serious, though, Mary. Why don't you come back with me? Hannah and Tilly are awful nice, and I'd be glad to have you. You wouldn't want for anything."

She looked at him for a long moment. "That's mighty nice of you, Lobo. It is. After my Tom died and I had my falling out with his people, I thought I'd live alone forever. And that's just what I've done for the last forty years."

"Doesn't mean you gotta keep living that way, you stubborn old bird." He had to talk her into coming with him. She was tough, but she couldn't last another winter here on her own. He hated to think of her dying alone in this forsaken place.

A defiant light came into her eyes. "You saying I need help? I was doing just fine before you came along, buster."

He raised his palms defensively. "Take it easy, Mary. I didn't say anything about you needing help. Though now that you mention it, you are getting up in years."

Mary gave another wild cackle. "Tell me something I don't know. You know when I was born? 1790. Next birthday, I'll be ninety-four."

"That young?" he said with a wolfish grin.

"Oh, you are a thorn in my backside, Lobo. What did I ever do to deserve such a troublesome visitor? And here I am, actually considering your offer." She shook her head with mock woe.

"I'm glad to hear it. I hope you will ride back with me. I'm serious."

Mary stared at the ground, nodding thoughtfully. "I'll think it over. You go see your long-lost family, and I'll make up my mind. But if I try riding a horse all that way, you'll be digging my grave along the trail. I'll be needing someone to pack my wagon for me."

"I might be willing to pack your wagon if you cook me supper again."

Mary spat a long line of tobacco juice into a thistly patch of weeds. "You drive a hard bargain, wolf man, but you might just have a deal."

CHAPTER 17

Two days later, Lobo reached Green Valley.

When he crested the hill and saw the valley spreading lushly away, Lobo was surprised to feel a lump in his throat.

This had been his home. Way back before the wolves, before anything, he had lived here.

A river split the valley, and several roads and paths seamed its vast acreage, which included neatly planted fields, expansive pastures, and broad tracts of fallow ground and untouched forest. Here and there, farms stood waiting, creating an idyllic picture almost too perfect for words.

I lived here, he thought, *among these people.*

With that happy thought, an old fear returned.

What if they didn't want him to return? What if they didn't believe his story? What if Mr. Smoger had been wrong, and this wasn't his family at all?

These daunting considerations stole his breath, asking

together the question that had haunted him since he had begun to understand that he was human…

What if I don't belong?

He sat there for a long time, pushed and pulled by conflicting emotions, wanting to ride down into that valley yet fearing what might happen when he did.

Finally, he chuckled, imagining what Crazy Mary would say if she could see him sitting here, hesitating.

Probably something like, *Quit wetting your pants worrying, sonny, and ride down there.*

Still chuckling, he started down the well-worn trail to the valley floor and passed through a stretch of woods before emerging into a large cornfield that sent a shiver down his spine.

That was just a dream, he told himself. *Don't go letting it spook you.*

He told himself that, but he didn't really feel better until he'd reached the other end of the cornfield and entered a recently cut hay field above which swallows dipped and whirled like otters in the sky, feeding on all the bugs displaced by the cutting.

Lobo filled his lungs with the good, green smell of fresh-cut hay and rode on, passing out of the stubble and entering the pleasant shade of a tidy apple orchard beyond which the land opened up again, revealing a neat-looking farmhouse and several outbuildings, all of them shining bright white in the sunlight.

His gaze locked on these buildings, especially the house. Again, he filled with conflicting emotions, but he kept riding forward, excitement winning out over apprehension.

Was this moment really possible? Was he about to meet his family?

And what if, despite his fears, they did welcome him?

The thought was too enormous to even consider, and as he left the orchard and entered the yard, he realized that some part of him didn't believe he even deserved such happiness.

He rode forward, delighted with every sight: not just the buildings themselves but also the three horses staring at him noncommittally from within the recently whitewashed stable, the plump chickens waddling in the vegetable garden, and the bright white sheets on the clothesline, undulating softly in the soft breeze.

It all looked so nice. It all looked like home.

"That's far enough, mister," a far-from-friendly voice declared to Lobo's right, and a boy a few years older than Tilly came out from behind the barn twenty feet away, pointing a revolver at him.

Lobo reined to a stop.

"Get down off that horse, mister," the kid said.

Lobo obliged, feeling rattled—not by the gun but because the boy looked a lot like Lobo minus the scars.

Despite the kid's physical appearance, however, the boy clearly had a much different upbringing than Lobo. He sure wasn't cut out for this moment, no matter what he thought.

"You just stand right there, mister," the boy said, a triumphant grin coming onto his face. "We got some questions for you."

The boy looked away for a long second, staring at the house as if he expected someone to join him, and Lobo, imagining the ease with which he could draw and fire his own weapons thought *dead, dead, dead.*

"You threaten a man," Lobo said, "don't take your eyes off him."

The boy snapped back around. The revolver shook in his hand. "Don't worry about me. I got you covered."

"All right. But just to be on the safe side, why don't you have me undo my gun belt?"

"I was just about to have you do that. Take it off and put it on the ground. Nice and slow, mister. I don't want to have to shoot you."

"Sounds good to me. Getting shot hurts." Lobo unfastened his belt and set it on the ground and put his hands in the air. "Now, have me step away from the guns so I can't pull a trick on you."

"Quit telling me what to do and get over here," the boy demanded. "That's it. Come a little closer. I want to get a look at you. All right, that's close enough. Keep your hands in the air."

"All right. You gonna ask me those questions or not?"

The boy stepped closer, studying his face. "Where were you last Friday just before sunset?"

"Two days' ride east of here, helping an old woman named Crazy Mary split firewood for the winter."

The boy made a face. "Sure you were. And I'm the king of France!" He jabbed the pistol in Lobo's direction as if to punctuate his disbelief.

"Quit pointing that thing at me, boy. And calm down. You get excited and shoot me, I'm gonna be sore."

"You don't tell me what to do," the kid said. "I'm the one with the gun, remember?"

When the boy looked away again, Lobo shot out both hands with lightning speed, seized the barrel, and twisted the revolver from the boy's hand before he even had time to pull the trigger.

The kid gave a yelp of surprise.

"Now, I'm the one with the gun," Lobo said without pointing the weapon at the kid. "Calm down now, boy. I am not your enemy, and I am not going to hurt you."

"Ma!" the boy hollered, his voice still full of panic. "Fetch the shotgun."

"That won't be necessary," Lobo said. He opened the gate on the revolver, let the cartridges fall to the ground, and handed the gun back to the boy, who stared at it with surprise. "Now, let's quit this foolishness and talk."

The door banged open and a dark-haired woman in her thirties stepped onto the porch, pointing a shotgun at him. Her hazel eyes narrowed—then flew wide open.

She lowered the barrel and stared at Lobo in bewilderment, an incredulous smile coming onto her somehow familiar face.

"Sebastian?" she said, leaning the shotgun against the wall and rushing down the steps, her eyes glistening with tears. "Sebastian, it's really you?"

She pushed past her son and reached up and took Lobo's face in her hands, staring at him with wonder, tears flowing freely now.

"You… know me?" Lobo asked.

She smiled through her tears and nodded. "It's been an awfully long time, Sebastian, almost twenty years, but of course I know you. You're my baby brother!"

CHAPTER 18

L obo reeled with emotion as his sister hugged him, sobbing happily.

For a few seconds, he was stunned into paralysis. Then his brain started working again, and he wrapped his arms around her and filled with overwhelming joy.

And yet, even now, holding his long-lost sister, part of him held back. It was all so big, so unexpected, that it felt unreal. He couldn't quite believe something so wonderful could happen to him.

She stepped back, wiped her tears away, and beamed up at him. "Let me see you, Sebastian. Oh, it's you. It's really you."

He smiled awkwardly, overflowing with emotion, not really knowing how to handle it and not knowing what he should do or say or think. Finally, he said, "It's good to meet you."

"Meet me?" she said. "Don't you remember me? It's me, Sophia. I practically raised you before... you went away."

Lobo frowned. "I'm sorry, Sophia. I don't remember anything."

Then she was crying again, crying harder than ever, but there was no joy in it, only loss, and Lobo felt bad, guessing she was pretty disappointed that he didn't remember her.

He stepped forward and wrapped her in his arms again and held her head to his chest. "Maybe it'll come back to me," he said. "One way or the other, I sure am happy to see you again."

"Yes," she said, nodding against his chest. "Yes." She squeezed him hard. "You're home now, Sebastian. You're finally home."

It was odd, hearing her call him Sebastian, but the name stirred something deep in his mind. The name felt right, just as Guerrero had felt right.

But there was one difference.

He had lived many years without a last name, so it was easy, letting Guerrero fill that void.

On the other hand, he'd had a name since the Padre rescued him. Maybe Sebastian had been his name long, long ago, but it wasn't anymore.

"My name's Lobo now," he told Sophia.

"What?" she said, leaning back with a confused look.

"I go by Lobo. It's the only name I ever remember going by. And lately, since I heard about you folks, I've been going by Lobo Guerrero."

Sophia blinked at him then nodded. "Okay… Lobo, then. So it's true? You were raised by wolves?"

He nodded again.

"And the rest of it?" she asked, tearing up again. "The sideshow, the brutal man?"

"Yes."

"I'm so sorry." She reached up and touched his face. "I'm so sorry for everything that happened to you."

Seeing the deep wells of love and compassion in her eyes, Lobo finally broke through the strangeness of the moment, finally understood it was all real.

This woman, Sophia, was actually his sister. He had understood that as a fact, believing her, but now, seeing that truth in her eyes and feeling it in his bones, he drew his big sister to him again, squeezing hard, and did something he never would have thought possible.

Lobo wept.

CHAPTER 19

Later, Lobo returned fully to himself.

He had moved through the shock and raw emotion, accepting this new reality, and settled into a solid happiness and burning curiosity.

His sister seemed to have made a similar adjustment. Her tears were gone, replaced by a constant smile and many, many questions.

Her boy, Davey, age fourteen, had been pretty sheepish at first, apologizing repeatedly for pointing a gun at his uncle, but Lobo smiled and shook the boy's hand and told him it was a good thing, defending the home, and promised to teach him how to do an even better job of it.

That made the boy happy. He volunteered to take care of Paddy then led the blood bay off to the stable.

"He's a good boy," Sophia said, leading Lobo inside. "He misses his father. Dave was killed by rustlers a few years back."

"I'm sorry to hear that," Lobo said.

They entered a neat little kitchen full of light.

"Thank you," Sophia said. "Dave was a good man. You would have liked him. And he would have liked you. Coffee?"

"Please."

"Have a seat," she said, indicating the small table near the window.

She made coffee. Then they sat, and she told him about his family and his past.

Lobo took it all in, recording the lost facts of his life more than feeling them. There would be time for feeling later. For now, he just wanted to know.

It turned out Lobo was older than he thought, almost twenty-three, born October 18th, 1860, in this very house, the second child and only son of Marco and Sylvia Guerrero.

"I was so happy when you were born. I was ten years old. All those years, I'd been alone. Then, you arrived. My very own baby brother. The next few years, we were very happy. You really don't remember?"

He shook his head. "Not yet."

She nodded sadly but did not cry. "Then, when you were four, you left with Mother and Father to see Mother's side of the family in Kansas. I stayed behind because Grandmother Guerrero was sick."

She shook her head, a slight smile coming onto her face. "How angry I was, having to stay. I'd been so excited to travel. It's a good thing I didn't, or I'd probably be dead now."

"What happened?" Lobo asked. "To our parents, I mean."

Sophia spread her hands and shook her head. "No one knows. Most people think they were murdered. Maybe by Indians, maybe by bandits. I used to wonder, but it doesn't matter anymore. They're gone—but you're here." She grabbed his hand and smiled.

He mirrored her smile but did not share her opinion. What had happened to his parents still mattered to him. Mattered very much, in fact. Somehow, coming here, meeting Sophia, and learning about his parents made the truth behind their deaths more important than ever.

"Tell me about your life," Sophia said. "Where have you been all these years? What have you been doing? Do you have a family? What's your profession? I want to know everything."

"Hold on," Lobo said, wondering how happy she was going to be once he started filling in the blanks.

Sophia was clearly a good, kindhearted woman, a widow raising her son as best she could. She had never given up hope that Lobo might still be alive and that they might someday be reunited. How would she react when she learned that her baby brother had become a hardened killer of men?

"I'll tell you everything soon enough," he said, "but first, tell me more. Are our grandparents still living?"

"Grandmother passed away years ago, but Grandfather Guerrero is still the bull of the valley." She smiled at this. "He will be excited to see you again."

"And I look forward to meeting him."

She studied Lobo for a second. "You look like him now that you're grown. In fact, you look even more like Grandfather than Father."

"What about our mother's side?"

"Oh, we have lots of relatives in Kansas. Grandmother and Grandfather are still alive, and we have loads of aunts and uncles and cousins. Mother came from a family of twelve. But truth be told, I only met them once, when I was very young. After that, Mother and Father died, so… well, I was busy here. First with Grandmother—she was sick a lot—and around the farm, of course, and then I met Dave and got married and had Davey, and I guess I've just been too busy all along to even think of visiting Mother's people. I was writing to one of our cousins out there, a girl named Martha, for quite a while, but the letters stopped a long time ago."

"What about on the Guerrero side?" Lobo asked. "Any other kin besides our grandfather?"

"Oh yes, lots of distant cousins. Grandfather came from a big family, but he only had three children, all boys. Uncle Sergio died before I was born, killed in a stampede. Father was the second oldest. Then there was Uncle Antonio. He and Grandfather had a falling out."

"Over what?" Lobo asked.

"I don't know. It was a long time ago. He moved out of the valley. I don't even really know him. Not really. But like I said, this valley's full of Guerreros. They're just not Grandfather's descendants like we are. So, tell me about yourself."

Lobo cleared his throat, not sure where to start or how much to tell her. Eventually, he'd probably tell her everything. She was his sister, after all. But first, he wanted to make sure his past didn't hurt her.

"Well," he said, "first thing I remember is the wolves. Even that's blurry."

"Do you remember anything about what happened to Mother and Father?"

He pictured the one-eyed man who haunted his dreams but shook his head. "First thing I remember is just living with the wolves. I don't remember them taking me in or thinking it was strange or anything. To tell you the truth, I don't remember thinking anything. Not in words, anyway. The first time I remember even thinking in words was after the Padre taught me. I mean, I understood words before he rescued me, the way a dog might. I figured out what Ahab Jackson—that was the sideshow man—wanted if he yelled certain things, but I didn't get a full grasp of language until the Padre saved me."

"Thank God for the Padre."

"Yes."

She laid her hand atop his again. "I'm so sorry that cruel man kept you in a sideshow. Have you reported him to the authorities?"

He shook his head. "He's gone."

"Dead?"

He nodded.

"Good," Sophia said. "Serves him right."

"Yeah," Lobo said and left it at that.

"It's strange, the way language left you," Sophia said. "You were a talkative kid. I guess maybe everything that happened was so traumatic that you just sort of forgot your old life?"

"Maybe. I was just a kid. Whatever the case, I made it. And here I am."

"Yes," she said with a smile. "Here you are. After the—"

But whatever she was going to say was cut off by a gunshot outside and a man's voice shouting, "Get out here!"

CHAPTER 20

"Is it from Lobo?" Tilly practically shouted when Mr. Pennsbury handed Hannah the telegram.

"Yes, dear, it is," Hannah said then thanked Mr. Pennsbury and went back out into the street, where Mr. Tuttle waited for them.

Hannah's heart sang as she read the message to herself.

HANNAH MILES, JASPER FLATS, COLORADO – SETTLED OLD DEBT in Slagville (stop) All is well (stop) Heading to Green Valley to meet my family (stop) Nearest town is Dunlap's Crossing if you want to reply (stop) Then I will come home (stop) Might bring a nice old lady with me (stop) Miss you both (stop) Lobo Guerrero, Redville, New Mexico

. . .

THEN SHE READ IT AGAIN AND SAID A PRAYER OF THANKS, HER mind whirling with all the telegram implied.

"What does it say, Miss Hannah?" the excited child demanded. "Is Lobo coming home?"

"Eventually. Here, read it yourself." She handed the telegram to Tilly.

Tilly's eyes whipped back and forth, a big smile coming onto her face as she read.

"He killed Jackson!" the orphan girl cheered, drawing strange looks from folks passing by. "And he has family?"

"Apparently."

Tilly smiled at that. "I'm happy for him. I wish we could be with him when he meets them."

"So do I," Hannah said, though she assumed his family was in for a surprise if they hadn't seen him since he was a baby. The man made an impression, that was for sure.

She felt a twinge of protectiveness. She hoped these long-lost relatives were kind to Lobo. And welcoming. But not too welcoming. Because the thought of his coming home—and she was so happy he had phrased it that way and had confessed to missing them—filled her with joy.

She was glad to see the telegram had been sent a few days earlier. That meant she was a few days closer to seeing Lobo and finally being able to tell him exactly how she felt.

The idea excited and terrified her. Mostly the latter. But that didn't matter. Because she didn't even have a choice in the matter anymore.

She needed to tell him how she felt, regardless of the consequences. His absence had removed any doubt. And her recent business dealings had emboldened her, giving her confidence and showing her what she was made of, which was tough stuff.

She just hoped it was tough enough stuff to handle his rejection if he did not return her feelings.

But now was not the time to think of such things. Now was the time to rejoice, because Lobo was alive. He'd dealt with Jackson and missed them and was coming home. And he had discovered his family.

Guerrero, she thought. *Lobo Guerrero.*

A good name. Solid and strong, like the man who bore it.

Then, she couldn't resist trying it on for size.

Hannah Guerrero.

It had a nice ring to it.

"I wonder who the nice old lady is?" Tilly said.

"I have no idea. But if Lobo wants to bring her back, she's welcome."

Tilly made a face at the paper, having already forgotten about the old woman. "Hold on… Lobo's last name is Gooey-rare-oh?"

Hannah laughed. "It's Guerrero, a Spanish name."

Mr. Tuttle smiled at that. "A fitting name for him. It means warrior."

"I like that," Tilly said. "It's the right name for him. If you two get married and adopt me, will my name be Tilly Guerrero?"

Instantly, Hannah's face set to burning, and she knew she was red as an apple with embarrassment. "Tilly, that is no way to talk."

"Sorry. But will that be my name?"

Hannah ignored her. Truth be told, she didn't even know

the answer. "Mr. Tuttle, I apologize for the delay, but if you'll excuse us, I want to go back inside and send a reply."

"You go on ahead, ma'am," Mr. Tuttle said, "and take your time. We got plenty of time. We aren't supposed to be at Tubbs's office for almost an hour."

Hannah nodded. She wanted to be early. It seemed only right, given that she was going to be interviewing prospective employees. But Mr. Tuttle was right. They had plenty of time.

She wondered again if the hands thought it strange, meeting at the marshal's office.

Well, if they did, they did. She felt safe meeting them there, and she sure wasn't going to conduct business in a saloon.

She and Tilly went back inside the telegraph station and sent a reply.

Back outside again, Hannah felt good. "All right, Mr. Tuttle. Let's go hire two new hands."

CHAPTER 21

L obo drew a gun and went to the door, ready for action. Sophia touched his arm, looking past him out the window. "It's okay, Lobo. It's only Jimmy."

"Jimmy?"

"Our cousin. Don't mind him. He can be a bit abrasive, even rude sometimes, but he doesn't know any better. He's not bad once you get to know him."

"All right," Lobo said and holstered his weapon, not liking the sound of this newcomer, kin or otherwise.

He followed her gaze to where a tall man around his age was climbing down from a wagon with a triumphant smile on his face.

She started to open the door but hesitated. "Oh, and one more thing. Don't let him get under your skin, okay? He's not one to tangle with. He has quite a reputation that way around here."

"I'll consider myself warned," Lobo said, and followed her

out of the house and into the yard, where their cousin was showing young Davey something in the back of the wagon.

"That's right," Jimmy was saying. "That's the thieving beast right there."

"Wow," Davey said. "He sure is big."

"That's right, boy," Jimmy said and clapped Davey's shoulder. "And he was coming right at me, baring his fangs. He jumped for my throat, but at the last second, I let him have it."

"Wow," Davey said, obviously impressed.

Coming closer, Lobo saw what was in the back of the wagon and gritted his teeth. It was a wolf, a medium-sized male a few years old, a once beautiful creature now covered in blood, its eyes frozen in death.

Repulsed, Lobo had to stop himself from growling.

"Jimmy," Sophia said, stopping several feet from their cousin, "I have someone I want you to meet."

"Huh?" Jimmy said. He turned from the wagon with an irritated expression and stared at Lobo, studying him.

Apparently, Jimmy didn't like what he saw because his eyes narrowed. "Who are you?"

"This is my long-lost brother, Sebastian," Sophia said, choking up a little. "My baby brother has come home again."

Jimmy's mouth dropped open. He shook his head emphatically. "That ain't right. That ain't even possible."

He took an aggressive step forward.

Lobo tensed, ready.

Jimmy lifted a hand and pointed at Lobo. "I don't know who you are, mister, but you'd best leave my cousin alone and clear out of here. Sebastian Guerrero is dead. He's been dead for twenty years."

Lobo said nothing. He just stared back at his cousin, not liking the man.

Jimmy was trying to make it sound like he was protecting Sophia from someone pretending to be Lobo; but Lobo sensed something else. The news of Lobo's survival had displeased Jimmy personally and extremely.

"I won't tell you again," Jimmy said, taking another step forward. "You clear out of here, you liar, and don't ever come back. Not ever."

"If another man called me a liar," Lobo growled, staring straight into Jimmy's eyes, "he'd already be dead. But because you're my cousin, I'll let you live today."

"Now, you men stop it this instant," Sophia said, stepping between them.

Jimmy looked around Sophia with blazing eyes. "You come here, to *my* valley, and threaten me? You got no idea who I am."

"Please calm down, Jimmy," Sophia said. "I know this comes as a shock, but this is Sebastian. I am one hundred percent certain. You were too young when he disappeared to remember him but look at him. Look at his hair, his eyes. Doesn't he look like Grandfather?"

"You're out of your mind, Sophia. He doesn't look a thing like Grandfather."

"Yes, he does," she said. "I'm telling you, this is my brother. I'll stake my life on it. If you just calm down, you'll see for yourself."

"I'll do no such thing," Jimmy said and glared at Lobo again. "I want him out of here. Now."

"Why?" Lobo asked calmly, studying the man, wondering about his desperate rage.

"Because you aren't who you say you are," Jimmy said. "Her brother's dead. You're just some imposter, trying to move in and looking to take what isn't yours."

"Enough, Jimmy. Not another word. I know just how to solve this situation."

"Kick him out," Jimmy said. "That's how."

"No. We'll take him to Grandfather Guerrero. Grandfather will recognize him."

Jimmy's eyes bulged. He looked almost panicked. "No, you can't do that. His heart couldn't take the shock, especially not so soon after what happened to—"

"Grandfather's still strong as a bull and you know it," Sophia said. "And as to that terrible business with Bannerman, this news will certainly lift Grandfather's spirits. His missing grandson has returned."

"He ain't your brother, and he ain't my cousin," Jimmy said, climbing back onto the buckboard. "Sebastian Guerrero is dead. Everybody around here knows that."

He started his mules and raced away, hollering something unintelligible as he trundled off, giving Lobo one last look at the young wolf he'd killed.

CHAPTER 22

W hen they rode into town, half of Slagville was
shuttered up. The saloons, the gambling hall, the
bordello, even the hotel. The place looked like cholera had just
paid a visit.

"What happened here," Laverne Chantilly asked an old man
standing on the sidewalk outside one of the darkened saloons.

"Jackson done got killed, that's what happened," the old man
said with a woeful shake of his snowy head. "Everything's shut
down while folks scramble, trying to figure out what to do with
everything. Man didn't have no kin, no will, nothing. From
what I hear, the big argument now's between Jackson's lawyer,
the town council, and a passel of painted ladies, all of them
trying to control his money and his businesses. In the mean-
time, a fella like me, he can't even get a drink."

"Tell me about the man who killed Jackson, and I'll give you
a drink."

The man's eyes lit up. "Name was Lobo, apparently. Blew

into town, killed a couple fellas over at the hotel, tied up the clerk. They say this Lobo's mean as a rattler and twice as quick. Orville, that was the constable—he's dead now, too, gunned down alongside Jackson, and let me tell you, mister, old Orville, he was nobody you'd ever want to mess with, that was for sure —but he came over to the hotel and took this Lobo into custody, locked him up, and they're saying he left for the night. Bad move on his part, because this Lobo, he got out. Busted right through the roof and climbed down on a rope he made out of blankets, believe it or not."

"Sounds like Wyatt Earp," Chester said.

"Uh huh," Laverne said.

"What's that?" the old man said. "You boys'll have to forgive me. I can't hear too good."

"Keep talking," Laverne told the man. "Tell me something I don't know if you want that drink."

The old man licked his lips. "Well, this Lobo, he went straight over to Jackson's house and gunned him down. Killed Orville, too, the constable, like I said. Yup, killed them both."

He stared up at Laverne with hopeful, thirsty eyes.

"All of that was in the papers," Laverne said. "Give me something new."

The man scratched his head, looking desperately thoughtful. "I don't know, mister. I just—"

Laverne started riding off.

"Wait," the man called after him. "Come back. I thought of something. I sure enough did. I thought of something that wasn't in no paper."

Laverne wheeled his steeldust and rode back to where the man stood, looking excited. "Bernie Karpotz, the hostler, talked with him. Man tried to give him Jackson's horse, but Bernie said thanks but no thanks. That's a fact. This Lobo, he showed up early, right after killing folks, I guess, and he woke up Bernie and told him he'd best fetch his horse if he knew what was good for him."

"Where is he?" Laverne asked.

"Who?"

"The hostler."

"Oh. Just down the street, mister. Just down the street on the left. You can't miss the place."

Laverne started to ride off again.

"Hold on now," the old man called. "You said if I told you something new, you'd give me a drink."

Laverne stopped and turned again. "Oh yes, that's right. I did, didn't I."

"Yes, sir, you did."

"Well, I'm a man who always does what he says he's going to do. A man who always pays his debts." He took out his pipe and sat his horse for a moment, packing sweet tobacco into the bowl with great deliberation.

The old man shifted from foot to foot with gleaming eyes, wanting the drink.

Laverne tucked the pipe stem between his teeth and struck a match and lit the pipe and puffed the tobacco to life, savoring its sweet, sweet aroma.

The old man, apparently growing cross with impatience, blurted, "Man could die of thirst waiting for you to get your pipe started."

Laverne smiled at that. Then, clamping the pipe in his teeth, he whipped a pistol from its holster and fired, smashing the silence of the shuttered street with the gunshot and the shattering sound that followed.

"Mother of pearl!" the old man shouted, hunching with fear, his hands gripping the top of his head. Wild-eyed, he whipped around and stared at the shattered glass of the saloon door. "What did you do that for?"

"I said I'd provide a drink. Go on inside and have one. Have two if you like. Drink yourself to death for all I care. My debt is paid."

The old man glanced at the broken window and licked his lips again. "I can't. That's Mr. Jackson's place and his whiskey."

"I'm sure Mr. Jackson will understand."

"Mr. Jackson's dead."

"Well, then, what are you worried about?"

"It's against the law."

"I'm sure the constable will understand, too," Laverne said, and rode down the street toward the livery.

CHAPTER 23

L obo, Sophia, and Davey rode to Grandfather Guerrero's
house on horses, not in a carriage, at Sophia's suggestion.
Lobo noticed his sister and nephew both rode well. Their
horses were fine creatures and obviously well cared for.

Apparently, he thought, loving horses was a family trait.

Nothing about Grandfather Guerrero's farm announced
him as the powerful, wealthy man who'd settled Green Valley.
In fact, his place looked almost identical to Sophia's, a neat yet
modest cluster of recently whitewashed buildings surrounded
by tidy fields, orchards, and pastures.

A shaggy mongrel barked as they approached, but when
they got closer, the dog quit barking and wagged its tail.

There was no sign of Grandfather Guerrero.

"That's strange," Sophia said, and Lobo heard worry in her
voice. "Grandfather always comes out to see us when Ranger
barks."

"Maybe Grandfather is out in the barn or something," Davey suggested as they reached the house.

Sophia shook her head. "Ranger would be with him." She cupped a hand to her mouth and called, "Grandfather?"

A soft breeze whispered through the shade trees near the house. The dog went from horse to horse, sniffing.

Off in the distance, from around the other side of the barn, came the squealing of pigs.

Then Lobo heard another noise and looked to the left just before a man's voice said, "Here."

He was tall with broad shoulders and a narrow waist. A lever-action Winchester was slung over one shoulder, and a revolver rode comfortably on his right hip.

Everything in Lobo sharpened, the enormity of the moment making everything stand out with absolute clarity.

This was his father's father, his grandfather, his blood, the patriarch of his people.

Despite his age—he had to be in his sixties—Grandfather Guerrero looked much younger. There was no weakness in him. Lobo saw that at once. He stood straight, radiating power, and his eyes, which were hazel like Lobo and Sophia's, shone with alert intelligence.

"You always come out when Ranger barks," Sophia said, sounding relieved. "When you didn't, I was worried."

"Things have changed," Grandfather Guerrero said. "I take a look before showing myself now."

As he said this, he studied Lobo.

A second later, one corner of his mouth lifted slightly in a barely perceptible smile. "I told them you weren't dead," Grandfather Guerrero said. "So you decided to come back to us, huh?"

Lobo nodded. "Yes, sir."

"Took your time about it." There was that slight smile again.

"Grandfather," Sophia said, "this is—"

"I know who it is," Grandfather Guerrero said, taking a step forward. "Get down off that stallion so I can get a look at you, Sebastian. You've changed a bit since I last saw you."

Almost smiling himself, Lobo climbed down, feeling something he'd never experienced before. He felt a deep, automatic respect for his grandfather. What's more, he wanted the man to like him, wanted his grandfather to approve of him. It was odd but primal, and Lobo didn't bother to question it as he stood face-to-face with the man and shook his hand.

His grandfather's grip was iron.

"I knew you were still alive," Grandfather Guerrero said. "I could feel it my bones. And now you're here."

He looked Lobo up and down and nodded, as if satisfied with something he saw.

Lobo, who'd never cared much what most people thought of him, couldn't help but wonder what that thing was.

"Isn't it wonderful, Grandfather?" Sophia said. She stood a short distance away from them with one arm around Davey's shoulders.

Grandfather Guerrero nodded. "It is. And what's more, it's right. It's right that you survived, and it's right that you came back to us. Nineteen years, I've been waiting for this moment. Nineteen years. I wish Ethel was alive to see you. For that matter, I wish your parents were alive. But I'm glad you're here. Let's all go inside and have some coffee."

"You two go ahead," Sophia said. "While you catch up, Davey and I will go home and get to work. When word gets around that Sebastian is back, folks will be coming from all over the valley. Tomorrow, we'll have a luncheon, give folks a chance to say hello."

Lobo flinched at the notion of meeting so many people at once, but he supposed there wasn't much he could do about it.

"Good thinking, Sophia," Grandfather Guerrero said. "You need anything?"

"I'll let you know. Let me go get started while you two talk. And Grandfather? He goes by Lobo now."

Grandfather Guerrero raised a brow. "Lobo, huh?" He nodded. "That works."

Sophia and Davey rode off.

"Let your horse into the corral before we go in. Fine stallion like that doesn't cotton to being hitched long."

Lobo nodded and did as he was told and took the saddle off Paddy's back and laid it on the top rail, along with the rest of the tack he removed.

Then they went inside.

Grandfather Guerrero told Lobo to sit at the table and got some coffee heating in an iron skillet on the stove. "So, where you been all these years?"

"All over. Mostly Colorado."

"You remember how it all started? Know what happened to your parents?"

"No, sir."

"I didn't figure. But I had to ask. Someone kills a man's family, a reckoning is in order."

"Yes, sir, it is."

Grandfather Guerrero looked at him again. "I can see you've

been around. Those two guns you're wearing tell me you've seen your share of trouble."

Lobo nodded. "And then some."

"That's all right. The goal of life is not avoiding trouble. It is doing the right thing, even when it's hard. Are you a good man?"

"I hope so. I believe I'm a better man now than I was."

"We all start from different places. It's easier for some to be good men than for others. But in the end, no matter where we start or how much trouble the good Lord lets us face, it's up to us, who we become. Are you married?"

"No, sir. I'd like to be."

"As a principle, or do you have someone in mind?"

"I want to marry a woman named Hannah Miles. And I want to adopt a little orphan girl named Matilda Frampton Kershaw."

"That's quite a name."

"And Tilly's quite a girl."

"How do you know her?"

"That's a long story."

"We haven't seen each other in nineteen years, not since you were just a little squirt. I reckon we got a lot of long stories to share. Do you remember me?"

"No, sir. I wish I did, but I don't remember anything before the wolves."

"So it was you out there in the mountains, huh? We heard something and went out looking for you a while back, but it came to nothing. Fella there said you'd been treated awful bad by a man who'd moved on but that a priest saved you."

"Yes, sir. That's how I came upon the orphan girl. I'd been

drifting here and there for a few years and stopped back to see the Padre, but somebody'd murdered him. He'd been tending to Tilly, so I kind of took her under my wing."

"All right. That wasn't such a long story after all, was it?" Grandfather Guerrero said with that hint of a smile again. He ladled steaming coffee into a pair of heavy mugs with chipped rims and brought them over and set them on the table, putting one down in front of Lobo.

"Thank you," Lobo said. The surface of the coffee swirled with bacon grease. He took a sip. It was hot and bitter and good, especially with the bacon flavor thrown in.

His grandfather sat there in silence for several seconds, studying him, then said, "You catch up with that man who hurt you?"

"Yes, sir, I did."

Grandfather Guerrero nodded and sipped his coffee. "How about the one that killed the Padre?"

"Yes, sir. All seven of them."

The slight smile returned. "Seven, huh?"

"And a few others who tried to help them."

"Well, a man's got to do what a man's got to do. As long as he tries to do what's right, no one can fault him for it."

"Yes, sir."

"Life is hard. A good man needs to be hard, too. It's only soft folks who don't understand that."

Lobo nodded, and they sat in silence for a spell, sipping their coffee and simply enjoying being together again.

No memories returned, but with every passing second, Grandfather Guerrero seemed more familiar to Lobo.

They talked for a long time.

Grandfather Guerrero shared his memories of Lobo, saying Lobo had been a downright nuisance, always wanting to shadow him everywhere and do everything he did.

He talked about Lobo's late grandmother and parents and about the valley, how he'd discovered it and staked his claim and worked hard to build a homestead and how he'd opened it to the family and how things had changed over the years, some of it for the better, some for the worse.

"That sister of yours is an angel," Grandfather Guerrero said.

"She seems very nice."

"Nice ain't the half of it. She's got a heart of pure gold. When your grandmother was sick…" He trailed off, shaking his head and staring into the dregs at the bottom of his coffee mug. "Well, I'll never forget it."

"She doing all right, raising the boy on her own?" Lobo asked. "She need money or anything?"

Grandfather Guerrero shook his head. "She's had it rough, but she's a Guerrero. She gets by. And as to money, no, I'll never let her want for anything. You need any money?"

"No, sir."

"All right. You strike me as a man who does what he has to do and takes care of himself."

"I try to be."

"This girl—Hannah, was it?—does she know you're planning on marrying her?"

"No, sir."

For the first time, Grandfather Guerrero seemed surprised. "Why not?"

"Haven't told her yet. Needed to set things straight first."

127

"Makes sense. But you're going to tell her?"

"Yes, sir. Soon as I'm done here, I'm going back and telling her everything."

"And what'll she say?"

"Yes, I hope, but honestly, I can't say, sir. She's too good for me, if you want the truth of it."

"But she has feelings for you?"

"I think so, sir," Lobo said, but something dark stirred within him, making him picture Brock Boone's handsome face. "I hope so, anyway. She's awful nice to me, and we've been through a lot together in a short time. She's watching over Tilly while I'm away."

"She sounds like a good woman."

"She is, sir. She surely is."

"I wish you luck, then. There is nothing this side of the good book that more greatly influences a man's life than his choice of a wife."

Lobo nodded. His grandfather's words made a lot of sense.

"Well, if she's waiting on you," Grandfather Guerrero said, "you'd best keep this visit short, then. You have time for the big shindig Sophia's planning for tomorrow?"

It was tempting to say no just to get out of the luncheon, but Lobo couldn't ride away from his family. Not yet. It was too good to meet them and talk with them. Doing so had opened a gaping void in him, a void he hoped to fill by hearing their stories and getting to know them.

"Good. Then you can head back and tell this Hannah how you feel. If you two get married and adopt the girl, bring them back here. We'll build you a house and get you started. You won't want for anything."

"Thank you for the offer, sir," Lobo said. The idea of bringing Hannah and Tilly here and making a life in Green Valley among his family had never occurred to Lobo, but it did appeal. It appealed very much.

But that didn't mean it was right. Or that it would even be his decision. Not solely.

"Hannah has a ranch outside of Jasper Flats," he said. "It was her father's before he died. Now she's running it alone."

"Cattle ranch?"

"Yes, sir."

"How many head is she running."

"Thirty-some."

Grandfather Guerrero nodded. It wasn't necessary to point out that thirty-some cattle made a small herd. "She doing all right with it?"

Lobo nodded. "She's a worker. Smart, too. And I've helped out a good deal." He didn't bother to mention all the money he'd sent her. That wasn't the point. "She's looking to expand. Before I left, I hired a couple of ranch hands."

"Good men?"

"Yes, sir."

"You trust them with her while you're away?"

"I do."

"All right. A man can never be too careful with the folks he hires. He's stuck with family. But hired hands, you gotta be careful."

"I did my best. I trust them. And I trust them to stand if there's trouble."

"Good. I employ a few people. I got a cook and a maid who come by a few times a week and a couple of hands who've been with me for a long time. I'm just hoping they stick around."

"Why wouldn't they?"

"We've had some trouble lately."

Lobo, who'd been piecing things together, said, "Something happened Friday?"

Grandfather Guerrero nodded. "You heard, huh?"

"Not really, sir. Mostly, folks have been dancing around it."

"For many years, my best employee was Lou Bannerman. He was a troubleshooter. He made some folks nervous on account of his past as a gunman, but all along, he was keeping them safe and keeping outsiders from running off with their stock."

"What happened to him?"

"Murdered," Grandfather Guerrero said bitterly. "Somebody dry-gulched him."

CHAPTER 24

"You'd best be going," Grandfather Guerrero said. "Your sister seems nice, but she'll nail your hide to the barn if you miss supper."

It was dusk. They'd talked for hours.

Lobo called Paddy and saddled the stallion.

Before mounting up, he turned one last time to his grandfather and held out his hand.

They shook again, staring into each other's eyes. "Thank you for the coffee, sir."

"It's good to see you again," Grandfather Guerrero said, still gripping his hand. "I'm happy you're alive. And I'm proud of the man you've become."

Then the older man hauled him into an unexpected embrace for several seconds.

Lobo said nothing. He didn't trust his voice not to crack in the wake of what his grandfather had said. It meant the world to him.

Grandfather Guerrero let him go and stepped back. "You know the way back?"

"Yes, sir. I think so."

"All right," Grandfather Guerrero said, and that subtle smile reappeared. "You get lost, come on back here, and Sophia will nail both our hides to the barn."

Lobo chuckled. "I should be able to find my way."

"All right, then. I'll see you tomorrow at the big shindig."

Lobo started to ride off, but his grandfather called to him before he'd gone far. "You be careful. Tonight, I mean, riding around. Keep an eye out, all right?"

"Yes, sir. You do the same."

From this distance, his grandfather looked smaller and somehow vulnerable. Lobo didn't like the image and waved and turned back around and rode off.

It had been a wonderful visit, so wonderful that he figured he'd still be unpacking just how wonderful it was even when he got home to Hannah and Tilly.

Sergio Guerrero was everything a man could want in a grandfather. He was a good man and strong, too, smart and wise and successful. Of course, observing these traits in their fathers and grandfathers helps boys become good men. But not all boys have this blessing. And Lobo was thankful that from now on, he would have Grandfather Guerrero to look up to.

As long as nothing happened to the man.

The thought troubled Lobo.

Lou Bannerman had been Grandfather Guerrero's employee. Why had someone shot him in the back?

Lobo had tried to get answers, but Grandfather Guerrero

wouldn't say much. Whether that was because he didn't know much or didn't want Lobo getting involved, Lobo couldn't say.

But it was too late for Lobo not to get involved. He was already involved. He'd been involved the second he learned a killer was on the loose here in Green Valley. Because even if he was only meeting these people for the first time in memory, they were his family, and he would protect them.

But how?

There was a killer on the loose, and no one seemed to have any idea who it might be or why he would have done it in the first place.

Bannerman had worked for Grandfather Guerrero for close to two decades. He was a quiet man, respected if feared in the valley, and had no entanglements or enemies.

It made no sense that anyone would kill him.

But they had. They'd shot him in the back as he was riding alone this time of night on the western edge of the valley by some place called Twin Rocks.

It was a sobering thought and Lobo did a slow sweep of the land ahead and behind. Seeing nothing alarming, he rode on, but the creep of menace remained.

There was a murderous back shooter somewhere in this valley, putting his whole family at risk. The killer had no apparent reason for murdering Bannerman, but that didn't mean he lacked motive. They just hadn't uncovered his reason yet.

In Lobo's experience, men always had a reason for killing. Men killed each other over women, money, land, or cards. Some men killed over an insult or even a glance they didn't appreciate. Men got drunk, angry, jealous, greedy.

But they had a reason.

And he was determined to figure out why someone might kill Bannerman. Then he would track down the murderer and stop him from killing again.

So much for a happy reunion. Green Valley was a mysterious and deadly place.

Then, as if voicing agreement, a lone wolf howled, long and mournfully, in the distance.

Lobo paused and listened as the wolf howled, filling the gathering night with her bottomless sorrow.

And it was a female. He could hear that, and he could feel it, too, as his grandfather had said, in his bones.

He waited, listening to her howl, feeling for her.

No other wolves howled in chorus or response.

Remembering the young male Jimmy had slaughtered, Lobo filled in the blanks.

The young male and the now howling female had paired off and pushed into this territory alone, meaning to make a pack.

Then Jimmy had killed the male and left the female all alone in the world. At least in terms of adult packmates.

"I'm sorry," he whispered in the night, feeling for this lone wolf crying out down by the river. "Do you have pups to feed out there?"

The only response was another long, soulful howl voicing all the pain and suffering in the world.

"Yeah, you do," Lobo said, nodding to himself, and suddenly realized he had more to do in this valley than simply catching a killer.

CHAPTER 25

H annah smiled, sitting next to Tilly in the front seat of the carriage, watching Mr. Tuttle, Plug, and the new hand, Desmond, escort the herd of four hundred head, mostly steers with a few dozen heifers and a new bull mixed in, across Hannah's property toward the swaying green grass of the land she'd leased west of the river.

Mr. Boone's men pushed the herd from either side and rode drag to keep them together.

"Thank you again, Mr. Boone, for helping us move the cattle," Hannah said.

Mr. Boone sat his horse on Hannah's side of the carriage, close enough that she could have reached out and touched the trouser leg of his plum-colored suit.

"My pleasure, Miss Miles," he said, showing her his deep dimples, "and it's no trouble at all. This is just business. I'm delivering my end of the bargain. And thank you again for the money. Are you certain you don't want to wait and pay me after we take these steers to market in the spring?"

"No thank you, Mr. Boone," Hannah said. "It's very kind of you to offer, but I'm happy to have paid you up front, as was good and proper."

Three thousand, two hundred dollars.

She had never handed someone that sort of money before. Never even a tenth of it. Never even a twentieth.

It was a truly mind-boggling sum.

And yet she had handed over the money without hesitation. Seeing the cattle mosey across her ground, hearing them low, Hannah felt zero qualms about spending the money.

Except it wasn't really her money. It was Lobo's.

Yes, he'd given it to her, but she felt strange spending it—especially so much of it.

At the same time, she thought Lobo would approve. He might even be impressed.

It was really happening. She was expanding the herd and putting herself in a position to make a great deal of money in the spring.

Even if the bottom went out of the beef market, as some said it would, she would still earn enough money to keep this ranch going for the rest of her life.

It was a staggering thought that made her very happy and, though she wouldn't have admitted it to anyone, proud of herself.

She was doing it. She was really doing it. She was building up the herd and securing her future. And not just her future. Tilly's future, too—and, she hoped, Lobo's future.

That was the one thing missing from this moment. She wished Lobo were here to see it.

Nonetheless, it would be wonderful when he returned and she was able to ride with him out to the thousand acres and show him these cattle and tell him, *Yes, I did this. I really did it.*

"There sure are a lot of them," Tilly said. "Can Mr. Tuttle, Plug, and Desmond really handle that many cows?"

"Yes," Hannah said, "once we get them there and settled."

"My men will help get the herd settled tonight," Mr. Boone said. "If you have any difficulty after that, I will happily help."

"Thank you, Mr. Boone," Hannah said.

Tilly picked up the spyglasses and studied the passing steers for a moment. "They look different than your old cows, Miss Hannah."

"My father believed in longhorns, dear. These cattle have been crossed with shorthorns. Do you remember Mr. Boone talking about the difference at supper?"

"Shorthorns have shorter horns?" Tilly said with a grin.

Hannah smirked at her. "What else do you remember, young lady?"

"There's more meat on them, so they bring more money at market, but they aren't as hardy and can't get by on the same forage as longhorns, which shouldn't be a problem, given all this grass."

"Very impressive, Miss Tilly," Mr. Boone said. "You sound like a bona fide cattlewoman."

They watched the herd reach the river.

Hannah tensed, knowing if there was going to be trouble, it would come now.

But the lead steer simply marched into the water, crossed the shallow river, and reached the other side without slowing.

Desmond stayed close, letting the steer lead but ready in case he veered to one side or another or got spooked by something. And Hannah was thankful for that because a stampede was the last thing she needed now.

"Your men work well," Mr. Boone commented as the herd streamed across the river. "I remember Mr. Tuttle and... what's the boy's name?"

"Plug!" Tilly said. "He's great!"

"That's it," Mr. Boone said. "Plug. Thank you, Miss Tilly. I remember him when I was rounding up the best hands I could find. I turned him down because of his age, and Mr. Tuttle refused to work for me if I wouldn't hire the boy." Mr. Boone smiled. "Looks like I made a mistake. And what about your new man?"

"Desmond," Hannah said. "I don't know much about him. Honestly, I hesitated to hire him. He came to the interview with a group of rough men."

"Is that so?" Mr. Boone said with a look of concern.

"Yes, there was a misunderstanding. They thought I was interested in hiring all four of them. When they found otherwise, they were angry. They used the coarsest language."

Mr. Boone's concern shifted to anger. "In front of you? That is inexcusable. Who were these men? Give me their names, please. I'd like to have a talk with them."

"Thank you for the offer, Mr. Boone, but that won't be necessary. There was no real harm done. I'm just thankful they revealed their true character before I made the mistake of hiring any of them."

"But you did hire their friend, this Desmond."

"Yes. He was still being respectful, so when I dismissed the other three, I asked him to stay."

"I'm thankful the three ruffians didn't start trouble."

Hannah smiled. "It helped that I asked them to meet me in front of the marshal's office. Marshal Tubbs is a friend of Lobo's. He helped me track down men looking for work."

"That was wise, meeting them there," Mr. Boone said, "but your friend, Mr. Tubbs, needs to work on his investigative skills. I'd expect better from a lawman."

"These men had just ridden into town. They stopped by the ranch of Mr. Tubbs's brother-in-law, so it was an easy connection for Mr. Tubbs to make. Unfortunately, there were no other hands looking for help."

"You should have told me, Miss Miles, and I would have lent you some of my men."

"Thank you, Mr. Boone. I do appreciate your generosity, but I am trying to do things on my own."

He smiled. "I see that. It's admirable. You are a strong woman, Miss Miles. Strong and intelligent and..."

He trailed off, and she felt herself blushing. She wasn't used to being complimented by men.

"Very capable," Mr. Boone finished. "But if anything changes, if this Desmond acts up or you need extra hands, let me know, and I will take care of everything."

"Thank you, Mr. Boone. Hopefully, that will not come to pass. I must admit that I am relieved to see Desmond work. He seems to know cattle."

"Yes," Mr. Boone said with a thoughtful look. "A lot of men know cattle. The trick is finding men who are also trustworthy.

But I don't mean to rain on your happy day. I'll stop. Because this is a happy day, Miss Miles. A very happy day. You could even say it's a triumph."

Yes, Hannah thought. *Today is a triumph. An absolute triumph.*

It was such a triumph, in fact, that she couldn't even imagine anything bad happening.

Of course, she could have no idea then just how wrong she was.

CHAPTER 26

L obo stood there, listening to the woman rattle on about people he didn't know, wishing he could just break through the crowd, saddle Paddy, and race out of Green Valley.

He'd spent a mostly pleasant morning with Sophia and Davey. Eating breakfast with them had set his nerves on edge, but he'd toughed it out and relaxed once the meal was over and they got to talking.

Then, he'd taken the boy outside and taught him a few things about firearms and facing threats.

Davey was attentive and appreciative.

So yes, overall, the morning had gone well.

But then everybody started showing up.

Despite the short notice, dozens of folks had flooded Sophia's property, set up tables, and filled them with food that visitors carted in from all corners of the valley.

There had to be a hundred of them, and they all wanted to

meet Lobo, to talk to him and touch him and ask questions and tell him all about themselves.

A red-faced man with a dab of sauce on one corner of his mouth stepped forward, smiling enthusiastically, and pumped Lobo's hand up and down.

"You probably don't remember me," the man said, smiling hopefully and filling Lobo's nostrils with the smell of raw onions, "but I'm your third cousin, Fred? Ben and Louise's son?"

The man kept shaking his hand up and down, up and down, smiling eagerly, his face seeming to get redder and redder as he launched into a detailed description of how, exactly, they were related and slid into a story of when they were kids.

"I'm a few years older than you, of course, maybe four or five, but who's counting, right? This one time, we played a trick on Sophia and made her think that—"

"Sorry," Lobo said, pulling his hand free and taking a step back. "I gotta get out of here."

Suddenly, he couldn't take it anymore. He turned and apologized as he struggled through the mass of people who were pressed close, close, close, making him feel like he couldn't breathe, like they were going to pounce at any second and rip him to shreds, maybe blatting on about relatives and old times as they ate him alive.

He finally broke through them and hurried away from their confused voices. It was all he could do not to run.

After all their talking and touching and pressing in from every side, his nerves were shot. He felt edgy, angry, defensive, desperate.

He had to get away from them.

"Lobo?" Sophia called from one of the serving tables. "Are you okay?"

"Okay," he called without turning and lifted a hand over his shoulder as he marched around the barn and hustled toward the stable.

Reaching the stable, he saddled Paddy, hurrying so no one would catch up.

He had to get out of here. At this point, he'd rather jump into a pit full of rattlesnakes than endure ten more seconds of small talk.

Coming here had been a mistake. It was good to meet Sophia and Davey and Grandfather Guerrero, but all these people and their babbling made him feel like he was covered in spiders.

He had changed mightily and believed he might even be able to start sitting down regularly to meals with Hannah and Tilly if they'd have him, but he would never adapt to crowds. He didn't even want to. Who in their right mind would?

As he was leading Paddy out of the stable, he slammed to a stop, having almost walked into someone coming the other way.

He tensed, wanting to leave without having to explain himself, then tensed again when the person said, "Whoa, buddy, where are you going in such a hurry?"

It was his cousin, Jimmy, the wolf-killer, who'd insisted the day before that Sebastian Guerrero was dead and Lobo was a liar.

With his nerves frayed as they were, Lobo said the first thing that came to mind. "What are you doing here?"

Jimmy didn't move. He just stood there blocking the way

and gave Lobo a big smile that didn't quite reach his eyes. "Felt bad about yesterday. It was a shock. I couldn't quite believe it was you, Sebastian."

"I'm Lobo now."

"Oh yeah. Lobo. Like wolf, right? Must've been a shock to you, too, meeting me when I'd just killed a wolf, huh?"

Remembering the bloody corpse of the young wolf, Lobo said, "Don't kill the female."

"What are you talking about?"

"The female wolf. You killed her mate. Don't kill her, too. Or the pups."

"Sorry, old buddy, but I have to think about the stock. Those wolves killed two calves. We can't afford to have them killing our animals."

"I'll pay for the calves. Don't kill anymore wolves. I'll take care of them."

Jimmy, still blocking the way, looked amused. "You gonna go talk to them, tell them to stop being wolves?"

"Don't worry about it. Just leave them alone, and I'll take care of it."

"You always were a bossy little cuss," Jimmy said with a light tone, but again, his smile didn't quite reach his eyes. "When we were kids, you were always following Grandfather around, trying to act like him, telling us other kids what to do and not to do." He shook his head. "I guess some things never change."

"I guess," Lobo said. "Get out of my way."

Jimmy's eyes flashed with anger, and Lobo saw his muscles tense. Sophia had warned Lobo that Jimmy was a fighter, and Lobo could see Jimmy was willing, anyway.

But he never quit smiling and did, after a slight hesitation, step to one side. "I just wanted to apologize for yesterday was all," Jimmy said. "For us, you know, getting off on the wrong foot."

"No problem," Lobo said, walking Paddy past him.

Jimmy patted him on the shoulder as he passed and held out his hand. "No hard feelings?"

Lobo shook his hand but minded his footing in case his cousin tried to pull him off-balance and attack.

"That's good," Jimmy said, shaking his hand. "That's real good. We're kin, after all. Right?"

Lobo said nothing and climbed into the saddle, aware that this encounter had honed his jagged nerves to a killing edge.

"Where you headed?" Jimmy said.

"Out."

"You'll miss the party."

"That's all right."

"But you're the guest of honor."

"They'll be all right."

"Okay. Suit yourself. Where are you going, though?"

"Why does it matter to you?"

"I'm just curious by nature is all. Hold on just a minute. I'll saddle my horse and come with you."

"No," Lobo said and rode off.

Still feeling Jimmy's gaze on his back, he glanced back when he reached the orchard.

There Jimmy stood, staring after him with that big, fake smile still plastered on his face. Jimmy waved.

Lobo did not return the gesture. Instead, he plunged ahead and disappeared into the orchard, happy to have the whole thing behind him.

CHAPTER 27

For a long time, Lobo just rode.

He felt ridiculous for having fled the party, but he couldn't change that now. He just had to avoid getting into a similar situation again.

Ever.

A man has to learn his limits and live by them, even if other folks don't understand.

He followed the main road west and crossed the river then took a smaller trail that branched off to the northwest, taking him not through fields but forest.

This side of the valley was wilder. Twice he startled deer that bolted off into the trees.

Drawing close to the high western ridge that hemmed in and defined the valley, he rode to the edge of the forest and saw through the thinning trees a herd of deer a hundred yards away, drinking and cropping grass at the edge of a small lake apparently fed by springs from the rocky ridge above.

Deciding to make himself useful, he climbed down from Paddy and pulled his Winchester from its saddle scabbard and walked over to a big oak and stood behind it and laid the stock of the rifle across a branch and shouldered the weapon and stared down its barrel and drew one of the deer, a nice-sized doe, into his sights.

The doe just stood there, broadside, chewing.

Lobo squeezed the trigger, and the gun banged into his shoulder, and the long flat crack of the rifle bounced off the western slope and rolled back across the valley.

The doe dropped.

The other deer streaked away, white tails bobbing.

The doe he'd shot staggered to her feet, stumbled a few steps, and fell again.

He waited. This time, she did not get back up again.

Lobo slung the rifle over his shoulder and walked toward the lake, leaving Paddy at the forest's edge, where the unflappable stallion had found some good forage. Lobo reckoned Paddy could use a drink but figured if the horse was thirsty, he'd smell the lake and come down on his own.

The doe was dead. He'd shot her through the heart.

Reaching the deer, Lobo laid his rifle on the ground, leaning it on a low rock to keep the muzzle clear of anything that might obstruct the barrel.

He pulled his knife from its sheath and went to work, opening the doe and removing her entrails, setting aside the heart and liver, which he would rinse and wrap in waxed paper once he whistled to Paddy and could reach his saddle bags again.

He stood, meaning to do just that, but hesitated when he

spotted two boulders sitting side by side two hundred yards away closer to the western slope.

They were huge and identical, looking almost manmade, sitting there flanking the old trail, which ran between them, angling toward a pass in the ridge to the north.

They had to be the so-called Twin Rocks.

Which meant this was where Bannerman died, shot in the back by someone who'd probably been lying in wait for him.

Lobo whistled for Paddy, who came trotting over and drank from the lake while Lobo took care of the organs and draped the deer over the stallion and lashed it in place.

Then Lobo mounted up and rode toward Twin Rocks, moving slowly and scanning everything.

The trail was old but still used regularly, judging by the number and age of hoofprints marring its surface.

He reached the twin boulders, marveling at their size and uniformity, and rode on, heading northwest.

A short distance later, he came to the spot where Bannerman had been killed. It was easy to identify, given all the tracks and the dried blood.

Lobo looked around and tried to recreate the murder in his mind.

He'd heard someone say Bannerman had been shot in the back while returning from town Saturday afternoon. Dunlap's Crossing was northwest of the valley. That meant Bannerman had been coming from up the trail, riding this way.

Which meant, Lobo thought, scanning the ground ahead and to both sides, *whoever shot him had holed up somewhere in this area.*

There was a lot of cover. Especially back among the talus at the base of the ridge eighty or ninety yards to the west.

He pictured it all happening, pictured Bannerman riding this way; imagined the crack of the rifle—how many shots had been fired? No one had said—and pictured Bannerman falling from his horse and hitting the ground and probably not getting far, given all the blood on the trailside grass.

As the scene came to grisly life, he tightened his focus. The killer had probably set up somewhere between that big pile of rocks to the left and the deadfall sixty yards on, closer to the trail.

He might have been hiding on the other side of the trail in those scrubby trees or hunkered down behind those smaller rocks, but Lobo didn't think so. Why would he go to the trouble when there was so much top-notch cover on the other side?

After all, setting up on the western side would have put him closer to the pass and the world beyond the valley, including Dunlap's Crossing, when he wanted to high-tail it out of there.

And that was just what he'd done, because the killer hadn't even bothered to rob Bannerman, who'd been found with twenty-some dollars in his pocket.

That puzzled folks. Why would someone kill Bannerman if they didn't care about his money?

It puzzled Lobo, too. But he reckoned it probably came back to money since folks said Bannerman had no enemies.

Someone had likely paid the shooter to kill Bannerman. He'd probably shot him, cleared out as fast as he could, and headed back to wherever he'd come from to collect his money.

Which still left big questions: who wanted Bannerman dead? And why?

With no way to answer either of those questions, Lobo

instead concentrated on what he could do: try to find where the killer had been hiding.

He rode to the base of the slope at the sharpest angle that made sense and started working his way slowly along the talus toward more likely ground.

There was a chance, of course, that the shooter had fired from somewhere on the slope, but Lobo doubted it. This was premeditated. No man, even a good shot, would choose to fire downhill when he had good cover and a straight shot on level ground.

A short distance later, his suspicions proved to be true.

A brass casing caught sunlight and winked at Lobo from the sandy wash behind a sizeable, flat-topped boulder.

Further back, behind a large pile of rocks, would have been a good place for the killer to hide his horse.

Lobo dismounted and looked around.

The murderer had waited here long enough to smoke a few cigarettes. Lobo discovered a pickle stem in the dust, too.

He found only a single casing, which made sense, given the size of the thing. It looked like a .50 caliber, and one decent hit from a bullet that big was all it took.

Lobo crouched and picked up the shiny cylinder and studied it for a moment.

He turned it over and read the butt of the shell and grunted at the discovery. "Interesting," he said aloud.

The cartridge was stamped .45-70-405, which meant the killer had used a .45 caliber rifle with a 405-grain bullet riding 70 grains of black powder.

Which furthermore meant he'd used an 1873 Springfield, otherwise known as a trapdoor rifle.

That was an army rifle. It wasn't all that uncommon to see civilians, especially old buffalo hunters, toting trapdoor rifles, but most folks now carried lever-action Winchesters because of their high capacity and rate of fire.

If you wanted to shoot somebody in the back and kill them with one shot, however, the '73 Springfield was a good choice.

Considering the rifle's range and power, he felt a prickle of apprehension and scanned his surroundings.

He was alone save for Paddy, the dead deer, and a large hawk wheeling on the currents overhead.

He slipped the cartridge into his shirt pocket and mounted up and started home, his mind full of questions.

Why would someone kill Bannerman?

Why now?

Was Lobo's family in danger?

And who in this region carried an 1873 Springfield rifle?

He was riding slowly, pondering the possibilities, and he felt a prickle of apprehension, scanned his surroundings—and spotted a lone rider sitting high atop the ridge, staring down at him.

At this range, with the afternoon sun dropping behind the rider, there was no way to make out his face or even the color of his horse. He was simply a silhouette staring down at Lobo from atop the ridge.

Whoever the man was, he'd seen Lobo examining the space behind the boulder.

Lobo raised a hand in greeting.

The man above did not wave back. He simply sat there atop his shadow horse, staring. Then, he wheeled and disappeared, riding down the other side, leaving the valley.

For where?

There was no sense giving chase. The man had a tremendous lead and could go in any direction—or set up an ambush in case Lobo did follow.

Besides, the man had done nothing wrong. Just because he'd spotted Lobo investigating the murder scene didn't mean the man was involved.

But if that was true, why did Lobo feel the cold fingers of menace tickling up his spine?

He headed back toward his family but stopped a short time later, when he spotted a track of interest cutting across the trail.

The print had nothing to do with the murder or the lone rider.

It was a wolf track.

CHAPTER 28

The she-wolf's tracks were perhaps a day old. By their long stride and the way they flanked the trail, running parallel to the path, Lobo knew she'd been heading home, not hunting.

So he was not surprised later when the tracks led him to the heart of the valley and angled to the right, leading him to a rocky meadow beside the river half a mile west of the trail.

Pawprints came and went along the bank, most of them leading to a cluster of rocks beside a fallen oak just this side of where the small meadow met thicker forest.

Lobo dismounted, ground hitched Paddy, and walked over to the rocks.

The mother wolf had been coming and going from the same spot for a while, meaning she had pups, and had made no attempt at stealth, which meant they had encountered no threats until Jimmy had killed the she-wolf's mate.

The den was between the stones in a hollowed-out space beneath the thick trunk of the oak.

Here, the ground was patterned with smaller pawprints.

The she-wolf wasn't home.

Lobo crouched beside the den, watching and listening and sniffing.

He smelled the pups and heard a whimper. A tiny growl sounded closer to the opening.

Lobo went back to his saddlebags and pulled out his leather work gloves and put them on, then went back to the den and balled his left hand in a tight fist and lowered it into the shadowy depression toward the tiny growl, which grew more insistent.

It was like fishing. And Lobo's gloved hand was the bait.

A second later, the pup struck. Lobo didn't draw back or struggle even when the tiny needle teeth sunk through the leather and into his hand.

Instead of shouting or pulling away, Lobo plunged his other hand into the hole, grabbed the little biter by the scruff of his tiny neck, and hauled him out.

He was a good-looking little pup, gray and brown with a white blaze on his chest, maybe seven or eight weeks old, judging by his size and teeth and the adult hair growing in around his nose and eyes. He released Lobo's hand and struggled mightily, kicking and growling, ears pinned back, as Lobo calmly examined him.

Making no vocalizations, Lobo finally held the pup in front of his face and looked him in the eyes.

The pup quit growling and looked away. He wriggled and

whimpered softly, the boldest pup of the pack finally realizing he'd bitten off more than he could chew.

Lobo shook the glove from his free hand and reached out and cupped the pup's jaw.

The pup didn't try to bite this time.

Lobo took his time examining him, then set him on the ground.

The pup slunk into the den, where his brothers and sisters yipped and whimpered.

Lobo shoved his gloves into his back pocket and walked over and got the deer and carried it back to the cluster of rocks and laid it on the ground about ten feet from the mouth of the den and sat down beside it.

The pups were probably mostly weaned by now. Soon, they'd learn to hunt, and their mother would move them away from this spot to a rendezvous point. For her sake, Lobo hoped these pups were ready for that soon. Otherwise, she would exhaust herself by feeding the litter all on her own.

He figured she and the male hadn't been together long and had probably moved into this valley recently. Otherwise, they would have had their pups months earlier. But the pups' age made sense if the two young adult wolves were new to one another and the valley.

Lobo's human side showed then. He couldn't help feeling sorry for the mother and even her dead mate. They'd had it made here in the valley. If Jimmy hadn't come along, they could have built a strong pack here, and—

He shoved this thinking from his head. It was all nonsense and besides, he couldn't fill his head with these types of thoughts, not when the wolves were tuned into his every move and even the slightest shift in his emotional state.

He had to keep his mind focused on the fresh meat. He forced himself to give the pups almost no thought at all, beaming only a paradoxical lack of concern bordering on contempt.

He took out his knife and inserted the tip beneath the soft hide on the deer's inner thigh and made an incision halfway along the leg. Then he worked the tip of the knife back along this incision, using his free hand to tug a little at the hide, peeling it away from the big muscle and exposing the fresh meat there.

He took his time with this work, knowing what would happen if he ignored the pups.

And sure enough, by the time he laid the haunch open, the pup he'd handled ventured out to sniff the venison.

There was no growling now. The pup inched closer, sniffing and licking his chops and looking from the meat to Lobo to the meat again.

Behind him, three less adventurous pups appeared, watching the scene with dread and fascination.

Lobo glanced at the pup, letting him know he saw him, and went back to work.

Every time Lobo tugged at the hide, the pup shied back. But after each of these incidents, the pup would grow bolder and come closer still.

Every now and then, Lobo would glance at him with little interest.

Lobo's apathy emboldened the pup, who got low to the

ground and leaned close and licked at the haunch, keeping his eyes on the human hunter the whole time.

Lobo sliced away a tiny sliver of venison and tossed it to the pup.

The pup grabbed it and retreated halfway to the den.

Another pup came forward and grabbed at the other end of the meat, and the first pup growled.

Lobo tossed another chunk down near them.

The second pup went for it.

The other two came out.

Five minutes later, he fed the alpha pup by hand.

After another five minutes, he was feeding and handling all four of them.

A short time later, they were crawling all over him, yipping with excitement the way pups their age did whenever the alpha returned from a successful hunt.

And when Lobo finally rode away, headed back toward the world of humans, the deer remained beside the den, and the pups were gorged with meat and covered in Lobo's scent.

CHAPTER 29

Tilly couldn't wait to see their faces. It was all she could do not to run to the bunkhouse, but Hannah had made her promise she wouldn't, so she crossed the yard in a fast walk, excited especially to see Plug's face.

Because Plug loved sweets almost as much as Tilly did, and that was saying something. When she grew up, she was going to have pie and cake for dinner and have a little meat and vegetables for dessert.

She lifted the warm bundle and put her nose close to the tea towel and inhaled, loving the smell of the sweet rolls. Then she really did want to run because she and Hannah would have sweet rolls themselves once Tilly had surprised the men. Would Mr. Desmond like sweet rolls? Probably.

Mr. Tuttle didn't really care for sweets, but Mr. Tuttle was old.

Mr. Desmond was pretty old, too. Maybe close to thirty?

She didn't know. But he wasn't as old as Mr. Tuttle, so maybe he still liked sweets.

Whatever the case, Miss Hannah sure was happy with her new hire. He'd worked hard, driving the cattle from Mr. Boone's property across Hannah's and onto the leased ground. Desmond had shown a lot of know-how and a lot of gumption, too, Hannah said, and he'd even offered to stay behind with the cattle when Mr. Boone had insisted on leaving a couple of his men with the herd "just to get them settled."

Tilly didn't know the first thing about cattle, but she was happy that things had gone well and that Miss Hannah was pleased, and she was looking forward to surprising the men with these sweet rolls then hurrying back to the house and having one herself.

Everything was coming together so nicely. Now, if Lobo would just hurry up and get home, everything would be perfect.

She reached the bunkhouse and paused outside the door, as Miss Hannah had also made her promise to do.

"That's their home, Tilly," Miss Hannah had said. "We can't just go barging in there any more than we would expect them to walk into our house without knocking."

"Yes, ma'am," Tilly had replied, figuring mostly Miss Hannah didn't want her walking in there if the men were cursing or didn't have their clothes on.

She clutched the sweet rolls to her chest and lifted her hand to knock on the door, which was slightly ajar, but hesitated when she heard Desmond's voice, sounding mean.

"What are you, afraid, boy? Take a drink."

Tilly leaned close and looked through the gap and saw Plug shake his head.

"No, thank you."

Desmond held out a bottle filled with clear liquid that Tilly, as a girl who'd grown up in a saloon, instantly guessed was liquor.

She felt a twinge of worry, remembering the trouble Plug had had in town and how he'd promised Miss Hannah to stay away from alcohol.

And then, as if Plug was reading her mind and wanted to put her at ease, the big fifteen-year-old cowboy shook his head again. "No, sir. I won't. Not here on the ranch. I promised Lobo and Miss Hannah that I wouldn't drink."

"Well," Desmond sneered nastily, now seeming very much like the three men with whom he'd shown up to the interview. "Aren't you just the good little boy? Let them run your life, huh, boy?"

Desmond took a pull off the bottle and winced at the stuff inside. He was a tall, lanky man with wide shoulders and big hands. His muscles weren't big like Plug's, but they looked hard and strong.

"It aint' about them running my life," Plug said, sounding defensive. Tilly hoped he didn't cave to the mean man's pressure. "Lobo and Miss Hannah gave me a chance."

"They gave you a job," Desmond sneered. "There are jobs everywhere. You get on the trail a while, you'll learn that. Right, Tuttle?"

"Not all jobs are the same," Mr. Tuttle said.

Tilly leaned a little and saw Mr. Tuttle sitting at the table near where the other two hands stood. Mr. Tuttle did not look happy.

Desmond waved him off.

"Lobo and Miss Hannah have been real good to me," Plug said. "I like it here. I want to stay for as long as they'll have me."

Tilly felt a little thrill at that. Miss Hannah had warned her not to get too attached to Plug because he would likely drift away sooner rather than later. But her friend wanted to stay for as long as they would have him!

Desmond held out the bottle again. She'd seen men like this before, in the saloon, men who wanted everyone to get drunk, men who got angry when anyone declined.

"This is the bunkhouse, boy. What we do here is our business, not theirs. I worked hard out there today. You did, too. We all did, ain't that right, Tuttle?"

Mr. Tuttle just stared.

"If I want to drink," Desmond said. "I'm gonna drink. That's what a man does. A free man, anyway. Come on, boy. You're a hired hand, not a slave. They don't run you. Now here, take a drink before you irritate me."

Plug made no move to accept the bottle. He shook his head.

Tilly knew Plug well enough, however, to see that Desmond was upsetting him. Plug was so big and strong and worked so hard, it was easy to forget he was only fifteen.

Meanwhile, Desmond was a man. A hard man who'd been around. A man who was pushing and pushing.

So no wonder Plug was upset.

It made her mad.

Then Desmond upped the ante, as her mother used to say. "You're a biggun, Plug, but you know what? I think you're nothing but a big old sissy."

"That's enough," Mr. Tuttle said from the table. His voice was low and dangerous. "Leave Plug alone."

Desmond took another drink and took his time, turning toward the table. Then he snorted at Mr. Tuttle. "Shut up, old man. You talk to me that way again, you'll wish you hadn't."

Tilly, who had, during her childhood in the saloon, preserved her life and the lives of others by recognizing moments like this, noticed Mr. Tuttle slip his hand under the table and understood instantly.

Desmond didn't realize what was going to happen if he kept pushing. He was drunk and mean, and if he kept pushing, he'd be dead, too.

And then Mr. Tuttle would be in big trouble.

He would have to run. And Plug would run with him.

Meanwhile, poor Plug, upset as he was by Desmond, was afraid to do anything because he didn't want to upset Miss Hannah or lose his job. But he was also clueless about Mr. Tuttle shifting his hand to the butt of his gun and didn't understand everything Tilly understood.

She didn't particularly mind the thought of someone plugging Desmond—he'd shown himself to be a nasty person—but she couldn't stand the thought of losing Mr. Tuttle and Plug.

So when the bully turned back to Plug again and pushed the bottle into his chest, demanding, "Now, drink up, sissy, or you're gonna make me mad," Tilly pushed the door open hard, making it bang against the wall and surprising the men.

Her eyes met Plug's. "Hit him, Plug."

"Hit me?" Desmond laughed. "I'd like to see this big baby try. I've been scrapping since he was just a glimmer in his daddy's eye. You couldn't hurt me with a sledgehammer, sissy boy. You want to try, go ahead, and I'll knock your teeth down your throat."

Plug glanced at Tilly with frightened eyes. She knew he wasn't scared of Desmond. But he was still scared of getting in trouble, losing his job, or disappointing Miss Hannah.

Meanwhile, Mr. Tuttle was pushing his chair back.

Tilly knew she had to do something. Right now.

"Hit him, Plug!" she shouted. "I saw everything. You won't get in trouble. Hit him as hard as you can!"

Plug raised his fists to his belly but hesitated.

Desmond slammed the bottle onto the table and raised his own fists. "Come on, then, dough boy. Hit me with your best shot."

But Plug hesitated, still afraid of the repercussions.

"You're being too nice," Tilly said, realizing that her friend was not going to swing—and understanding she had to change that. She took a step forward. "Just because Desmond is an old, weak sissy doesn't mean you can't hit him."

The drunken man whipped his head around, eyes blazing with fury, just as Tilly had hoped. "What did you say to me, you little brat? I'll teach you to talk to me that way!"

Desmond took a step toward her but jerked to a stop when Plug seized his arm—again, just as Tilly had known he would.Cursing, Desmond pulled his arm free, lurched toward Plug, swinging a wild haymaker...

And walked straight into Plug's big fist.

There was a meaty thump, like someone hitting a boiled ham with a bat, and Desmond fell back onto the floor and lay there, motionless, arms flung wide, completely unconscious.

CHAPTER 30

"D id you practice with that six-shooter the way I showed you, Davey?" Lobo asked the boy.

"Yes, sir."

"Good. Something else I want you to do. Work on your reloading speed. The more you do it, the faster you'll get, and the more likely your hands will do their job if you're under a lot of pressure."

The boy's eyes glittered with interest. "You mean like in a gunfight, Uncle Lobo?"

"That's exactly what I mean."

Sophia frowned at him from across the table.

"Not that a gunfight is something to hunt for," Lobo said to appease her.

"I know, sir," Davey said. "You sure made that clear when you were teaching me to draw faster."

"Well, it's worth saying twice. Gunfights are a last resort." Then, wanting his sister to hear the whole truth, Lobo added,

164

"but this is the West, and a lot of men end up in situations of last resort. I sure would hate for you to be in that position and not know how to win."

"Yes, sir."

"All right," Sophia said. "Let's hope the gunfights hold off till tomorrow, at least, because it's time for you to go to bed, young man."

"Aw, Ma, do I have to? I want to talk to Uncle Lobo."

"No, son," Sophia said. "It's past bedtime. Get on up there. You're supposed to help your great-grandfather tomorrow, and you know he will expect you to work hard."

"Yes, ma'am," the boy said. "Goodnight, then." The boy stood and held out his hand. "Goodnight, Uncle Lobo."

"Goodnight, Davey. I'll see you in the morning."

As the boy's footsteps trudged upstairs, Lobo said, "You're doing a good job with him, Sophia. He's a good kid."

"Thank you, Lobo. I know he is, but that's nice to hear. I'm so glad you're here. Not just to see you. But for Davey, too. It's been hard for him, not having a father."

Lobo nodded. "At least he's got Grandfather Guerrero."

This made Sophia smile. "Yes, that's true. And of course, Grandfather has taught Davey a lot, and Davey thinks the world of Grandfather, but it's different with you. Davey is impressed. You're younger, and you've seen the world."

"Well, I'll do my best not to lead him astray."

"May I ask you something, Lobo?"

"Go ahead."

"What happened today? At the luncheon, I mean. I looked up, and suddenly, you were pushing through everybody like you were going to be sick. The next thing I knew, you were long gone."

"Sorry to leave so abruptly. There were just too many people, too much talking, too many folks getting in close. I struggle with that."

"Are you okay now?"

"Yeah, I'm okay."

They were quiet for a moment.

Then Sophia asked, "Is that from living with the wolves?"

"Yes."

"I can't imagine. But I'm sorry I put you in the situation."

"It's my fault. You had no way of knowing. I should've said something. I thought maybe I could get through it, but then…"

"I'm sorry, Lobo."

"Don't apologize. You went to all that time and trouble, and I ran out on the party. Were people upset?"

"Confused, I guess. Then Cousin Jimmy came in and started stirring the pot."

"I don't like him."

Sophia frowned. "I'm sorry. But you didn't threaten him, did you?"

"No."

"He said you threatened him."

Lobo felt a fire light in his chest. "I never threatened him. Why would he lie like that?"

"I have no idea. Jimmy's different. Seems like he's always mixing it up with somebody."

"Well, if he's fixing to mix it up with me, he's barking up the wrong tree," Lobo said, remembering the dead wolf and the way Jimmy had blocked his path, smiling, trying to get him going.

"Don't do anything. He's a fighter."

"So am I."

"But if you do anything, he'll sic the sheriff on you."

"That sounds like something he'd do. What does Jimmy have against me, anyway?"

"I don't know. Maybe it's just because he wants to be the center of attention. He came here yesterday, wanting to impress us with the dead…" she trailed off, looking uncomfortable, then said, "with the animal he killed. But you were here, so it ruined his surprise. Plus, you weren't afraid of him."

"Why would I be?"

"Most folks are around here. Not Grandfather Guerrero, of course, but everyone else treads lightly around Jimmy. He's got a reputation. He's no one to mess with."

Picturing the cartridge in his shirt pocket, Lobo said, "Has he ever killed anybody?"

Sophia frowned. "I've heard stories."

"Oh yeah? What kind of stories?"

"I've heard a couple of them. About Jimmy fighting with other men. Not here in the valley. But in town, at the saloons. Folks say he got in a fight with one man and knocked him down and kicked him in the head a bunch of times, and the man was never right again."

"Why would he kick the man if he was already down?"

Sophia looked frightened. "Jimmy's got an awful temper."

Lobo's hackles rose, seeing her fear. "He ever hurt you?"

She shook her head. "He's knows if he did, Grandfather

Guerrero would kick him out of the valley. And that would be the end of his dream."

"Which is?"

"To replace Grandfather Guerrero. Jimmy wants to own the valley and wants everyone to respect him."

"Good luck with that. He could own the whole United States, and folks wouldn't respect him. No one respects a man who can't control his temper. They might fear him, but they never respect him."

"Just be careful around him."

"I can handle myself."

"I know you can. Or at least it seems that way. I just don't want anything to happen to you."

Lobo looked at her. For a second, he considered telling her everything, explaining all that he'd been through, all the men he'd killed, but he decided against it.

His showing up here had been a big shock to his sister. A good shock, but a shock all the same. And at this point in time, she seemed to think he was a good man.

But if he told her everything he'd seen and done, she might not feel that way anymore. He wouldn't do that to her. She'd waited all this time for him. He couldn't stand the thought of hurting or disappointing her.

"So where did you go, anyway?" Sophia asked. "When you left the luncheon, I mean. Where did you ride off to?"

Lobo considered telling her about the wolves but decided against it. She wouldn't understand. People understood nothing about wolves, and he didn't want to scare her.

"Cut across the valley," he said. "Came across the spot where Bannerman got killed and had a look."

Sophia looked sick. "All by yourself? That's dangerous, Lobo. Don't look at me that way. I know you can take care of yourself, but Mr. Bannerman was tough, too. Lot of good that did him."

Remembering the man on the ridge, Lobo nodded. "Whoever killed him waited behind some rocks with a powerful rifle."

"How do you know that?"

"Because I found the spot… and this." He reached in his shirt pocket and showed her the casing.

Sophia shuddered. "Is that what the killer used?"

Lobo nodded.

"Put it away, please. I don't even want to see it."

He dropped the casing back in his pocket. "I'm trying to figure out why someone would have killed Bannerman, but no one has any idea. Apparently, he had no enemies, and the killer didn't even rob him."

"I have no idea. I don't even like to think about it."

"Well, we have to think about it. I got a feeling whoever did it isn't done yet. And I don't want anybody else getting hurt."

Sophia's eyes bulged at the thought. "You think he might shoot somebody else?"

"I have no idea. But unless we come up with a good reason for someone to kill Bannerman, we have to assume the killer will strike again. Did Bannerman have a woman?"

"Not that I heard of. Nobody in the valley. In town, maybe? But again, not that I know of. You could ask Grandfather Guerrero. He and Mr. Bannerman were together every day for years and years. Since around the time you disappeared. I can't remember exactly when Grandfather hired him, but it was around that time."

"Exactly what sort of work did Mr. Bannerman do for Grandfather?"

"Different things down through the years. He did some hiring for him and handled all of his firing. He delivered messages and escorted people and things and cattle back and forth from different places. He ran down rustlers a couple of times. A couple of times that I know of, anyway. Probably it was more than a couple of times. But mainly, he was a bodyguard."

"Bodyguard? Why would Grandfather need a bodyguard?"

"I don't know. Truth be told, I never even really questioned it. Grandfather does what Grandfather does. He's a very powerful man, very important. Not just here in the valley but in the region. So it never seemed strange, him having a gunman around."

Lobo nodded, taking everything in. There was a puzzle here. He just couldn't see all the pieces yet.

"There's a chance Mr. Bannerman was killed by the Triple G boys," Sophia said. "That's what I heard at the luncheon today. Folks are talking about it."

"Who are the Triple G boys?"

"The Triple G is a ranch west of here, just the other side of the valley."

Remembering the ridge rider, Lobo said, "Why would they kill Bannerman?"

"I don't know. Some cattle dispute, probably. Men are always ready to fight over cattle."

"Or anything else."

"Yeah," Sophia said sadly.

"How come you didn't mention the Triple G before?"

"You asked about enemies. I never heard of Mr. Bannerman having trouble with anyone over there. Besides, Grandfather already went to town and told the sheriff everything. He's looking into it."

"Sounds like I gotta talk with Grandfather again."

"Just be careful, Lobo."

"Talking to Grandfather?"

Sophia laughed through her worries. "No. Just be careful, I mean. I already lost you once. I don't want to lose you again. So just be careful, okay?"

He could see she was holding back and that there was more to it. "Why should I be careful, Sophia?"

"Because not everybody will be happy that you're back."

"Why not?"

"Because when Grandfather dies, Green Valley is all yours."

"What?"

"Uncle Sergio, Grandfather's oldest son, died young. He had no children. So Father became Grandfather's heir. Father died. You were Father's heir. So that makes you Grandfather's heir."

"Me? I can't be the heir."

"You are."

He shook his head. The notion was ridiculous. "I can't inherit this valley. I never put in even a single day's work making this place what it is. Who's been the heir all along? Since everyone thought I was dead?"

"Grandfather Guerrero never thought you were dead. He always said you were alive."

"Well, who would have inherited everything if I was dead?"

"Nobody knows."

"Would it have been you?"

She shook her head. "Maybe it would have passed to my husband if he was still alive? But no, it wouldn't come to me. It would pass to a male."

"Davey, then?"

Sophia shrugged. "Maybe? I really don't know, Lobo."

Lobo thought about it. He and Sophia were their father's only children. That left only one other possibility he could think of.

"What about our uncle, Jimmy's dad?"

Sophia shook her head. "Not after Grandfather and Uncle Antonio argued. Grandfather ran him out of the valley. Uncle Antonio has lived up in Dunlap's Crossing for a long time. Grandfather would never give him the valley."

"Maybe I'll track down Uncle Antonio when I'm in town and talk to him."

Sophia looked frightened. "You're going to Dunlap's Crossing?"

Lobo nodded.

"Well, I'd steer clear of Uncle Antonio. He's a hard man."

"Maybe I will," Lobo said, and thought, *and maybe I won't.* "But I still have to go to town. I'm hoping for a telegram."

"From that woman you told me about, Hannah?"

He nodded.

"I'm happy for you, Lobo. You're a good man. You deserve a good woman. I hope I can meet her someday. Tilly, too."

"I hope so, too," he said, picturing the smiling face of Brock Boone. "I really hope so, Sophia."

CHAPTER 31

Sitting at the table, waiting for Tilly to return, Hannah peeled away the tiniest fragment of a sweet roll and tucked it into her mouth, where it melted on her tongue. She smiled as the lovely tastes of sugar, dough, and cinnamon all blended together. Then she said a quick prayer of thanks, not only for the delicious treat but also for the wonderful day and what it meant.

She had done it, praise God. With the help of Mr. Boone and several hired hands, she had secured a large enough herd to change her and Tilly's lives forever.

Four hundred new shorthorn crosses now grazed just across the river on ground she had leased. The herd was no longer a dream, an idea, or even a plan.

The herd was real. And it was hers.

Or rather, she supposed, it was Lobo's, since all the money had come from him, but she knew Lobo well enough to guess what he would say about that.

I gave you that money. You bought the cattle. It's your herd.

She smiled, loving him.

It didn't matter who owned the herd, Hannah or Lobo. Either way, she had made the deal and seen it through, and she hoped that Lobo would return soon and that they would throw together, herd and all, forever and ever.

The thought made her smile.

Because suddenly, it was easier to believe.

After all, if she had the vision and spirit to buy four hundred head of cattle, if she, a young woman with no experience in such matters, could turn that dream into reality, why couldn't she tell Lobo how she felt and help him to understand that they could have a wonderful life together?

The door banged open, and Hannah leaned back with surprise, her hand going automatically to her dress pocket and the derringer she kept there.

"Come quick, Miss Hannah!" Tilly said. "There's trouble in the bunkhouse."

Hannah jumped up from her seat. "What sort of trouble?"

"Come on," Tilly said, starting out the door. "Mr. Desmond got drunk and tried to hurt Plug."

"What?" Hannah called, hurrying after her. She had heard the girl perfectly fine; but her mind was having a hard time making the words real.

Desmond had gotten drunk? And he'd tried to hurt Plug?

Running after Tilly, Hannah felt a rush of dread and disappointment.

It had all been going so well. Everything had been going perfectly. But now this.

Doubt whispered in her mind, *You were so proud of yourself. Now what?*

Hannah caught up with Tilly as they raced around the barn then pulled away from her and was through the door of the bunkhouse.

Hannah gasped at the sight within.

Desmond sat on the floor with his hands behind his back, a dazed expression on his battered face. He was bleeding from the nose and mouth and from a nasty gash across one eyebrow. That eye was swollen shut.

Mr. Tuttle sat a short distance away, holding a revolver in one hand.

Plug gave a start when Hannah came through the door and looked at her with an expression of panic. "I'm so sorry, Miss Hannah. I didn't want no trouble. But he kept pushing, and—"

"Plug didn't do anything wrong," Tilly said loudly, coming in behind Hannah. "I saw everything, Miss Hannah."

Desmond touched his split brow and cursed loudly. Then he set to struggling. "Untie me, boy, and we'll see what's what."

"You work your wrists loose and do anything stupid," Mr. Tuttle told Desmond with icy calm, "and you'll die with a slug in your guts. Begging your pardon, ma'am. But men such as him don't understand any other way."

Hannah, still badly surprised, still trying to adapt to what had apparently transpired, still reeling with disappointment, and feeling a rush of self-doubt, latched onto Mr. Tuttle's tone of calm confidence. "What happened, Mr. Tuttle?"

"Big ox hit me," Desmond said, "because I wouldn't share my bottle."

"That's a lie, Miss Hannah," Tilly objected.

"Shut up, you little…" Desmond sneered and finished by calling Tilly a vile name that no man should ever call a woman, let alone a child.

Hannah gasped.

With a roar of indignation, Plug stepped forward, grabbed Desmond by the shirt front, jerked him off the floor, and lifted him into the air in a display of almost superhuman strength. "You never talk to Tilly that way again!" he bellowed, giving Desmond a shake.

Desmond spewed curses and drove a knee into Plug's gut.

Plug didn't so much as grunt. He rushed forward and slammed Desmond's back into a vertical post with such force that Hannah was surprised the bunkhouse didn't collapse. "If you ever talk to Tilly that way again, I'll snap you in half! Do you hear me?"

Plug seemed to have finally gotten through to the drunken cowboy, who cried out with pain and then stared at the incredibly strong boy still holding him up by his shirt front and demanding an answer. "Yeah, I hear you."

Plug set Desmond on his feet but stayed close, watching the belligerent man like a hawk.

He's protecting us, Hannah realized. *That's why he's staying so close. So Desmond can't do or say anything to hurt Tilly or me.*

Through her pain and disappointment, she felt a wave of affection for her young cowhand and for Mr. Tuttle, who still sat there, solid as a rock, pistol in hand.

"Thank you, Plug. And thank you, Mr. Tuttle. And thank you, too, Tilly. Let's start over from the beginning, shall we? Desmond, I would ask you to refrain from cursing or saying anything at all until I've asked you to speak, please. Now, let's start with Mr. Tuttle. What happened?"

Hannah listened as Mr. Tuttle, Plug, and Tilly all gave exactly the same statement.

After getting drunk, Desmond tried to force Plug to join him. Plug refused. Things escalated from there. Finally, Desmond threatened to hurt Tilly, and Plug stopped him by grabbing his arm. Desmond swung at Plug and missed, and Plug knocked him cold.

"Desmond," Hannah said, turning to the glowering man, "would you like to say anything for yourself?"

"They're all a bunch of dirty liars! They all ganged up on me. I don't know why. But they're lying! I didn't do nothing!"

"It's clear to me," Hannah said, clasping her trembling hands behind her back and trying to keep her voice as calm as Mr. Tuttle's had been, "that hiring you was a mistake."

"You're firing me?" Desmond raged.

"That is correct. You are fired, sir. Plug, Mr. Tuttle, gather his things and escort him off the ranch, please. Before you leave, I will go into the house and fetch two dollars. I won't have anyone saying I didn't pay for his time."

"You'll regret this!" Desmond said. "All of you. I'll get you and you," he promised Plug and Mr. Tuttle, then swept his gaze over Hannah and Tilly. "I'll get all of you. I got friends in town. This is gonna cost you a lot more than two dollars!"

CHAPTER 32

Lobo woke early and slipped out of the house while Sophia and Davey were still sleeping. He saddled Paddy and rode out into the valley, got into position at the edge of a fallow field, and killed another deer just as the sun was coming up.

He field dressed the doe, took her back to Sophia's, and had her skinned and quartered before Davey came outside and asked what he was doing.

"Fresh meat," Lobo explained. "A man's gotta put meat on the table. That and protecting his family are a man's two biggest jobs."

The boy nodded solemnly. "Can I go with you next time?"

"Hunting? Sure. Be good to have you along. But you're gonna have to get up earlier."

"I'd like that, Uncle Lobo."

"All right, then. Next time I go out, I'll take you with me. Here, take these in to your mother."

He handed the boy the heart and liver and tongue.

"Yes, sir," Davey said but hesitated, watching Lobo wrap a haunch in the bloody hide. "What are you doing, Uncle Lobo?"

"I'm taking a quarter someplace."

"Where?"

"Don't worry about it," Lobo said. He hadn't told anyone about the pups. People wouldn't understand what he was fixing to do. "Give that stuff to your mother. I'll be back after I finish up in town."

"Yes, sir." The boy hurried off toward the house.

He was a good kid. Lobo was glad to know him.

As he lashed the hide-wrapped haunch onto Paddy's back, Lobo considered the possibility that, if things worked out as he hoped they would, Hannah and Tilly would want to move here to Green Valley and live among his family.

Don't forget me, sonny, he imagined Crazy Mary saying then letting go with another stream of tobacco juice.

How nice it would be, living with Hannah and Tilly—and yes, Crazy Mary McGee—building a life together alongside Sophia and Davey and Grandfather Guerrero.

But first, he would have to take care of these wolves, of course. And catch a killer. And convince Hannah to marry him and move here...

He shook his head, wondering again how, exactly, he had come to entertain such fantastical thoughts. Better for a man to keep his eyes and ears open and his nose to the ground.

He rode across the valley again, left the road near the river, and tethered Paddy in a meadow halfway to the wolves.

Moving silently, he walked the rest of the way to the den with the rolled-up hide over one shoulder.

Normally, with pups being as old as they were, the she-wolf would be out hunting by now. But Lobo was counting on last night's deer changing that.

Approaching the cluster of rocks, he saw crows working at the deer's largely stripped carcass and figured he was right.

When he was forty feet away, the crows took flight.

The she-wolf's head emerged from the den.

Lobo dropped his grisly package on the ground and crouched beside it.

The she-wolf disappeared into the den again. He knew that in a gorged state, she would be holed up with her pups and also knew she would be less curious and less malleable, so he couldn't hope to win her over by tossing her some scraps.

His plan was going to take time.

She knew who he was. She smelled him and knew he was the one she'd smelled on her pups, the one who'd brought the meat.

And here he was, carrying fresh meat again, something she would associate with him and his smell.

That's just what he wanted for now.

Over time, the wolves' curiosity would outweigh their caution, and they would come out to sniff him.

He would know exactly how to act then—strong, confident, mildly interested—and this would embolden them as days passed.

He would continue to bring them meat. And eventually, he would lure them out on a nighttime hunt.

Once they had killed and eaten together, he would become pack.

Then he could lead them out of this valley, away from men

like Jimmy, to a safe place where the she-wolf could hunt game, not stock, and the pups would be free to grow up and live as wolves should.

Content with this plan, Lobo did exactly what he knew he should do next, one of the things his sister and nephew would never understand. He tore away a bit of venison with his teeth, making a show of feeding, then stretched out in the morning sun and fell asleep on the ground.

He woke to something cold and wet tickling his forehead.

Opening one eye, he saw the bold, little, brown and gray pup leaning forward to sniff him.

Lobo looked at him then shut his eye again and pretended to go back to sleep, showing the pup what he thought of him.

A second later, the pup yelped.

Lobo opened his eye once more and saw the she-wolf trotting away, tail low but not clamped, the adventurous pup gripped in her jaws by the scruff of his neck.

She disappeared into the den, taking the misbehaving pup with her.

Lobo sat up, scratched himself all over, stood, stretched, and then plodded off, leaving the meat and his scent behind.

Things had gone well here. Perfectly, in fact, and he was confident that he would be able to escort the wolves to safety in a few weeks.

But now, it was time to go to town, where he would check the telegraph station, drop in on the sheriff, and maybe even look for this uncle of his who'd had such a severe falling out with Grandfather Guerrero years ago.

CHAPTER 33

Lobo rode into Dunlap's Crossing, hitched his horse outside the telegraph station, and went inside.

As he'd hoped, there was a telegram waiting for him.

LOBO GUERRERO, DUNLAP'S CROSSING, NEW MEXICO – So good to hear from you (stop) Happy to know you dealt with Jackson (stop) Best of luck with family (stop) We are well but miss you terribly (stop) You will be surprised when you come home (stop) Big changes here (stop) Hope to see you soon (stop) Hannah Miles, Jasper Flats, Colorado

LOBO LEANED THERE AGAINST THE STORE FRONT AND REREAD THE telegram several times. How he missed Hannah and Tilly.

Some of what Hannah had written filled him with hope. She'd been excited to receive his telegram and was interested in his family. She said they missed him terribly and hoped to see him soon and referred to his return as coming home.

These things filled his chest with a strange heat and made him want to hurry up and catch this killer and head home as quickly as possible.

He didn't like the end of the telegram, though, the part about big changes and how he would be surprised.

Was that Hannah's way of hinting that she was engaged to Brock Boone? Was the rest of her message, the part about missing him and hoping to see him soon, just her treating him as a cherished friend?

The notion sickened him, and for the hundredth time, he wished he had told her how he felt before leaving on this trip.

But of course, he could not change the past, so he folded the telegram and stuck it in his pocket and went next door to the mercantile, where he bought two large panniers, which he filled with things he thought Sophia and Davey might appreciate, mostly food and coffee and a box of ammunition for Davey's revolver.

He asked the merchant to put the loaded panniers behind his counter and told him he'd be back for them.

"All right, sir. You take your time. I'm open until five."

"I won't be long. Which way to the sheriff?"

"He's just down the street, sir. Take a left and he'll be three blocks down, across the street, just past the gun shop."

Lobo thanked him and left and went outside and took a left, a new idea coming into his mind.

A short time later, he spotted the gun shop and crossed the street and went inside.

A man with a neatly trimmed goatee looked up from an old

revolver he'd stripped atop his counter. "Howdy. What can I do for you?"

"You got any .45-70-405 ammo?"

The man nodded. "Sure do. Always keep some in stock."

"I'm glad to hear that. Didn't know if you would."

"Oh yeah. Couple fellas around here tote 73s."

Lobo knew he had to play this next part carefully, so he forced what he hoped looked like an incredulous smile onto his face and what he hoped sounded like idiotic good cheer in his voice. "You don't say. Well, those are men of high intelligence. I might just know them. What are their names?"

"Fella named Jimmy carries a Springfield," the man said.

"Jimmy?" Lobo said, shocked by this discovery. "Jimmy Guerrero?"

Instantly, Lobo realized his mistake. At the mention of the name Jimmy, he'd accidentally dropped his happy hayseed act and let something show in his face and voice that made the shopkeeper pull back.

Suddenly cagey, the man licked his lips. "He a friend of yours?"

"Oh yeah. Me and Jimmy go way back."

"But you don't know what rifle he carries, huh?" the man said.

It was all Lobo could do not to growl at himself. That was twice he'd messed up. "I was away for a while."

"Uh huh," the man said. "I don't remember seeing you in here before."

Realizing he'd fumbled his act, Lobo just looked at the man and let his voice go flat. "Who's the other one?"

"Sir?"

"You said two men carried Springfields. One is Jimmy Guerrero. Who's the other one?"

The man shook his head and took a step back from the counter. "Sir, I ain't at liberty to be giving out folks' names. Now, did you want some of that .45-70-405 ammo or not?"

Lobo stuffed his hand in his pocket and came back out with four greenbacks. He laid them on the counter. "What I want is the other man's name."

The shopkeeper showed him his palms and shook his head again. "I'd rather stay out of trouble than have a few extra bucks if it's all the same to you, sir."

"Tell me his name."

"Look, mister. Why don't you just forget I said anything, all right? I'm trying to do you a favor."

Grab him by the ears and bounce his face off the counter a few times, Lobo thought. *That'll make him talk.*

But at that moment, the little bell over the door rang as a father and his young son entered the store, talking and laughing.

"Hi, Steve," the shopkeeper said. "Junior. Good to see you both. What can I do for you today?"

"You go ahead and help this gentleman," the father said.

"Oh, that's all right," the shopkeeper said, drifting away from the counter. "We just finished up. I don't have anything else to say to him."

Frustrated, Lobo swept the money from the counter and went back outside.

He paused there on the wooden planks and stared out at the town, not really seeing it, his mind gnawing at this new information.

Two men around here carried Springfields.

He didn't get the second man's name, but that probably didn't matter, since he did get the other's.

His cousin Jimmy carried a '73.

Suddenly, he wanted to get back to the valley and talk with Grandfather Guerrero. It sure would be interesting to know where Jimmy had been when Bannerman got killed.

But first, he needed to go next door and speak with the sheriff and see how his investigation was going. For all Lobo knew, the sheriff had already arrested someone from the Triple G outfit and Jimmy's rifle choice was a mere coincidence exaggerated by Lobo's dislike of his cousin.

Maybe. But Lobo didn't think so.

As it turned out, he was left to stew in his suspicions, because when he went next door, the sheriff's office was locked up and a note on the front window read *CLOSED*.

That was it. No *"Be back soon"* or any indication of when the sheriff might return.

Lobo wasn't willing to waste his day waiting here. He needed to get back to the valley and see what his grandfather had to say.

CHAPTER 34

F rom the second story of his office, the sheriff watched the stranger emerge from the gun shop and come walking this way, his scarred face set with determination.

The man was tall and lean with broad shoulders and narrow hips, and he wore two revolvers in the style of a gunfighter.

He came down the sidewalk straight toward the office.

The sheriff thought of the *CLOSED* sign downstairs and started to turn from the window, meaning to go down and open the door before the man saw the sign and left.

But the sheriff hesitated and turned back to the window.

Why had he hesitated?

Because, he realized with surprise, this man had awakened something within him.

Caution... or perhaps even alarm.

Which made no sense.

The sheriff was a big, tough man who never ran from trouble. He feared no one.

And yet…

Something about the man on the street was familiar.

And menacing.

He chuckled at the absurdity of his hesitation and hitched his pants, meaning to go downstairs but suddenly paused again, nailed in place by a troubling thought.

Recently, he'd been hearing stories about a man named Lobo.

Could this be him?

Lobo.

What if…?

He tried to laugh off the chill that followed but couldn't.

Lobo.

Wolf.

Could it be… him?

No.

That wasn't possible.

But what if it was?

The man was walking away now, moving with deadly grace down the street, heading where?

Green Valley?

The sheriff had the sudden urge to fetch his rifle, throw open the window, and put a bullet through the man's spine.

He shook his head.

An absurd notion. One stemming from an equally absurd fear.

Right?

He searched his mind and heart and realized he wasn't sure.

Which meant he had to do some investigating.

He had to return to Green Valley.

With that thought, a terrible grin split his graying beard.

Because new possibilities were presenting themselves.

Yes, he had been rattled by the appearance of the man.

But if that really was Sebastian Guerrero down there, every-thing had suddenly aligned in a way he couldn't have anticipated.

Sebastian might be the answer to all his problems, the key to everything he ever wanted.

CHAPTER 35

Crazy Mary was outside, sharpening her axe, when she saw them coming out the trail.

Visitors again, so soon after her first guest in years?

It didn't seem possible.

Unless, of course—and she realized instantly, when the men rode into view and she saw their rifles and hard faces and strange attire, that this was the case—these visitors were following her former guest.

The lead rider drew close, his face partially obscured by a cloud of pipe smoke. As he reined in, the smoke wafted across Mary's face, nearly choking her with the sickly-sweet smell of death.

For a wild moment, she was convinced the rider was none other than Death himself, come at last to fetch her away to the shadowlands beyond this torturous, beautiful thing called life.

But then the smoke cleared, and she saw beneath the crumpled top hat not the grim reaper but merely one more brutish man with the soulless eyes of a hardened killer.

Behind him, the other man—obviously a brother, despite his ridiculous mountain man attire—grinned... an unsettling expression from someone so clearly devoid of humor or humanity.

"Hello, Mother," the man in the top hat said.

Mary steeled herself. "If I was your mother, I'd haul you down off that horse and cut your hair off. You look terrible."

Silence reigned for several thudding heartbeats.

Despite her terror, she held her ground, determined to die in defiance if die she must.

But the man merely said, "We're looking for someone."

"Yeah?"

"Yes." He stared at her, his soulless eyes full of menace and calculation. "A man named Lobo. Have you seen him?"

Mary spat a line of tobacco juice on the ground between them.

"Yeah, I saw him," she said. "He was here."

There was no sense hiding that fact, she knew. Because men like these weren't really men at all. They were demons. And they knew Lobo had been here.

If she denied that fact, they would hurt her. Or maybe even kill her.

And recently, she'd decided that maybe she did want to live a while longer. Lobo's offer to take her away to live with his ladies and him had rekindled a fire within her, bringing warmth and light to a life that had long ago gone cold and dark.

So she did not deny his having visited.

Besides, if she had lied, she would have lost the opportunity to talk about Lobo… and to help him.

"When?" the man in the top hat asked.

"Oh, I don't know. A week ago? My memory ain't what it used to be." She shook her head, thinking, *Careful now, Mary, you crazy old bat. Careful now, or you'll get yourself killed and never get to meet that little pistol, Tilly.*

Everything in her sharpened. She said, "About a week ago, I reckon, maybe less. Stayed here with me for a spell. Left two, three days ago."

The man in the top hat stared at her, filling the air with another gagging wave of sweet smoke. "Why did he stay here? Was he injured?"

"Not a scratch."

"Then why did he stay here so long?"

"Because I hired him to do some work."

The man studied her. His gaze was cold, reptilian. "You hired him."

She spit again and nodded. "That's right. Paid him in ham and beans. You boys looking for work?"

"No. We're looking for Lobo."

"You friends of his?" she asked, knowing exactly what they were.

"That's right," the one in the fur cap said, speaking for the first time. "Old friends."

"Did he say where he was headed?" Top Hat asked.

"Well," she said, and hesitated, looking from one man to the other, pretending uncertainty. "I suppose if you're friends of his, it can't hurt."

"That's right, Mother. We just want to help him."

"Well, if that's the case," she said, and smiled conspiratorially, "I'll tell you. Lobo said he was playing a trick on anybody who was after him."

That got their attention.

"What sort of trick?" Fur Cap asked.

"Wait till you hear this," she said. "He went north toward the Gillespie Trail. He's taking that east. The sly fox is heading back to Slagville."

"Slagville?" Fur Cap said with obvious surprise. "What for?"

"You boys might not know it, but I guess I'll tell you, seeing as you're friends of his. Lobo got into some trouble back in Slagville."

"We heard something about that," Top Hat said, "which is why we're surprised he's riding back."

"Well, apparently, he had a mix-up with a fella by the name of Jackson back there. This Jackson, he owned half of Slagville. Had a whole bunch of money. Get this. Jackson had twenty thousand dollars' worth of gold bars."

She paused, letting them chew on that for a moment.

"No sense riding back after the gold," Top Hat said. "Whole town's fighting over Jackson's money."

Mary spit tobacco juice and let go with a wild cackle. "Not this money, they ain't! It's hidden where they'll never find it. But Lobo knows where it is. He got it out of Jackson before he killed him."

"Where's the gold?" Fur Cap asked.

Mary made a show of looking back and forth between them a couple of times. "You boys promise you're friends of his?"

"Oh yeah," Fur Cap said. "We go way back."

"All right, then," she said, and laughed again. "Are you ready for this? Jackson buried the gold in a little stone sarcophagus five feet under the outhouse cesspool!"

She threw back her head with a fit of wild laughter and was still cackling when they rode off, heading east for Slagville and the disappointing excavation awaiting them there.

Hopefully, she'd bought Lobo enough time to see his family and clear out of Green Valley before these bounty hunters caught wind of him.

And hopefully enough time for him to come back and get her before these wicked men returned, or Crazy Mary McGee was in for a world of hurt.

CHAPTER 36

W hen Lobo rode up to his grandfather's house, he saw
Grandfather Guerrero and Davey stacking firewood
under the porch up close to the house, where it would be easy
to reach after the snow started falling in a few months. It was
good work for a cool, bright day like today, and Lobo was
happy to see his young nephew sweating and smiling.

Grandfather Guerrero was, indeed, teaching Davey to be a
man. Stacking a neat woodpile months before the first snow
was a perfect example of preparing the boy for manhood.

But Lobo didn't like the fact that neither Davey nor Grandfather Guerrero had spotted him until the dog, who'd taken his
own, sweet time noticing Lobo's approach, had finally barked.
Remembering Davey's awkward attempt at holding him pris-
oner, Lobo reckoned that Grandfather Guerrero, while smart
and good and likely tough as nails, hadn't done a lot of
gunwork.

Which helped to explain why he'd hired Bannerman in the

first place. And laid bare the fact that Bannerman's death had left Grandfather vulnerable.

This in no way lessened Lobo's respect for his grandfather. Most men had never faced a gunman, let alone done the sort of work Lobo had.

But it did leave him feeling uneasy about Grandfather Guerrero's safety and reminded him to spend more time with Davey, teaching him to handle his firearms and himself.

"Hi, Uncle Lobo," the boy said, beaming up at him.

"Davey," Lobo said with a nod. "Grandfather."

"Good to see you, Lobo," Grandfather Guerrero said. "Why don't you climb down and give us a hand?"

"I'd be happy to help later, sir," Lobo said, "but I have to take care of something."

"All right," Grandfather Guerrero said. "You need a hand?"

"No, sir. But I do have to ask you something."

"All right. Climb down. Give that horse a break."

Lobo hesitated for an instant, because he wanted to take care of business, but then nodded and said "yes, sir" and climbed down and did as his grandfather suggested.

"You wanted to ask me something," Grandfather Guerrero said after Lobo shook hands with Davey and him.

"Yes, sir."

"Is it something you can say in front of Davey?"

Lobo glanced at the boy, who watched him hopefully.

"By the time I was his age, I'd killed deer with my teeth and fought grown men in a sideshow. I reckon Davey can handle anything, so long as it's the truth."

Grandfather Guerrero nodded. "All right, then. Ask."

"Where was Jimmy when Bannerman got killed?"

Grandfather Guerrero's pupils swelled, but his voice stayed level. "I think he was hunting."

"Hunting, huh?"

"You don't think he had something to do with it, do you?"

"I don't know."

"I heard you two didn't really hit it off."

"No, I don't like him, but that's not why I'm asking."

Lobo fished in his pocket and came out with the killer's casing and handed it to his grandfather.

"What's this?" Grandfather Guerrero said.

"Casing."

"I see that. Chambered in .45-70-405. So a trapdoor gun."

"Not just any trapdoor gun. The gun that killed Lou Bannerman."

Grandfather Guerrero frowned at the casing. "You're sure?"

Lobo nodded, then told them about his trip to the western edge of the canyon, explaining how he'd discovered where Bannerman had fallen and where the killer had hidden. He also told them about the rider atop the ridge but did not bother to tell them about the wolves, knowing they wouldn't understand.

"Now I see why you asked about Jimmy," Grandfather Guerrero said. "You know he totes a trapdoor?"

"I do. Stopped by the gun shop in Dunlap's Crossing, and the man said Jimmy carried a '73."

"Did Uncle Jimmy kill Mr. Bannerman?" a frightened-looking Davey asked.

"No," Grandfather Guerrero said. "We're not saying that. A lot of folks carry trapdoor rifles."

"According to the man at the gun shop," Lobo said, "only Jimmy and one other man around here carry '73s."

"That he knows of," Grandfather Guerrero said.

Lobo nodded, wondering why his grandfather seemed so rattled. Probably because Jimmy was also his grandson. No man wants to think his descendants are capable of cold-blooded murder.

"Fair enough," Lobo said, "but I'm going to ask Jimmy where he was Friday."

"Like I said, he was hunting."

"I'm gonna go ahead and ask him anyway. I want to look him in the eyes when he tells me."

"You think he's lying, Uncle Lobo?" Davey asked.

Lobo laid a hand on the boy's shoulder. "I'm not saying he's lying. But whenever you talk with a man, you make sure and look him in the eyes. Sometimes, his eyes tell you more than the mouth."

The boy nodded solemnly.

"Don't go over there and stir things up, Lobo," Grandfather Guerrero said.

"I'm going to ask him. That's all. If that stirs him up, so be it. I'm not going to tiptoe around Jimmy."

Grandfather Guerrero frowned. "He's got an awful temper on him."

"I'm not afraid of him."

"No," Grandfather Guerrero said, and his frowned deepened. "I don't suppose you're afraid of anybody."

"No, sir," he said, but his mind conjured the image of the one-eyed man from his dreams. "Not particularly."

"Well, I hope you two don't have trouble. I surely do. You're both my grandsons. It ain't right, cousins fighting."

"I don't want to fight."

"Good. Promise me you won't shoot him?"

Now, it was Lobo's turn to frown. "I'm afraid that's a promise I can't make, sir."

"Sure you can."

"Won't, then. You start promising not to shoot somebody," he said with a glance toward Davey, wanting the boy to hear and remember this, "sooner or later, your promises will get you killed. I don't want to shoot anybody, but if he tries to shoot me, I will put him down."

Grandfather Guerrero nodded, looking thoughtful, and Davey stared at Lobo with bulging eyes.

A short time later, Lobo left them and rode south to Jimmy's house, near the river at the center of the valley.

Wanting to keep his family safe, Lobo was ready to ask Jimmy the hard questions and ready, as he'd said, to handle whatever came his way, but when he rode up to the house, he discovered that Jimmy wasn't home.

There was no way to know where Jimmy had gone, but Lobo was determined to interrogate him, so like any good hunter, he settled in to wait.

CHAPTER 37

⚜

Brock Boone sat his horse alongside a dozen of his men, hidden within a grove on the land Hannah Miles had leased from Curtis Baldwin.

The herd had bedded down all around them, just as Brock had hoped.

A hundred yards to the southwest, the boyish voice of Jamie, his youngest hand, crooned to the drowsing cattle.

Brock knew that Cecil, the only other hand outside the grove, would stick close to Jamie as directed, just as he knew that if trouble came, it would come from the opposite direction, the northeast, and the road to Jasper Flats.

Trouble seemed unlikely—and yet, he expected it all the same, and he was glad Miss Miles had contacted him.

He was not surprised that her new man, Desmond, had caused such a stir.

As a cattleman, you grew to understand men like this Desmond. They knew the work but sooner or later—and usually, it was sooner—they showed their true colors and did something abominable.

And since he knew Desmond associated with coarse punchers in Jasper Flats, Brock expected they—

"Sir," Two Hawks said, slipping silently back into the grove. "Riders approaching."

Brock nodded, smiling grimly, thinking yet again how glad he was to have employed the Mescalero scout three years earlier. Two Hawks could move through the night like a patch of shadow and had saved Brock countless times on both the trail and the ranch.

So they were coming. Just as his gut had told him they would.

Brock's men stood ready but understood that they were to do nothing until he gave the command.

And he must be absolutely certain before he did that.

He didn't have to wait long.

Soon, the riders came into view, trotting toward the cattle as silently as coyotes. With the bright moon overhead, they were easy to count.

He'd been expecting three or four rustlers. But Desmond must have had more friends than the ones they'd known about, because eight men circled around the herd.

He eased his horse forward, heart pounding with excitement. He loved to fight. There was no better measure of a man than combat, and time and time again, Brock Boone had successfully answered the demands of battle.

"We gonna go get them, Mr. Boone?" Drayton asked eagerly.

"Not yet," Brock whispered. "I want to catch them red-handed. Let them start cutting out cattle, and we'll reveal ourselves."

"If you say so, sir. But they're already trespassing, sir, and we all know what they're up to."

All around him, men nodded. They were good men and ready, too, just as he had known they would be. That was why he'd chosen them to ride along tonight.

"Soon enough, men," Brock said. "Soon enough."

But the rustlers didn't do what he expected. Instead of cutting out the closest cattle, they spread out a little and kept riding south, sticking to the western edge of the herd.

Brock watched them for a few seconds then frowned, understanding that things had changed.

"What's keeping them?" Drayton asked.

"Time to move, men," Brock said. "They aren't cutting out cattle. I was wrong about their plan. They mean to stampede Miss Miles's herd."

Most rustlers tried to be stealthy. But these brutal men wanted to get behind the cattle, stampede them toward town, and gather up a bunch on their way back to Jasper Flats.

They didn't care about Hannah Miles's men hearing them. They were here not only to steal cattle but also wreak havoc and scare Miss Miles.

Savages.

Seeing only two night guards, Desmond and his friends were probably hoping for some trouble, too.

Well, they'd have that. Yes, they would have plenty of trouble.

"Drayton," Brock said, then named three other men. "You

head out their back trail. Find some cover. When they run, don't let them past you."

Drayton smiled in the gloom. "Yes, sir, Mr. Boone."

Brock sent four other men south to protect Jamie and Cecil in case the rustlers rushed them. "If there's shooting, you men come fast and hit hard."

Turning to Two Hawks and the others, he said, "Come on, men. We're going straight at them."

The plan was bold and simple—two elements shared by the best battle plans.

"Let's ride," he said, and all three groups left the grove at the same time.

Brock rode at the front of his spearhead, of course. Not only did he plan to lead by example; he meant to do the talking.

Despite his love of battle, he hoped to take these men without a single shot being fired, knowing that bloodshed would disturb Miss Miles, who had no idea that he and his reinforcements were even here, waiting for the rustlers he'd been certain would come.

So yes, he planned to talk to Desmond and these other men, to explain that—

One of the rustlers spotted them and opened fire before Brock could so much as wish them a good evening.

An instant later, the night thundered with gunfire. Fifty yards away, muzzle flashes spangled the darkness.

Cries of pain and anger sounded on both sides.

Heart thumping with excitement, Brock shouldered his carbine, picked out one of the shadowy rustlers, and pulled the trigger.

The man fell from his saddle.

A moment later, Brock flinched, struck in the arm.

He snarled in the darkness, a fearless warrior transported by that blend of joy and rage known only by combat veterans, and knocked another rustler from his mount.

For several seconds, chaos reigned.

Then, Brock's riders rushed in from the south and smashed into the rustlers, breaking them apart, and the fight was over. A few rustlers streaked toward town as Brock had known they would, but they soon reached Drayton, whose men greeted them with hot lead, ending the whole affair.

Four of Brock's men were wounded, not counting himself. One of these men, a well-liked German named Krupp, was hit hard and would need a doctor. Another had fallen from his horse and broken an arm. The other wounds were superficial.

The other side hadn't fared so well. Six, including Desmond, were dead. The other two were in bad shape but would likely survive long enough to be hung, anyway.

What concerned Brock more was the cattle. The crash of gunfire and screaming of men had stampeded them.

The faster his men gathered the herd the better. Any lost cattle he would replace from his own herd. He wanted Miss Miles's first foray into the beef business to be a big success, after all.

His voice full of command, Brock congratulated his men on their victory and explained what needed to happen.

Excited by the action, the men set immediately to work.

Brock put Drayton in charge and then turned toward the east on his own mission.

Miss Miles would have heard the commotion. Now, he needed to set her mind at ease.

CHAPTER 38

L obo dozed in the shadows beneath an apple tree just outside Jimmy's house. Resting, but never deeply, some part of his mind remaining aware, in the manner of wolves in new territory.

He had picketed Paddy behind Jimmy's house, reckoning that when his cousin returned, he would be traveling on the well-established path and therefore miss Lobo's stallion behind the house.

But as the night wore on, Lobo's half-sleeping mind went from thinking in terms of *when* and started thinking in terms of *if*. Because it no longer seemed certain that Jimmy would be coming home at all this night.

Maybe he was staying with someone in the valley. Friends, family, a woman.

Or maybe he'd gone somewhere outside the valley. Maybe he was spending the night in Dunlap's Crossing.

The delay gave Lobo time to consider these things and other

things, too, such as the possibility that Jimmy had run out altogether.

What if the lone rider atop the ridge had been Jimmy? Or someone aligned with Jimmy?

Or maybe Jimmy had gone to town and spoken with the gun shop owner.

The longer the night dragged on, the more convinced Lobo became that Jimmy was the killer. If that was true, and he knew Lobo suspected him, Jimmy might try to kill him before he could spread the word.

Lobo welcomed that turn of events.

Or maybe Jimmy would run away. Somehow, that didn't seem likely.

Jimmy was too bold, too confident, to run. This was his home. Folks in the valley knew him, and that would matter if Lobo, a stranger with a scarred face, started accusing him of murder.

So Lobo lay there in the dark, dozing and waiting, still expecting to hear the rhythmic clopping of hoofbeats.

But hour after hour, no hoofbeats came.

Had Jimmy run out?

And, if so, what would that mean?

Lobo's inability to answer these questions made it painfully clear just how little he knew.

Someone had killed Bannerman and might strike again. This put his family at risk.

And because Bannerman had been his bodyguard, these facts mostly put Grandfather Guerrero at risk.

Why else kill a bodyguard? There seemed to be no other reason for someone to kill Bannerman, so Lobo had to assume that someone had removed Bannerman to get at Grandfather Guerrero.

This thought lifted his hackles, bringing him to full wakefulness. If anyone tried to hurt Grandfather Guerrero...

But he reined in his rage.

He didn't know who had killed Bannerman, let alone why.

For all he knew, it was someone from the Triple G ranch. The next day, he would head back to Dunlap's Crossing and talk to the sheriff. Maybe he would have some information about the Triple G gang.

Maybe. But his gut told him Jimmy was the killer.

Why, though? Why was he so certain?

Yes, Jimmy carried a '73. But they weren't exactly scarce. You couldn't convict a man for simply owning one.

Then there was the question of motive.

Did Jimmy have a reason to kill Grandfather Guerrero? Did he think by killing him, he would inherit the valley?

Sophia did say that's what Jimmy wanted, to replace Grandfather and run the valley.

But that didn't mean he'd kill for it. Or that, if Grandfather Guerrero died, Jimmy would inherit the valley.

According to Sophia, no one had known who the heir might be. Not until Lobo showed up, anyway. And apparently, everyone in the valley would understand that Lobo would now be the heir.

Of course, the murderer couldn't have known, when he killed Bannerman, that Lobo would show up a few days later.

Now, though? Lobo was here. The heir had returned.

Did that mean Grandfather was safe, at least unless someone took out Lobo?

He hoped so. But he was still determined to get to the bottom of this and make the killer pay.

Again, his mind went to Jimmy.

Was it possible that Lobo suspected his cousin not because of overwhelming evidence but because he simply didn't like him?

Yes, of course that was possible. Likely, even.

But Lobo was rallying a lynch mob. He just wanted to confront Jimmy with some hard questions and watch his cousin closely when he answered.

Then what? What if Jimmy failed to confess, but Lobo knew he was lying? What if he was all but certain that Jimmy had done it?

Again, Lobo was a stranger here. If he rode into town and explained to the sheriff the subtly incriminating tells of Jimmy's voice and facial expression, would the lawman put Jimmy behind bars? Or would he lock up Lobo as a lying troublemaker?

Based on his experiences with lawmen in other small towns like Dunlap's Crossing, Lobo didn't like his chances.

If he wanted to convict Jimmy—or at least stay out of jail himself—he would need a confession, a witness, or some undeniably hard evidence against his cousin.

He wasn't likely to get any of those things tonight. In fact, the longer this dragged on, the more it felt like a wild goose chase.

He sat up and stretched and was about to go check on Paddy when a low, sad song rose to the west.

The howling hit him right in the heart.

208

Half a mile away, the she-wolf had come out of her den to howl at the moon, expressing her bottomless grief.

A lump closed Lobo's throat.

Maybe he would forget Jimmy and saddle Paddy and ride over to the she-wolf and—

A gunshot cut the night, and the howling sliced away forever.

CHAPTER 39

Tilly awoke to the sounds of boots and muffled voices and slipped from bed and went to her door and listened with alarm.

A man's voice spoke out there.

What was a man doing in her home in the middle of the night?

She wished she had a gun, but she didn't. All she could do was warn Miss Hannah, who kept a gun on her nightstand.

But then, as Tilly came to full wakefulness, she realized there was another muffled voice in the mix. A softer voice, lilting with hushed concern.

Tilly couldn't make out the words, but she knew the voice belonged to Miss Hannah, just as she knew that something was wrong.

Had Desmond come back? Was he making good on his promise to hurt Miss Hannah?

Tilly threw open the door, ready to charge hades with a bucket of ice water if anyone was trying to hurt Miss Hannah.

Standing in the kitchen, however, was not Desmond or one of his foul-mouthed friends but rather Mr. Boone.

Miss Hannah had been looking at him with concern, her eyes large, her mouth slightly ajar, and reaching out to touch his arm—which Tilly now saw was soaked in blood.

Now, Miss Hannah's hand fell away, and she and Mr. Boone looked at Tilly.

"What's wrong?" Tilly asked. "What happened to your arm, Mr. Boone?"

Mr. Boone smiled. "A mere scratch, my dear. Nothing to trouble you."

"I'm sorry we woke you, Tilly," Miss Hannah said. "Now, go on back to bed."

Tilly didn't budge. "He came back, didn't he?"

"That's right," Mr. Boone said. "He came back. But you don't have to worry. He won't be bothering you."

"What about his friends?"

"They won't bother you, either."

"Did you kill them?"

After a slight pause, Mr. Boone nodded. "It was a fair fight, but yes, my men and I got the best of them—and the rascals got what they deserved."

"Good," Tilly said, feeling better. "Thank you for killing them, Mr. Boone."

Mr. Boone gave a little nod, but Miss Hannah stared at Tilly with that strange look she sometimes gave her, an expression of confusion or wonder... or maybe both.

But Tilly could see that, despite Mr. Boone's good news, Miss Hannah remained upset.

Tilly crossed the room.

"Tilly," Miss Hannah said weakly, "I asked you to—"

"It's okay, Miss Hannah," Tilly said, taking Miss Hannah's hand. "Don't worry. Mr. Boone took care of them like Lobo would've done if he was here. Everything's going to be all right."

"Yes," Miss Hannah said, her eyes sliding out of focus, "I suppose you're right. It's just... I fear... perhaps... I mean, I just wonder if maybe..."

Mr. Boone stared at her, waiting for her to finish.

But Miss Hannah seemed to have slipped into a stunned state. She just stood there, saying nothing and staring at nothing.

Tilly gave her hand a squeeze. "Miss Hannah?"

Miss Hannah snapped out of it and offered an unconvincing smile. "I'm sorry, Tilly, and I do apologize, Mr. Boone. I'm not handling this very well, am I? It's just been a lot, I suppose. I mean, I had been so worried about the cattle, but then everything went so smoothly, and it seemed like everything would be okay. Then Desmond started that trouble in the bunkhouse, and I started worrying again. But we ran him off, and you told me not to worry, Mr. Boone, so I didn't, but now this has happened." She shook her head. "Eight men, you said? Eight men dead?"

Mr. Boone nodded somberly. "I am afraid so, Miss Miles. I do hate to be the bearer of this news, but yes, eight bad men have been killed tonight."

"On my property?"

"On the ground you leased."

"I'm responsible."

"There is no question of responsibility, Miss Miles. You've done nothing. If anyone was to be questioned, it would be I, and I assure you that I will lose no sleep over that possibility. These men were the worst sort, and we've improved Colorado by sending them to their rewards."

"Tomorrow," Miss Hannah said, her eyes sliding out of focus again, "I will go to town and tell Marshal Tubbs everything."

"I will come with you," Mr. Boone said.

Miss Hannah shook her head. "That's all right, Mr. Boone. I'm certain I can handle this at least. And I've been relying on you far too much lately."

"Not true, Miss Miles," Mr. Boone protested. "I remain your faithful servant."

Miss Hannah shook her head again, more emphatically this time, looking deeply troubled. "No, I have. The funny thing is, I had almost convinced myself that I had been doing great things. Buying cattle, leasing land, moving toward some bright future..."

"And you have," Mr. Boone said.

"No, I haven't. I've been playing a game. Letting you help me and taking credit for it. You sold me cattle for a song, pushed them onto the ground I leased, and had your men watch them. Meanwhile, Desmond, the one man I actually hired—Lobo hired Mr. Tuttle and Plug, you understand—didn't last a day. Then he came back with a gang of thugs, and now you and some of your men have been shot..."

Tilly hugged Miss Hannah, seeing she was close to tears.

"My dear Miss Miles," Mr. Boone said, taking Miss Hannah's hand in his, "might I recommend that we forgo further discussion so you can get some rest? Everything is all right, and contrary to what you seem to believe, you have been doing an impressive job of expanding your herd and creating opportunities. Desmond was a bad apple. That was all. Anyone could have made the mistake of hiring him."

"You wouldn't have."

"No, likely I wouldn't have. But with all due respect, ma'am, I've been a cattleman for years. You're a bit newer to the business. It is my heartfelt belief that you are being far too hard on yourself."

Miss Hannah blinked at him. She had made no move to pull her hand from his, Tilly noticed with a twinge of irritation. "Thank you, Mr. Boone. Thank you for everything."

"I'm just happy that my men and I were here," Mr. Boone said. "The cattle stampeded of course."

"Oh no," Miss Hannah gasped.

"Don't be concerned, Miss Miles. My men have already started rounding them up. They will gather the entire herd by morning."

"It's overwhelming," Miss Hannah said, smiling but looking like she might burst out crying at any moment. "Thank you, Mr. Boone. Thank you so very much. I just don't know how I can ever repay you. You've given me the chance of a lifetime and saved the herd and the ranch and got shot in the process. What can I do for you? How can I possibly repay your unbelievable kindness?"

Mr. Boone shifted his weight, seeming momentarily uncomfortable, a thing Tilly had never seen from the cattleman. It might even have been endearing to her if he hadn't still been holding Miss Hannah's hand. But he was. In fact, now he had wrapped both of his big hands around hers, making it disappear altogether.

"There is one thing you could do for me, Miss Hannah," he said, "though I hate to ask the favor of you."

"Anything," she said. "Please tell me how I can repay you. Whatever it is, it won't be nearly enough."

"Well, I believe I mentioned an upcoming party at the Masterson estate. It's tomorrow afternoon, and I am embarrassed to attend alone. If you really would like to do something for me—and I assure you, that is not necessary—would you consider attending the party with me? As a friend and business partner, of course."

For an awkward second, no one said anything.

Tilly went cold with dread.

"I apologize, Miss Miles," Mr. Boone said, releasing her hand. "I've overstepped my bounds. I never should have suggested—"

"No," Miss Hannah said, seizing his hand in hers. "You did nothing wrong, Mr. Boone. If I can make you feel less awkward at this party, I would be happy to attend with you. As a friend and business partner, like you said."

And with that, Tilly felt all her hopes and dreams crumbling away.

CHAPTER 40

Lobo sprinted toward the gunshot, knowing he could run the half mile faster than he could fetch and saddle Paddy.

And he wanted to get there as quickly as possible because while he was certain he was too late to save the she-wolf, he had to rescue the pups.

It took him a moment to get his bearings, especially when passing through a dark patch of forest, but a short time later, he charged into the meadow and saw, to his great horror, the she-wolf lying dead on the ground. A short distance away, Jimmy Guerrero kneeled at the edge of the river, holding something underwater.

"Stop!" Lobo bellowed, running straight at his cousin.

The shout startled Jimmy, who shot to his feet, still holding a dripping sack in his hands.

A sack that wriggled and whimpered...

"What are you doing?" Lobo demanded, grabbing the sack from him.

"Wiping out vermin," Jimmy sneered.

Lobo crouched and yanked the cord from the top of the sack and opened it and released the pups, who spilled onto the riverbank in a whimpering, sopping-wet mass and struggled to their feet and scampered toward the corpse of their mother.

"Question is," Jimmy said, "what are *you* doing here? This is my property, and I didn't give you permission to—"

Lobo jumped to his feet. "I told you not to hurt the she-wolf."

"Why should I listen to you? We're farmers here, in case you haven't heard. These wolves are predators."

"I told you I'd take care of them."

"Well, I saved you the trouble. I already took care of her. And I would've taken care of them, too, if you hadn't shown up."

"What kind of a monster drowns puppies?"

Jimmy grinned at him. "The kind who doesn't want to waste ammo. But now you give me no choice." He looked past Lobo toward where the pups surrounded their dead mother, nuzzling her and licking and whimpering. The little gray and brown pup with the white blaze on his chest pointed his nose toward the dark sky and howled, filling the night with agony. "Step aside, and I'll kill them, too."

"No, you won't," Lobo growled.

Jimmy grabbed the butt of his revolver and yanked it from its holster. "Oh yes I will."

He lifted the barrel, swinging it toward the pups, but Lobo lashed out, chopping Jimmy's wrist.

The gun fired into the forest and fell to the ground.

Jimmy cursed and threw a punch.

At this range, Lobo couldn't get out of the way.

Jimmy's knuckles pounded into his jaw.

Lobo jerked his head at the last instant and turned with the punch, taking most of the steam off it, but it was still a decent punch, and then they were scuffling, going at it toe to toe, both men punching and taking punches for several brutal seconds.

But although Jimmy was strong and fast and willing, and despite his reputation as a fighter, he was no match for Lobo, who caught his cousin clean with a wicked left hook that staggered the wolf-killer. At almost the same instant, Lobo's right fist crashed into Jimmy's temple and sent him sprawling.

Lobo pounced, ready to keep hammering away, but saw his cousin was already unconscious.

His first thought was to draw his Bowie and finish the job, but he would not stoop to murder, no matter how much Jimmy deserved to die.

For that much was clear now. Even if Jimmy had had nothing to do with the murder of Lou Bannerman, he had killed this she-wolf in front of her young then tried to drown those same pups in a burlap sack.

It filled Lobo with such rage that it was all he could do not to kill the man.

Instead, he decided to give him a taste of his own medicine. And then he would ask Jimmy all those hard questions that needed to be answered.

He rolled Jimmy onto his stomach and grabbed the cord he'd tossed away and lashed his cousin's wrists tightly behind his back.

Jimmy started coming around.

Lobo pinned him to the ground with one hand and one knee. "What are you doing?" Jimmy demanded.

"Letting you see what it feels like," Lobo said, and slammed the sack over Jimmy's head.

Jimmy roared in protest as Lobo dragged him down the bank to the water and shoved his head underwater.

He held it there for several seconds then jerked Jimmy's head out again.

Jimmy gasped and sputtered. "Let me go!"

"Not until you see what it felt like for those pups," Lobo said.

Jimmy struggled, but Lobo was supercharged with rage and had him pinned on his chest with his wrists tied.

"I'll kill you for this," Jimmy promised.

Lobo shoved his head underwater. This time, he held it for thirty seconds.

Jimmy struggled wildly beneath him.

Lobo yanked Jimmy's head out of the water again.

Jimmy gasped for air.

"Where were you Friday afternoon?" Lobo demanded.

Jimmy cursed at him.

Lobo plunged his head under water again.

Half a minute later, he pulled it out again and repeated his question.

"I was hunting," Jimmy snarled.

"Hunting Bannerman?"

"What?" Jimmy said. "No, I wasn't hunting Bannerman. What are you talking about? Are you crazy?"

Whatever else Jimmy was, he was a great actor. He sounded sincere.

Lobo shoved his head underwater again.

Jimmy struggled mightily but to no avail.

Lobo pulled his head back out. "Why did you kill him?"

"Didn't... kill... him," Jimmy panted, gasping for air. "You're... crazy!"

"You're gonna pay for what you did," Lobo said. "I ought to just kill you right now."

He shoved Jimmy's head underwater again but was badly startled a second later.

"Sebastian!" Sophia's terrified voice cried. "What are you doing?"

Lobo whipped his head around and beheld a terrible scene illuminated by lantern light that in his rage he hadn't even noticed approaching.

Sophia stood there, sobbing, looking at him like he was a monster.

Beside her, young Davey's shaking hands were pointing his pistol straight at Lobo. "Let him go, Uncle Lobo," the terrified boy pleaded. "Don't make me shoot you, sir. Please let him go!"

"Davey," Lobo said, "Sophia, it's not what it looks like."

"Davey? Sophia?" Jimmy cried. "Help me, please! He's gone crazy! He's a savage! He's trying to drown me!"

CHAPTER 41

⚜

The disappointment on Grandfather Guerrero's face pierced Lobo's heart like a dagger made of ice.

"I just don't know what to say," Grandfather Guerrero said after he—and the dozens in attendance—had heard both sides of the story.

Or, more precisely, they had heard the awkward truth from Lobo and Jimmy's wild lies.

It was mid-morning, the next day, and Green Valley's citizens had gathered outside Grandfather Guerrero's home to hear their patriarch pass judgment on the previous night's strange and shocking events.

Lobo sat to his grandfather's left, facing the crowd.

By the way they stared at him, he knew they believed Jimmy's wild exaggerations.

Jimmy sat on Grandfather Guerrero's other side, a good distance from Lobo.

Grandfather Guerrero had asked both men to leave their firearms and other weapons at home—or, in the case of Lobo, on Sophia's property.

He had spent the night in her barn, not wanting to frighten her or Davey anymore than he already had. That was the worst part of it. He didn't particularly care what most of these people thought, but it killed him to know his sister, nephew, and grandfather suspected Lobo was a crazed killer.

"He kept saying he was gonna kill me," Jimmy said again. "It was terrible. He would hold my head under, then pull it up and yell at me, telling me this was it, he was fixing to murder me."

"That's a lie," Lobo said.

"Sebastian," Grandfather Guerrero said in a stern voice, "I would ask you to refrain from speaking until we've heard from your cousin."

Lobo shut his mouth and waited.

"I'm not lying," Jimmy lied. "Ask Sophia and Davey. They heard him."

Everyone turned to Lobo's sister and nephew.

"Is that true, Sophia?" Grandfather Guerrero asked. "Did you hear Lobo threaten to kill Jimmy?"

Sophia wiped at her tears again. She hadn't quit crying since the riverbank. "I don't know. I don't even know anymore."

"Davey?" Grandfather Guerrero said. "What did you hear?"

Davey looked small and sheepish. His eyes went from Grandfather Guerrero to Lobo to the ground. "I heard Uncle Lobo say something."

"And what was that?" Grandfather Guerrero asked. "What did you hear? You don't have to be afraid, Davey. You're safe here. All we want is the truth."

"Well," Davey said, sneaking a nervous glance at Lobo and looking rapidly away again, "I heard Uncle Lobo say something about..."

"Yes?" Grandfather Guerrero coaxed.

"About killing Uncle Jimmy."

The crowd murmured, staring at Lobo the way folks used to stare at him when he was a wild thing locked in a sideshow cage.

"Ha!" Jimmy crowed. "I told you! He said he was gonna kill me. And he would have, too, if Sophia and Davey hadn't heard the gunshots and come running."

Lobo knew, because they'd spelled it out the night before, that Sophia and Davey had come running because of what Lobo had said before leaving Grandfather Guerrero's place, Lobo telling his grandfather and nephew that he wasn't afraid to kill Jimmy if there was trouble.

Now, Jimmy pointed across the gap at Lobo. "He is a wild animal raised by wolves. If you don't believe me, ask him. He'll tell you himself. For years, he lived with them, killed with them, ate raw meat."

Folks groaned and made faces.

It was nothing Lobo hadn't seen before.

He sat there with his mouth shut and his jaw muscles working hard. He should never have come here. He couldn't stand Jimmy and had no use for most of these people, even if they were kin.

But he cared too much for Sophia, Davey, and Grandfather Guerrero to stand up and make a scene, proclaiming those things.

"Sebastian," Grandfather Guerrero said. "What do you have

to say about all this?"

"First of all," Lobo said, "I didn't threaten to kill him. He said something about killing me, and I told him I *ought* to kill him. Which yeah, I felt like doing. Because like Jimmy said, I was raised by wolves. That was a long time ago. But wolves are special to me. And he was wiping out the pack. I told him not to shoot the she-wolf. I told him I'd take care of everything."

"What were you gonna do?" Jimmy interrupted. "Go talk to them? Take off all your clothes and run with them and kill—"

"Jimmy," Grandfather Guerrero cut him off. "I would ask you to hold your tongue until Sebastian has his say. Go ahead, Sebastian."

Lobo went ahead and did his best to explain everything that had happened, but the longer he talked, the clearer it became that his testimony was a lost cause.

These people had sided with Jimmy, and nothing this wild stranger could say would ever sway them.

The only thing that hung in the balance, the only thing Lobo cared about, was what his loved ones—Grandfather Guerrero, Sophia, and Davey—thought of him. That and, of course, catching the killer before he struck again.

But he wasn't about to start pointing fingers at Jimmy and accusing him of Bannerman's murder now. His evidence was thinner than thin—a single casing and his own gut feeling—and everyone would think he was just trying to fire back at Jimmy for everything that had happened, perhaps even trying to exonerate himself by accusing his cousin of an even worse crime.

Besides, something about Jimmy and the Bannerman murder still bothered him.

As Jimmy went on, playing up his innocence and piling wild

fabrication upon wild fabrication, Lobo could hear and see his lying plain as day.

Couldn't everyone hear and see that Jimmy was lying?

Apparently not.

But Lobo could.

Which stood out in stark contrast to the night before. Because, although it was inconvenient to admit, Jimmy had sounded honestly confused when Lobo had questioned him about the Bannerman murder.

That didn't mean Jimmy was innocent, of course, but he had sounded a lot different than he did now, when he was clearly lying, so Lobo wouldn't feel right accusing him perhaps falsely.

He needed to get this over with, apologize or whatever, and get back to hunting the killer... who might, he realized, be any one of the folks now looking at him like he had two heads.

"What I'd like to know," Jimmy said, "is where Sebastian was Friday night."

The crowd murmured with surprise and stared suspiciously at Lobo.

"I was two days' ride east of here," Lobo said.

"Can you prove that?" Jimmy asked, "because I gotta tell you, Sebastian, it looks mighty strange, a killer like you showing up right after Mr. Bannerman was murdered in cold blood. Especially when Bannerman was Grandfather Guerrero's bodyguard... and you stand to inherit this valley if something happens to Grandfather!"

By the gasps and fiery stares of those in attendance, Lobo knew this destroyed his half-formed dreams of possibly settling here in Green Valley with Hannah and Tilly.

These people would never accept him. And he would never accept them.

Grandfather Guerrero scowled. "I don't for a second believe my grandson had anything to do with the murder of Lou Bannerman."

By the stares and muttered objections of the crowd, however, Lobo saw they very much suspected him of Bannerman's murder.

A gloating Jimmy said, "Well, I do. I'm going to tell father, too."

People nodded and voiced their agreement.

But Jimmy's proclamation made no sense to Lobo. After all, what good would it be, Jimmy reporting his suspicions to his father? Uncle Antonio didn't even live in the valley. Grandfather Guerrero had kicked him out years ago.

"That will be enough of that sort of talk," Grandfather Guerrero said, an edge coming into his voice. "I run this valley, and I will handle this situation. I don't need the sheriff's help."

Jimmy leaned back, crossed his arms over his chest, and gave Lobo a satisfied smirk.

So Jimmy's dad, Lobo's exiled uncle, was also the sheriff whose office had been closed the previous day?

Folks set to whispering.

Lobo could tell by their eyes that they had convicted him not only of threatening Jimmy but also killing Lou Bannerman.

Fine. He was done with them.

He was going to solve the murder, stop the killer from striking again, and ride out of here. He would keep in touch with Grandfather Guerrero, Sophia, and Davey, but the rest of these people were nothing to him.

And in a day or a week or a month, however long it took for him to catch the killer and protect Grandfather Guerrero, Sophia, and Davey, he would be rid of Jimmy and these others.

Grandfather Guerrero cleared his throat. "Well, I've made up my mind. Jimmy, you've always had a mean streak."

Jimmy uncrossed his arms and sat up, looking shocked.

"You like to stir things up," Grandfather Guerrero said. "You're a troublemaker, and I know you have given Sebastian a hard time since the moment he showed up here."

"What?" Jimmy protested. "He was the one who—"

"No," Grandfather Guerrero said, cutting him off, the edge in his voice sharper than ever now and hard as tempered steel. "You had your say. Now, I will pass judgment."

Jimmy just stared at him.

Lobo felt a glimmer of hope. Maybe Grandfather Guerrero had indeed seen through Jimmy's lies.

"I'm through with you stirring up trouble," Grandfather Guerrero told Jimmy. "You're my grandson, but Jimmy, if you stir up any more trouble, you're going to have to leave the valley... forever."

Jimmy's mouth dropped open, and his face went red. He stared at Grandfather Guerrero like he wanted to tear his throat out, but he restrained himself and said nothing.

Then Grandfather Guerrero turned to Lobo.

Again, pigs squealed in the distance.

"Sebastian, I'm glad you came back to the valley. It is so good to know you are alive."

Lobo nodded at that, relieved that his grandfather had indeed seen the truth.

"However," Grandfather Guerrero said, "you are clearly a

violent man with a dangerous temper. I don't know exactly what happened down by the river, but everyone, even Davey, heard you say something about killing Jimmy. I'm afraid you'll have to leave. I want you out of Green Valley by sundown."

CHAPTER 42

A s they entered the mercantile, Miss Hannah said, "Are you all right, Tilly? You don't look well."

Tilly, who indeed felt horrible, merely shrugged her shoulders.

What else could she say? What else could she do?

Because it wasn't illness making her feel so horrible. It was their reason for coming here.

Miss Hannah was buying a dress. She was buying a fancy dress to attend the party with Brock Boone. And regardless of what Miss Hannah said, Mr. Boone wanted to marry her.

Worse, with all the time they'd been spending together and all the business they'd been doing and Mr. Boone coming over and fighting the rustlers, it seemed to Tilly that Miss Hannah and Mr. Boone were drawing closer and closer.

And wasn't that what people did when they fell in love?

What if tomorrow at the party, Mr. Boone asked her to marry him?

What if Miss Hannah said yes?

All of Tilly's dreams would come crashing down. Because all she wanted in this world was a loving family. But not just any family. She wanted to be the daughter of Miss Hannah and Lobo, and she wanted them to have children who would be her brothers and sisters.

Was that too much to ask?

No.

But now, everything was in danger. If Miss Hannah agreed to marry Mr. Boone, Tilly would never be happy again.

Never, ever, ever.

But Tilly could do nothing to change things. Miss Hannah had promised to attend the party out of indebtedness to Mr. Boone.

Tilly could do nothing to change Miss Hannah's mind. Miss Hannah would never break a promise over the objections of a child, especially when Miss Hannah wouldn't understand any of Tilly's objections anyway.

Miss Hannah had no intention of marrying Mr. Boone. But what if, at the party, swept up in all the money and splendor and music and good food and interesting people, she changed her mind?

Miss Hannah touched Tilly's forehead and frowned. "You don't have a fever. But no, you don't look well. I will pick out a dress as quickly as possible, dear. Then we can head home."

Tilly nodded. "Yes, Miss Hannah."

But the mention of picking a dress sickened her. She had to get out of the mercantile. She couldn't watch Miss Hannah choose the dress she might very well be wearing when Mr. Boone proposed and ruined everything Tilly wanted in life.

"Miss Hannah," Tilly said, "would it be all right if I waited for you outside?"

Miss Hannah frowned. "You really are feeling sick. I'm so sorry, Tilly. And yes, certainly. Plug, would you stay with her, please?"

"Yes, ma'am," Plug said, "I'll keep her safe."

Miss Hannah smiled. "I know you will. Thank you, Plug. I'll be out soon, Tilly."

"Take your time, Miss Hannah," Tilly said. Despite her fears, she felt bad for worrying Miss Hannah.

"Thank you, Tilly. I just need the dress and a few other items. It shouldn't take more than fifteen minutes."

As Miss Hannah went off to pick her dress, Tilly felt worse and worse.

Why were these things happening?

If only Lobo would come home.

He could stop all of this by simply telling Miss Hannah how he felt. If she knew he loved her, she wouldn't marry Mr. Boone for all the cattle in the world, no matter how many fancy parties he took her to.

But Lobo was far away with his long-lost family near some town called Dunlap's Crossing.

Plug held the door for her, and they went out onto the boardwalk.

He patted her shoulder gently. "I'm sorry you don't feel good, Tilly."

"It's okay, Plug. Thanks for coming out with me."

"Sure thing."

"Can you keep a secret?"

"You know I can."

"I'm not really sick."

Plug nodded. "It's on account of the party, ain't it? On account of Miss Hannah's going with Mr. Boone?"

Tilly was impressed by Plug's perceptiveness. "You're right."

"I guess you're hoping Lobo will come home before Mr. Boone asks Miss Hannah to marry him?"

"That's right, Plug. That's exactly right. I just wish there was some way to bring Lobo home faster."

Plug shrugged. "You could send him a telegram."

For a second, Tilly just gaped at the boy. "Plug, that's a great idea. Come on!"

"Huh?"

She grabbed his hand and pulled him across the street, dragging the rugged cowboy toward the telegraph station. "That's exactly what I'm going to do. I'm going to send Lobo a telegram. But I need you to help me."

All the color drained from Plug's face, but he let her drag him across the street. "Me?"

"That's right, Plug. I need your help. Do you have a dime I could borrow?"

"Sure, but—"

"Great. Don't worry about Mr. Pennsbury. He knows me. Just let me do the talking." She stopped abruptly and impulsively hugged Plug. "You're wonderful, Plug. Thank you so much!"

And then they were hurrying down the street, rushing to take care of this before Miss Hannah came back out of the mercantile.

CHAPTER 43

The pups whined as Lobo stood and stepped out of the box and replaced the board, blocking them from following him and trapping them inside the stall again.

He felt bad for them but knew they would be all right eventually.

Wolves are nothing if not resilient.

"I'll be back," he told them. "Just gotta go to town, get supplies, and talk to somebody. Then I'll come back and throw you in the panniers, and we'll go for a long ride together."

The gray and brown pup rocked his head back and howled.

"I feel the same way, buddy," Lobo said and left them.

His grandfather's decision to exile him had rattled Lobo. He'd never seen it coming because his grandfather seemed like a wise, down-to-earth man and because Lobo knew he had done nothing wrong. Not really. Everything he'd done was justified. What had swayed everyone was Jimmy's lies.

Because of those lies, Lobo wouldn't be able to set things right with his family or catch the killer.

But he would honor his grandfather's wishes and leave.

Before leaving the valley, however, he would stop by Grandfather Guerrero's and warn him about the killer. Because the more Lobo thought about it, the more he reckoned the killer had murdered Lou Bannerman in order to get at Grandfather Guerrero.

It could very well be, in fact, that Lobo's appearance had stopped the killer from striking—and that his disappearance might leave his grandfather open again.

Maybe, if Lobo warned him, Grandfather Guerrero would at least hire another bodyguard.

He hoped so.

But first, town.

As he was saddling Paddy, Davey showed up, looking younger than his fourteen years. His eyes were puffy and red. He stopped several feet away and stared at Lobo, looking like he might cry.

"Hello, Davey," Lobo said.

"I'm sorry, Uncle Lobo."

"You got nothing to be sorry about, Davey."

"I never meant to get you in trouble."

"You didn't. I got myself in trouble. But just so you know, I really wasn't going to kill your Uncle Jimmy."

Davey nodded, looking relieved.

Which struck Lobo as strange, but then again Davey was just a boy, and he'd led a somewhat sheltered life here in Green Valley. Which didn't make him a bad kid. But it did allow him to cling to childish notions, like the idea of violence never solving anything.

Violence solved a lot of problems. And if folks were judicious in its implementation, it generally did a better job of fixing things than any amount of talking ever could.

"When Great-Grandfather Guerrero asked me what I heard, I told him the truth. But I didn't expect him to... you know."

"Kick me out?"

Davey nodded, looking miserable.

"Davey, don't apologize to me. Never apologize for telling the truth. And that's what you did. You told the truth. What folks do with the truth, that's up to them, not you. They're wrong about me, but I won't argue. I'll just move on. I have places to go and folks to see. Man can drive himself crazy, trying to fix the wrong problems."

He had planned on doing whatever he could to find and stop the killer of Lou Bannerman, but if Grandfather Guerrero wanted him to leave, what could he do about it?

Nothing, that's what.

He would honor his grandfather's wishes, leave the valley, and never come back.

"I just feel bad that—"

"Hey, Davey? Enough. Don't apologize to me again. I mean it. Stand up straight."

The boy did as he was told.

"Now look me in the eyes, young man," Lobo said. He remembered how hard it was for him, having been raised by wolves, to look a man in the eyes.

The way he'd been raised, locking eyes was a sign of aggression, and an invitation to fight. But here, among men, it was expected.

The boy looked him in the eyes.

"A man who won't look you in the eyes is either a coward or a liar. And I won't have the world thinking either of those things about my nephew, do you understand?"

"Yes, sir."

"A man only needs to say something once. Apologize once, thank somebody once, warn them once. You live your life that way, folks will take you at your word. And that's important. Folks don't take you at your word, they're gonna test you left and right. And that's how a man gets in trouble."

"Yes, sir."

"I wish I could stick around and teach you a thing or two, but Grandfather Guerrero has spoken, and I will respect his wishes."

"You're leaving then?"

"Of course. He told me to, didn't he?"

"Yes, sir."

"Maybe someday, if your mother wants, the two of you can visit me."

Davey's big smile brought his whole face to life. "I'd like that, sir."

Lobo clapped him on the shoulder. "So would I, Davey. So would I. Now, I gotta go to town and get supplies for my trip."

"You'll be back for supper, won't you, Uncle Lobo? Ma is making you something special."

"I wasn't planning on hanging around that long."

Davey frowned. "All right. Ma will be sorry. She feels real bad about everything."

"She didn't do anything wrong."

"No, but she feels like I do. I mean, everything happened so fast. When we were over at Great-Grandfather Guerrero's—you and me, I mean, before everything went wrong—I got scared, hearing you talk about facing off with Uncle Jimmy. And then, when we heard the gunshots and went out there and saw everything—"

"Forget it, Davey. Neither one of you did anything wrong. Tell you what. If your mama can put supper on the table a little early, I'll stick around. But then the pups and I are riding out of here. Grandfather Guerrero wants me out by sunset, and I won't be hanging around longer than I'm wanted."

The boy brightened again. "I'm glad you're staying for supper, Uncle Lobo. Ma will be real happy."

"All right," Lobo said, wishing he could spend more time with the boy and work some of the excitability out of him. He held out his hand.

Davey straightened and shook his hand and looked him in the eyes.

"It took guts, coming out here to talk to me," Lobo said. "That's good. Life's hard. You want to make it, you're gonna need plenty of guts."

CHAPTER 44

"Lobo, huh?" the man at the Dunlap's Crossing telegraph station said. "Yeah, I think maybe I do have something for you."

He turned and plucked a telegram from its cubbyhole. "There you go. A telegram from a Mr. Horton."

Mr. Horton? Lobo thought, feeling a twinge of dread. *Who's Mr. Horton?*

"Nothing from a Miss Miles?" he asked.

The man took another look. "No, sir. This is the only one with your name on it. Hope everything's okay."

"Me, too," Lobo said. He took the telegram and strode from the station and read the note on the boardwalk outside.

Lobo Guerrero, Dunlap's Crossing, New Mexico – This is Tilly (stop) Come home fast (stop) Miss Hannah is attending

a party with Mr. Boone (stop) I love you (stop) Tilly (stop) Plug Horton, Jasper Flats, Colorado

LOBO STOOD THERE FOR A MOMENT, STUNNED BY THE MESSAGE.

He was relieved that Mr. Horton was just Plug. He'd never heard the boy's last name before and had feared the message might be from an undertaker or blackmailer. But this relief barely registered.

Because Brock Boone was courting Hannah. And she was attending a party with him.

Which meant Hannah had feelings for Boone and must be planning to marry him. Otherwise, she would never attend an event with him.

Lobo felt like he'd been punched in the stomach.

Grandfather Guerrero had kicked him out of the valley. Hannah was marrying Brock Boone.

Suddenly, he was all alone again, a wolf without a pack.

The realization settled over him like a killing frost, ending all dreams and happiness.

Not that he was surprised.

He supposed he'd always known things would end this way. He'd let himself believe otherwise for a time, but now, he realized that all along, he'd known that Hannah would marry Brock Boone, adopt Tilly, and leave Lobo alone again.

Maybe it was for the best.

Not for him, of course. He couldn't think of anything worse.

But for Hannah. And Tilly. Boone was a good man. Wealthy, generous, stable. He had an estate, a fortune, and a big enough staff to provide a life of luxury for Hannah and Tilly.

Meanwhile, Lobo's quest to set things right had sputtered and died. His own family had rejected him, and he hadn't even been able to protect them from the killer.

Now, he was completely alone again.

Well, almost.

You have the pups, he told himself.

The thought brought no joy, only a sense of responsibility. Without Hannah and Tilly, without family, he could never experience joy again.

So be it. Some folks aren't slated for joy. And he was chief among them.

But the responsibility remained. It was up to him to help the pups.

He would not fail them. Nor would he fail Crazy Mary. He had promised to help her and help her he would.

She was expecting to travel with him to Hannah and Tilly, but he wouldn't ask them to put up Crazy Mary if he wasn't going to live there anymore.

And he could not stay there, could not bear to see Hannah with Brock Boone, could not bear to see Tilly call Boone *Daddy*.

He was glad that Tilly would have a stable home and all the things money could buy, but he would miss her.

Would she miss him?

Yes.

Of that, he was sure.

Would Hannah miss him?

As a friend, perhaps. But Brock Boone had apparently swept her off her feet.

Tilly asked him to come home fast.

That would be a mistake. It would only upset things. If Hannah had chosen Brock Boone, then Lobo should just—

Fangs within him snapped that line of thinking in half.

It was the old wolf in him, the wolf that had made it so hard to merge his life with humans, the wolf whose thoughts he'd battled against as recently as that night in the hotel, just before he'd squared off with the Hatley gang.

But now, the wolf's voice surprised him.

Hannah is yours, the wolf growled. *Tilly is yours. They are your pack.*

A man passing by gave him a strange look and stepped from the boardwalk into the street.

Lobo realized that he had been growling.

Which made sense. Because this time, the wolf was right. This time, he and the wolf were one.

Hannah and Tilly were pack.

His pack.

Brock Boone had moved into Lobo's territory. He was trying to take Lobo's pack.

And while there was enough human left in Lobo to know he couldn't just go back and kill Boone, and enough love in his heart for Hannah that he wouldn't force her to choose him, he would not give up his pack without a fight.

He was going home fast, as Tilly had directed. Unless Hannah was already married, he was going to tell her exactly how he felt and exactly what he wanted.

And woe to Brock Boone if he tried to stand in the way.

CHAPTER 45

B efore heading home, Lobo had one last bit of business
here in Dunlap's Crossing.

He had to report what he knew to Jimmy's father, his Uncle
Antonio, the sheriff.

He started walking in that direction.

He'd been surprised to learn Jimmy's father was the sheriff.

It still didn't sit right. Lobo didn't know why, exactly, and no
matter how much he scratched his head, it didn't become any
clearer.

Maybe it was because he didn't like Jimmy. Or maybe it was
because the first thing he'd known about Uncle Antonio was
that he'd clashed with Grandfather Guerrero and gotten kicked
out of the valley years ago. Or maybe it was just a gut feeling.

Whatever the case, it didn't sit right.

That being said, he had to speak with the man.

It was a risky move, since Lobo's evidence all pointed

toward the killer being the sheriff's son, but Lobo had to do the right thing, had to hope that the sheriff would put law over family, set aside the old grudge with Grandfather Guerrero, and do his best to stop the killer from striking again.

Lobo understood his uncle might not do these things, but that didn't matter.

Lobo still had to do the right thing, still had to try to protect his family. And having been exiled from the valley, this was the only chance he had now of doing that.

But yes, it was a risk. And not just because he would be asking Uncle Antonio to investigate his only son.

Also, Jimmy had made it clear after the trial that he was riding straight to Dunlap's Crossing to share his suspicions about Lobo with his father.

Those suspicions were absurd, of course, but you never knew about small towns.

If Lobo marched into the sheriff's office now and shared his suspicions about Jimmy, Uncle Antonio might throw him straight into jail.

And folks around here would believe Lobo was the killer. That much was clear from this morning's debacle at Grandfather Guerrero's.

These people were ready to believe he was some half-wolf savage who'd come back to Green Valley to kill Grandfather Guerrero and claim his inheritance straightaway.

And if Lobo was charged with Bannerman's murder, it would leave Grandfather Guerrero wide open. Nobody would even be looking out for the killer, not with a convicted Lobo behind bars or dangling from a rope.

Reeling with these terrible thoughts, Lobo finally reached the sheriff's office.

Once again, the CLOSED sign hung in the window.

He stood there for a moment, blinking at the sign, feeling like he was missing something, feeling like the key to everything was dangling just out of reach.

Why was Jimmy pushing like this?

Why was he trying so hard to rile people up and make them believe Lobo was the killer?

Of course, if Jimmy really was the killer, framing Lobo for the murder would be the perfect move. It wouldn't just protect Jimmy from suspicion. It would also open the door for him to get exactly what he wanted.

In fact, if Jimmy acted now, while Lobo was still on the loose, mere hours after Grandfather Guerrero had exiled him…

Lobo stopped walking and froze in place, his heart suddenly hammering in his chest.

Lobo didn't need to be convicted of anything.

Jimmy had already put the idea of Lobo's guilt in people's heads.

And if someone murdered Grandfather Guerrero mere hours after he'd banished Lobo, everyone would assume Lobo had done it.

They would hunt him down and string him up, no trial necessary.

And Jimmy would likely inherit Green Valley. Though maybe he'd have to kill Davey and Sophia to get it.

Lobo's blood froze.

Not for his own safety. But because Grandfather Guerrero was in danger. Now, more than ever. This very hour.

Lobo hurried down the street.

He had to warn Grandfather Guerrero before Jimmy murdered him.

CHAPTER 46

S equestered by several bachelorettes, Hannah sipped her
tea, hoping it would settle her stomach. She'd only
nibbled at the pastry, which was flaky and beautiful and far too
sweet, much like the young women smiling at her now. They
surrounded her with eager expressions, reminding her of
predators encircling wounded prey.

They all looked so young and beautiful and soft, and seemed
so natural together in this opulent mansion, finishing one
another's sentences and tittering with laughter that would have
seemed as out of place on the ranch as Hannah felt here among
Jasper Flats' elite.

It was terrible. She felt ridiculous with her tanned face and
forearms and big farmgirl hands among these pale, thin girls
and their soft hands and hard eyes.

Because despite their smiles, their eyes glittered, looking as
hard as diamonds.

Mr. Boone and the other men at the party, including the

host, Mr. Masterson, all seemed to think Hannah looked nice this afternoon. They smiled and bowed and kissed her hand and snuck appreciative glances.

But Hannah knew the truth.

And these girls, being female, also knew the truth.

She looked ridiculous. She *was* ridiculous. She did not belong here. And never would, no matter how many cattle she bought or how much money she earned.

"So," a big-eyed girl with a head full of luxurious, brunette curls asked, "how did you manage to capture Mr. Boone?"

The other ladies leaned in conspiratorially, their smiles stretching tight as bowstrings.

"Capture him?" Hannah said. "I didn't capture him."

"Of course you have, silly," a blonde said. "You're here, aren't you? And with him."

"Besides," a girl with glossy black hair remarked, "he can't stop looking at you. He's clearly enamored."

They glanced toward Mr. Boone, who stood a short way off, talking to a group of men in expensive-looking suits. The men were all older than Mr. Boone and smaller. They all seemed to be focused on him, even when someone else was talking, as if they cared more about his reactions than whatever the speaker had to say.

Mr. Boone noticed the females looking, smiled at Hannah, and lifted his glass.

The girls turned from his stare, tittered gaily, and drew closer to Hannah, making her want to run out the door, hitch up the wagon, and speed home. What strange creatures these wealthy town girls were.

"He positively adores you," one of them said, laying a soft

hand on Hannah's work-hardened arm, right where the ridiculous tan line from her dress began.

"Yes," another agreed. "He can't keep his eyes off you."

"I keep asking myself the same thing," a red-haired young beauty said, so flustered with the state of things that she was clearly struggling to remain polite. "I don't know your family name. How did you manage to land the most eligible bachelor in the territory?"

"I didn't," Hannah said, starting to feel irritated. She'd already told them that. Why wouldn't they believe her? Were they calling her a liar? "He invited me here as a friend and business partner."

For some reason, this made them all laugh like they had never heard anything so funny.

Hannah frowned, loathing them and wishing she could escape. Yes, everything here was beautiful—the estate, the food, the guests, everything—but she just wanted to be back on the ranch with Tilly.

"Pardon my intrusion, ladies," Mr. Boone said, sidling up next to Hannah and taking her arm gently in his, "but I was hoping for a word alone with Miss Miles."

"Certainly, Mr. Boone," one of the girls said with a shadow of a curtsy. "Don't let us keep you from your friend and business partner."

The girls tittered again, staring at Hannah with glittering eyes, hating her.

Hannah turned her back on them and allowed Mr. Boone to escort her through a set of tall double doors onto a stone veranda overlooking a wide bed of colorful zinnias, still standing straight and bright despite the cold nights they'd been having.

"I'm terribly sorry to have left you alone with them," Mr. Boone said, once they'd separated themselves from the others. "That's all right," Hannah said, pulling free and glancing back in their direction. "Thank you for rescuing me."

The girls clustered together near the door, talking rapidly. Catching her glance, they twiddled their fingers and giggled.

"They are strange and clannish creatures," Mr. Boone said, nearly echoing Hannah's earlier thoughts. "I should have known that you would not enjoy their company. Truth be told, I rarely attend such events. But being new here, I felt obliged. Also, business often begins at events like this. A mildly unpleasant afternoon affair might lead to a million-dollar deal months later."

Hannah nodded, not budged an inch by his mention of million-dollar deals. Still, she didn't want to seem rude. "It's a nice house," she said lamely.

Mr. Boone chuckled. "Yes, it is a nice place. And the food is good. That being said, I'm happy to finally have a moment alone with you, Miss Miles."

He was looking at her strangely again, and his voice was thick with some mysterious emotion that made her feel more uncomfortable than she'd felt among the silk-clad, lily-white idiots.

She took an involuntary step away from him. "You are?"

"Yes," he said, stepping forward and staring into her eyes. "Seeing you among these loathsome bachelorettes underscores something I've known since I first laid eyes on you. You are special, Miss Miles."

Hannah blinked at him, nearly frozen by the awkwardness of it all. She wanted to leap over the wall and flee through the zinnias but couldn't be so rude to Mr. Boone, who had done so very much for her. "I am?"

"Yes," he laughed. "You don't even see it, do you?"

She shook her head.

"My dear Miss Miles," he said, capturing her hand in his. "You are the most exquisite, the most fascinating, the most alluring woman God ever fashioned upon this Earth."

She just stared at him. "I... um..."

And then, to her immense terror, she saw that he was taking a knee before her... in front of all the guests now staring out the double doors and windows, the tittering girls and the men in their expensive suits and their dried-up wives, who'd stared at Hannah upon her arrival with all the cool calculation of hawks hunting a winter field.

Mr. Boone seemed completely unaware of the onlookers. He stared up at her, his blue eyes sparkling with emotion. "I have never met anyone like you in my life, a life I now understand will never be complete without you in it." His deep voice throbbed with passion. "Miss Hannah Miles, will you make me the happiest man in the world by—"

"Don't, Mr. Boone," Hannah said sharply, wanting to save him the embarrassment of completing a question to which there could be only one answer. "Please stand up. I don't wish to be rude, sir, and I do not wish to humiliate you."

Mr. Boone's hopeful expression crumbled into one of hurt dismay.

She slipped her hand from his.

He came to his feet and stared at her with pained eyes. "Miss Miles, I wish you would allow me to—"

"No," she said firmly. "I don't want you to ask me any questions, Mr. Boone. It was terribly nice of you to invite me here as your friend and business partner, but I do believe I should be going. Tilly will be missing me."

"Yes, of course," he muttered, seeming confused. "I understand. But Miss Miles, I really must insist you allow me to—"

"No," she said, drilling her gaze into his eyes. "They're looking at us."

"I don't care about them, Miss Miles. I care only about you. In fact, I love—"

"I love the fact that we are such good friends, too, Mr. Boone," she interrupted, "but I must insist you stop making a scene. I'm growing uncomfortable."

"Oh, I… I'm terribly sorry. That was horribly insensitive of me, Miss Miles. I'm so enamored with you that I didn't even consider—"

"That's quite all right, Mr. Boone," she said, "but I would be obliged if you would take me home immediately."

"Yes, of course," he said. "I will express my regrets to the host and send for the carriage, and we will be on our way." He seemed to brighten abruptly. "Perhaps we will be able to speak in peace on the way home."

"I would enjoy that, Mr. Boone," Hannah said, knowing she had to make things completely clear to spare this man's pride and keep him from hating himself and her alike. "And since we are such good friends now, I am hoping to speak to you concerning matters of the heart."

His dimples appeared. "Yes, Miss Miles. I have the same hope."

"Oh good," Hannah said. "Because I've had no one else to share my secret with. I've been harboring it for so long."

"Yes?" he said hopefully.

"Yes," she said and hated that she had to do this to such a nice man. It was like putting down a good horse with a broken leg. "You see, I'm deeply in love."

Boone brightened further still. "You are?"

"Very much," she said, and pulled the trigger. "Do you remember Lobo? You met him once, just before he left. I love him with all my heart, and he should arrive home soon, and I'm hoping that he's going to ask me to marry him."

CHAPTER 47

L obo pushed Paddy, streaking back to the valley, not even slowing when he passed the place where Lou Bannerman had been killed.

Having recognized the dynamics of the situation, he was certain that Grandfather Guerrero's life was in danger.

It was obvious now.

Jimmy planned to kill Grandfather Guerrero, blame the murder on Lobo, and seize the valley.

Lobo hoped he wasn't too late.

He hoped Grandfather Guerrero was still alive.

As he drew close to the ranch, Lobo spotted a terrifying sight: Grandfather Guerrero's dog lay dead just outside the whitewashed house, shot through the heart.

Rage roared up inside Lobo. Why kill a friendly dog?

But this rage barely registered, given the overwhelming fear gripping him now.

Was he too late to save his grandfather?

He pulled his Winchester, slowed Paddy, and scanned his surroundings.

An unfamiliar black stallion was hitched outside. To Lobo, the big horse looked like the midnight steed of Death himself.

Jimmy had come for Grandfather Guerrero.

He dismounted, rifle at the ready. Seeing nothing, he listened hard.

A soft breeze whispered across the yard, rattling leaves.

Otherwise, all was silent.

He moved toward the door of the house, ready to spring if someone opened fire from inside.

But no gunshots broke the eerie silence.

The door was ajar.

He leaned close, listening hard, but heard nothing inside save for the rhythmic ticking of a clock marking the disappearance of precious seconds.

Then he heard the squealing.

It was back toward the barn. High and wild and hungry, the squealing split the air, shattering the still and covering Lobo in goosebumps.

The pigs were ready to feed.

He rushed forward, the terrible squealing filling the air like he was charging straight into the heart of a nightmare.

And when he reached the hog pen, that nightmare swelled, nearly choking him.

A bloodied Grandfather Guerrero lay beside the feeding trough, struggling fruitlessly against his bonds. His legs were tied. His wrists were also bound by metal handcuffs like lawmen sometimes used.

Twenty feet away stood not Jimmy but the lawman who'd

used the handcuffs, Jimmy's father and Lobo's uncle, Sheriff Guerrero.

A tin badge shone dully on his chest. His hand rested on the latch to the gate between the pig wallow and this feeding area.

On the other side of that gate, pigs squealed, ready to feed.

Lobo barely registered these things because he was shocked by the man's face. A sneering grin split the silver-streaked, black beard.

It was a face Lobo knew, even though he couldn't remember ever having met the man.

Not in real life.

But he had met him, over and over. In his dreams. In his worst nightmares.

Because he would recognize that face, that smile, that eye patch anywhere.

Lobo's uncle, Sheriff Antonio Guerrero, the man who killed Bannerman and who was now preparing to feed Grandfather Guerrero to the hogs, was none other than the one-eyed man who had haunted Lobo's dreams all these years.

CHAPTER 48

B rock Boone marched across his property, his big hands balled into fists.

He had never been so humiliated, so gutted, in all his life.

Miss Hannah Miles had crushed his hopes and his heart.

Not that he harbored any resentment toward his precious neighbor.

She had been predictably wonderful about everything, even as she dashed his dreams. She had even stopped him before he could make his proposal, wanting to save him that indignity.

For that, he would be forever indebted to her.

But the moment branded his soul with the mark of something Brock had never experienced: unforgettable failure.

He was a man who always got what he wanted. Always pushed and worked and fought until he achieved his every goal.

Now, however, this thing, marriage to Hannah Miles, was suddenly out of reach… or so she believed.

She said she loved Lobo, which boggled his mind. It truly

did. And yet, it explained so much, explained why Miss Miles had spurned Brock's advances like no other woman.

Brock knew he was handsome. Hadn't everyone always told him that?

He was also well-formed, tall and muscular, and had worked hard to perfect his physique through rigorous daily exercise.

What's more, he had graduated from West Point, served honorably in the United States Army, attaining the rank of captain—a thing he never lorded over people, carrying his rank among civilians the way some officers did after leaving the service—and had gone on to make a fortune by working tirelessly and taking calculated risks. He'd built something in Texas and was building something here, something sweeping and solid, a foundation upon which he and the right woman could build an impressive life and legacy.

And that woman could only be Miss Hannah Miles. He loved her, as he had tried so desperately to tell her, but she claimed to love another.

Brock would not accept that.

How could she possibly love Lobo? He was an ugly man in dusty clothes, rail thin with a face full of scars.

What sort of life could she hope to build with Lobo? From everything Brock had heard, Lobo was a gunman who'd started tracking outlaws, the way so many violent men did sooner or later.

How could she possibly fall in love with a man like that? What could he offer her that Brock couldn't provide in spades? What possible future could she hope to build with someone that was supposedly raised by wolves?

It was absurd, and Brock refused to believe it.

Not that his precious Hannah Miles would lie. No, she was above all deceit.

But clearly, she was confused. Somehow, this Lobo had deluded her.

Well, Brock would not surrender without a fight.

In fact, given that Miss Miles was clearly poised to ruin her life, it was nothing less than his duty as a gentleman to save her from this Lobo.

Always a man of action, Brock quit marching away from his estate, turned, and started heading back toward everything he worked so hard to build.

He had decided what he must do.

He would post guards along the road that ran between his ranch and Miss Miles's place.

The very second that Brock learned of Lobo's return, he would ride straight there, declare his undying love, and stop Hannah Miles from ruining her life.

And if Lobo had a problem with that, Brock would do whatever it took to win the hand of Miss Miles.

CHAPTER 49

L obo was stunned.

For a moment, he just stood there, unable to do anything but watch and listen.

"You were right all along, Pa," the one-eyed man said. "I was the one who killed Marco and Sylvia. I thought I'd killed the boy, too, but apparently, he somehow survived. And that's the best thing that ever happened to me. Because you kicked him out of the valley, and now, everyone will think he did this to you. The crazy wolf-boy returns to seize power the only way he knows how... through brutality."

"I knew it was you who killed your brother and his wife," Grandfather Guerrero said, still struggling to no avail. "I should have killed you when you came home with that grin on your face."

"Yes, you should have. But you didn't. Because you're weak. Unfortunately, my own son shares that weakness. Which is why

I have to do this. Jimmy's too soft to kill you. Oh, a stranger in a bar, sure. Jimmy will beat a man to death if he has to. But he never would have killed you just like he never would have killed Bannerman. He's too soft, too sentimental, and too scared of his almighty grandfather. But now, you're gonna die, my boy will have the whole valley, and I'll be moving right into your house. Though I don't think I'll be having any bacon here. You say I'm a monster, but even I can't eat the pigs who ate my daddy."

The one-eyed man threw back his head with a burst of rich laughter that finally snapped Lobo from his paralysis.

He shouldered his rifle and stepped into view. "Leave that gate shut, or I'll kill you."

If his uncle was surprised, he didn't show it. His smile remained, and his one eye stared straight at Lobo, twinkling with humor.

"So it really is you, eh, Sebastian?" the one-eyed man said. "I saw you the other day, checking my office and walking down the street, and thought it was you, but I just couldn't bring myself to believe it. The wolves were so close when I laid you on the ground. You were in shock, of course, after seeing what happened to your parents. You didn't even put up a struggle. I wonder if that's why they didn't rip you apart. Whatever the case, my nephew, I wouldn't fire that rifle unless you want your precious grandfather to be eaten alive. You've killed enough men to know they don't just stand still when the bullet strikes. You shoot me, I open the gate."

He jiggled the latch.

The pigs squealed and shoved, fighting among themselves, wanting the fresh meat.

"Don't listen to him, Sebastian. Shoot him dead. He's pure death with that six-shooter."

The one-eyed man laughed. "Don't listen to him. Don't let him boss you into doing something you don't want to do. Why would you want to save him? You stand to gain more than anyone from his death. You're the heir of Green Valley."

"I heard everything," Lobo said. "I know your plan. I knew it even before I heard you tell Grandfather. Though I didn't know it was you. I thought it was Jimmy."

The one-eyed man snorted. "Jimmy is soft. Not strong like you and me. Come on, lower the rifle. Let's put our troubles behind us. You can have the valley. Just let me move back. I'm getting old and want to be with family. Look, I know you think I'm a bad man, but you're confused. Your grandfather kicked you out, just like he kicked me out. He doesn't care about family, so why should family care about him?"

"You tried to feed me to the wolves," Lobo said, rubbing his fingertip back and forth across the trigger, ready to fire... but wanting to know more.

"You should thank me," the one-eyed man said. "I could have killed you. Just like Marco tried to kill me out in those woods. And just like he killed your mother when she confessed her love for me. You see, son, I'm your real father."

The man's wild claim staggered Lobo. Was it true? Was the one-eyed man his real father?

"Don't listen to him, Sebastian!" Grandfather Guerrero shouted from beside the feed trough. "He's a liar. Your mother loved your father very much. Antonio went out there to kill his brother, thinking to inherit this valley."

"Shut up, old man, or I'll open this gate." The one-eyed man lifted the latch and grunted, using his great bulk to brace the gate against the squealing pigs pushing from the other side. "Now, put down that rifle, Sebastian. What are you going to do, shoot your own father? Is that the thanks I get for sparing your life?"

Facing any other man on the planet, Lobo would have acted decisively. But the one-eyed man had stepped straight out of his nightmares and wasted no time jumping straight into the great questions Lobo had pondered since before he even had the words to analyze them.

Or rather, after he'd lost those words and before he'd regained them.

Because the trauma of what had happened to him in the forest that day had wiped away his words, his memory, and his life, leaving him a hollowed-out shell of a boy, a hollowed-out shell that was rescued not by a human but by wolves, wolves that taught him the value of the pack.

"I could have killed you that day, Sebastian," the one-eyed man said, "but I gave you a chance instead. And look what you made of it. Your time with the wolves made you strong, much stronger than your father or my son or your beloved Grandfather Guerrero. You know it's true. You're strong like me. Strong men know how to forgive. Strong men like us aren't afraid to give second chances. Now, I'm asking you to give me a second chance just like I gave you a second chance all those years ago."

Lobo stepped closer, judging distances and time, finally clear-headed enough to see everything.

His uncle eyed him, some of the confidence going out of his face. He studied Lobo's face, saw something, and suddenly started begging. "You don't understand, Sebastian. I created you. Made you what you are, a survivor."

"You killed my parents and left me to die. You thought the wolves would eat me."

The one-eyed man grunted again, leaning into the gate with all his considerable weight, his boots digging into the ground. He offered a wriggling smile. "I gave you a chance. Now, it's your turn. Give me a chance like I gave you."

"All right," Lobo said, putting his sights on the shoulder of his uncle's shooting hand. "I'll give you a chance just like you gave me a chance. You tried to feed me to wolves. Now, I'll…"

With a wild cry, his uncle grabbed for his gun.

Lobo pulled the trigger.

Struck in the shoulder, the one-eyed man twisted with the impact. He dropped his revolver, and his feet shifted, bringing most of his weight off the gate.

His blood rained down on the squealing pigs, and they went wild, shoving through the gate and knocking him to the ground.

Lobo charged into the feeding pen to his grandfather.

The one-eyed man bellowed with rage and struggled onto all fours, grabbing once more for the six-shooter he'd dropped, but a second later, a dozen mud-covered hogs piled on top of him, squealing with rage and hunger and bloodlust as they ate him alive.

Lobo picked up his grandfather, hurried out of the enclosure, and closed the gate behind them.

For a terrible moment, the one-eyed man's angry bellow became a high-pitched scream of pain and terror, but it soon cut off altogether, and all that was left was the horrific sound of the pigs devouring him, a fitting end to the man who'd killed Lobo's parents, tried to feed him to wolves, and then haunted his nightmares all these years.

CHAPTER 50

⁓

"I'm so glad you were here," Sophia told Lobo after Grandfather Guerrero, wearing a clean shirt and bandages, had left to spread the news.

"So am I," Lobo said. "If I'd arrived five minutes later, it would have been too late."

Sophia shuddered at the thought. "Does Jimmy know yet?"

"No. We came straight here. Grandfather will spread the word first, then get a few men to ride with him before he tells Jimmy."

"Do you think Jimmy will try to hurt him?"

Lobo shook his head. "I doubt it. But there's no telling how a man will react to the death of his father, so better safe than sorry."

"I'm going to miss you, Lobo."

"I'm going to miss you, too."

"Please promise me you'll come back to us."

"I'll try," Lobo said, "but I'm not making any promises. To

tell you the truth, after spending a couple of days here, I won't be in any hurry to return. Folks were awful quick to turn on me."

Sophia nodded sadly. "They aren't bad people. It's just—"

"I'm not cut out for big groups, Sophia. Probably never will be. But wherever I land, though, you and Davey and Grandfather are always welcome."

Sophia smiled and took his hand in hers. "Then this isn't goodbye. Only goodbye for now."

"Sounds good to me," he said, and hauled her into another hug. "It's awful good to know you, big sister."

This got her crying again.

He didn't mind. He held her there, knowing he was going to miss her terribly once he was back on the trail, which he would do as soon as he took care of one last thing.

"You think Davey's got them pups ready to go yet?" he asked.

"I'm sure they're ready. He's a good boy."

"I know he is. Once I get settled, send him my way for a while. I'll make him a good man."

"He'd like that," Sophia said, "and so would I."

"Good. I'll count on it, then. But here, there's one more thing before I go." He reached into his shirt pocket and pulled out the paper he and Grandfather Guerrero had signed and unfolded it and handed it to her.

"What's this?" Sophia said and set to reading it. Her mouth dropped open.

She glanced up at him then read it again and looked again and shook her head. "You're giving me Green Valley?"

"I'm not," Lobo said. "Grandfather Guerrero is."

"But you're surrendering your claim?"

He nodded. It hadn't been easy, getting Grandfather Guerrero to agree, but in the end, Lobo had convinced him.

They both knew Lobo was right.

Grandfather Guerrero just didn't want him to leave.

But Lobo had to. And not just because folks here had turned on him.

He didn't want Green Valley. Having his grandfather's apology and acceptance was enough.

He had finally settled his past. At long last, he could move into the future.

"I don't deserve this valley," Lobo said. "You do. This is your home, not mine."

"Oh Lobo," Sophia said, and embraced him again, crying harder than ever. "Thank you, dear brother. But this is your home, too, if you want it to be."

He shook his head.

"Where is your home, then?" she asked. "With Hannah and Tilly?"

Lobo twisted the knob and opened the door to leave. "That's what I'm fixing to find out."

CHAPTER 51

Two days later, Laverne Chantilly reined his steeldust to a stop within the shadowy grove.

He had been dreaming of what he would do to the old woman when he saw her again. He had considered many things since they had dug out the privy to discover nothing but the old woman having played a grand joke on them.

Mere death was far too good for her, considering what she had done. Currently, Laverne was torn between burying her neck deep in sewage or simply torturing her, Apache style.

Whatever the case, she would die regretting ever having sent the Chantilly brothers on a wild goose chase.

As soon as they tracked down Lobo, they would ride back and drop in on her.

And peering out of the trees at the man sitting in front of the house yonder, Laverne reckoned they had just taken a big step toward tracking down their prey.

Chester drew up beside him.

Laverne wrinkled his nose, catching a whiff of his brother. "You still smell like that privy."

"You don't exactly smell like a rose yourself, brother."

Laverne grunted, wondering if he smelled as bad as Chester. He pulled his pipe from his hatband and his tobacco pouch from his coat pocket and set to packing the bowl, wanting to smother his brother's stench with sweet, sweet smoke.

"You reckon that's him?" Chester asked, nodding toward the man sitting all alone on his front step.

Laverne lit his pipe, drew deeply, and exhaled smoke from his nostrils. "That's him."

"Think he'll talk?"

"He'll talk. I guarantee it."

Chester grinned. "I mean without us having to work on him."

Laverne puffed at his pipe. "From what folks say, Lobo killed his father. He'll talk, all right."

"What if he doesn't know where Lobo went?"

"Even if he doesn't know, he'll get our answer for us. Someone kills your daddy, you do whatever you gotta do to get them."

Chester grinned at him and cocked a brow. "Laverne, you killed our daddy."

Laverne nodded and exhaled a cloud of pale, sweet smoke. "Yeah, but that was different. Come on. Let's go meet Jimmy Guerrero."

CHAPTER 52

"Took you long enough, didn't it?" Crazy Mary said, stepping out of her cabin with a grin on her face and the flintlock pistol shoved through her belt. "I figured they'd take one look at you and kick you out."

"They did kick me out," Lobo said, "but then they changed their minds."

Crazy Mary chuckled. "This I gotta hear."

"Well, we'll have plenty of time to share stories. Are you ready? I'd hate to have to wait for you to pack. I want to get home."

"You know, this whole time you been gone, I been waiting for you to come back and ask if I had made up my mind."

"I knew you'd come with me. Let's go."

Crazy Mary shook her head, feigning disgust, and spat a long stream of deep brown juice into the dying weeds to Lobo's left. "You can't just go supposing such a thing, whippersnapper. A lady likes to be courted."

"My apologies. Are you coming or what?"

"Well, it's your lucky day, Lobo. Because I do want to go. I'm sick of this place. Hitch the mules, and we'll load the wagon. And don't go whining. Most of what I got is food. Hams and such."

Lobo grinned. "You're gonna have a time keeping the pups away from those hams."

"Pups?" Crazy Mary said, looking around. "What pups?"

Lobo climbed down from Paddy and led her to one of the panniers and lifted the lid.

The pups blinked up at them, whining happily. A gray and brown head popped out and licked Mary's hand.

Crazy Mary squinted. "Those aren't pups. They're wolves."

"They're wolves and pups."

Crazy Mary shook her head. "Traveling with wolf pups. I can see you're determined to ruin my reputation."

"The only reputation you've got is the crazy old hermit lady who lives on the mountain."

"You're darn right! And I cherish that reputation. Worked hard to earn it. Now what will people call me? The mildly antisocial wagon lady who travels with wolf pups and weird men?"

Lobo chuckled. It felt good. He was glad Mary was coming with him.

Suddenly, she grew serious. "Couple of fellas came by here, looking for you."

"Oh yeah?"

She nodded.

"Friends of mine?" he asked, knowing they weren't.

She shook her head. "No, I can't say they seemed particularly friendly. In fact, I'd have to say they seemed downright unfriendly. I'd bet my best ham that they aim to kill you."

"Lot of that going around. Did they give their names?"

"No, and I didn't ask. I got them out of here as fast as I could. I believe they're bounty hunters."

He grunted at that. He hadn't looked for paper since taking out Hat Hatley and his gang.

Was there paper on Lobo now?

Perhaps.

But based on what?

It would have to be Jackson. Or the constable, whatever his name was. Orville something.

That's the only thing he could think of, unless his cousin Jimmy had somehow convinced the law that Lobo had killed his father unjustly.

Could be.

"How long ago did they stop here?"

"Few days back. Shortly after you left."

Lobo nodded. Not Jimmy, then. Must have to do with Jackson and the constable.

"I played a little trick on them," Crazy Mary said, and showed him her mostly toothless grin.

"What did you do to them?"

"I'll tell you on the trip. For now, let's just say I used what they wanted to give them what they deserved."

Lobo shrugged, not knowing what she meant and not much caring at the moment. He wanted to get on the road.

He had to think, too. If there was paper on him, getting home might not be so easy. And he might be putting Mary at risk.

"You might not want to come along if bounty hunters are tracking me," he said.

"Pshaw! You think you can get rid of me that easily, sonny, you're in for a surprise! I can't stay here anyway. Those two come back, there's no telling what they'll do to me. And truth be told, they don't look like nobody you'd want to mess with."

"What did they look like?"

"Strange," Crazy Mary said. "One of them had a top hat and smoked the worst-smelling pipe I ever smelled."

Suddenly, Lobo felt as if he'd plunged into an icy pool.

Crazy Mary said, "The other one wore—"

"A fur cap," Lobo said.

"That's right. You know them?"

Lobo shook his head. "I know of them. Every bounty hunter, outlaw, and gunman knows about them. We've had a change in plans. We're only grabbing what we need and getting onto the road as quickly as possible. You had a visit from Laverne and Chester Chantilly, the most dangerous bounty-hunting team in the territory. We gotta put some miles between them and us... pronto."

CHAPTER 53

"I gotta say you're looking pretty chipper all of the sudden," Crazy Mary said a few days later as they rolled down the road south of Jasper Flats. "I assume we are getting close."

"Yes," Lobo said, driving the wagon. "It's not much farther now."

"Well, then," Crazy Mary said and spat the chew from her mouth. "There. I don't want Hannah and Tilly thinking I'm not a lady."

He glanced at her with surprise. "You aren't gonna chew in front of them?"

"Not gonna chew? Sacrilege! Of course, I'm gonna chew. I just didn't want them to meet with an old chew in my mouth. I'd been working that last cud forever."

She threw back her head with a characteristic cackle.

Crazy Mary had held up well during the trip.

So had the pups. Lobo had found a wooden box in Mary's barn and put it in the back of the wagon and lined it with some old blankets that Mary didn't want and put the wolves in there, and they'd been happy enough, especially as they had bonded so well with Lobo, accepting him as their new alpha.

The mules were also doing well, but not as well as Paddy, who'd been trailing beside them with only a saddle for a load. Lobo wished he could leave the saddle off the stallion's back, too, but every now and then, he stopped the wagon and rode Paddy out to scout their back trail, not wanting the Chantilly Brothers to sneak up on them from behind.

He didn't know much about Laverne and Chester Chantilly but knew enough to understand that he was in deep trouble if he let the brothers pin him down. They were hardened killers with a reputation for always getting their man—and for shooting him all to pieces when they did. In fact, whenever a bounty hunter brought in a particularly mangled criminal, folks said he'd "Chantilly-ed" the outlaw.

Of course, there was a chance the bounty hunters had given up their search. But Lobo doubted it.

As they were rolling alongside Brock Boone's sprawling property, Crazy Mary said, "You're doing it again."

"Huh? Doing what?" Then he realized he'd been growling as he stared past Boone's fence in the direction of the man's home.

Was Hannah there now?

He shoved the thought from his mind. He had to get home, had to see Hannah, had to tell her what he thought.

"That the fancy cattleman's property?" Crazy Mary guessed.

Lobo nodded—and in that instant spotted a rider up ahead, off to the left, just north of Boone's gate.

The man saw Lobo, too. In fact, he scoped him with a

spyglass for a moment. Then he wheeled his bay and charged off across the range toward Boone's estate.

He was waiting for me, Lobo thought. *Boone had him posted there.*

Why?

Had Boone heard about the bounty? Was he planning to collect it?

Sure would be a convenient way for Boone to eliminate him if Hannah still had feelings for Lobo.

The wolf in Lobo snarled, *Let him try.*

He was ready for Boone. But at the same time, he knew his troubles were heaping up.

Yes, he was almost home. Yes, he had done everything he had set out to do, killing Jackson and reuniting with his long-lost family. And yes, on top of all this, he had also managed to put down his own personal bogeyman, his Uncle Antonio, the one-eyed man who'd been haunting his nightmares for two decades... all while making his family safer.

And yet, suddenly, he was in more trouble than ever.

The bounty hunters might be just back around that bend, coming fast. Other bounty hunters might be scoping out Hannah's ranch, awaiting his return. Brock Boone might be rallying a posse to bring Lobo to justice.

Beyond all that—and this concerned Lobo more than all those other threats put together—Hannah might, in just a matter of minutes, spurn his love and crush his soul forever.

They passed Boone's gate. The road to his place had seen a lot of traffic. Wagons, horses, cattle. That was no surprise since Boone was a wealthy cattleman making a name for himself in the region.

What was a surprise was the wide swath of chewed-up ground stretching away from Boone's gate, over the road, and across Hannah's property.

Someone had driven a lot of cattle, likely hundreds of head, from Boone's place onto Hannah's.

Why?

Lobo's stomach sank.

Had Hannah already married Boone and invited her new husband to graze cattle on her ranch?

As they rolled on toward whatever fate awaited him, he glanced at the side of the road, remembering how he had pitched the plain, little doll into the brambles on his way out of town. It had been a foolish thing to do, perhaps, but he'd been so disappointed when Brock Boone had revealed the fancy doll for Tilly.

But he couldn't change the past, so he let go of his mistakes and focused his eyes on the road ahead—after one more quick glance over his shoulder.

There was no sign of Boone or the bounty hunters or anyone else.

Good.

Because he was almost home. This was the moment he had been waiting for, the moment upon which his future hinged.

If Hannah accepted him, everything would be perfect. Yes, he would still have to deal with the bounty hunters and other problems, but he wasn't hoping for a trouble-free life. He was hoping to face those troubles beside the woman he loved, Hannah Miles.

As they entered Hannah's property, Lobo's heart galloped like a wild stallion.

The house came into view.

He'd never been more excited or terrified.

This was it, the moment that would change everything forever.

He stopped in front of the cottage and called out.

There was nothing. Silence and stillness reigned.

Feeling disappointed, Lobo spoke briefly with Mary then hopped down from the wagon.

Where were they?

Then a blond-haired bullet raced around the stable and charged straight at him, a most unexpected doll clutched to her chest.

CHAPTER 54

"L obo!" Tilly cried. "You're home!"

Spilling over with happiness, Lobo crouched down and spread his arms.

Tilly pounded into him, laughing joyfully as she squeezed his neck and peppered his stubbled cheeks with little kisses. "Oh, Lobo, I'm so happy you're home!"

"I'm happy to be home, Tilly," he said, holding her tight. "I sure did miss you."

"Not as much as I missed you!" she said, and squeezed his neck so hard he thought she might be trying to collect the bounty herself.

"Where did you get that pitiful doll you're holding?"

"Faith is not pitiful," Tilly said, stepping back and holding the shabby doll up for him to examine. "I take good care of her. Which is more than I can say for you. That was a stupid thing to do, leaving her out there in the scrub."

"Yes, it was," Lobo said, drinking in the sight of the little girl he yearned to make his daughter. "But I'm done leaving folks behind."

Tilly beamed at that, but then he couldn't see her anymore because his eyes were locked on the smiling woman who had just come around the corner of the stable.

Heart hammering in his chest, Lobo stood.

Hannah froze in place and stood there, clutching a fistful of carrots and staring at him. She looked beautiful in her plain blue dress and her hair coming undone and her hands dirty halfway to the elbow with mud that had somehow managed to leave a streak on one rosy cheek.

"Hello, Hannah," Lobo said, his voice quavering with emotion.

For a fraction of an instant, she remained frozen there, and Lobo was gripped by a terrible tension, everything he wanted, everything he could ever want, his whole life hanging in the balance, waiting for her response.

And then Hannah dropped the carrots, ran straight at him, and cried out his name, pounding into his embrace just as Tilly had.

They hugged, laughing, and without even thinking about it, he kissed her soft cheek. She kissed his cheek in return, and their eyes met for a fraction of an instant, and they turned their heads, bringing their lips together, and suddenly, they were kissing for the first time.

Lobo was vaguely aware of Tilly squealing with delight and clapping her tiny hands, but mostly, he was swept away into the sweetest, most glorious moment he had ever experienced, a moment that dismissed all his fears and brought his hopes and dreams and desires to fruition as they held each other kissing and kissing and kissing.

Lobo finally broke the kiss, panting for breath, and stared at Hannah's beautiful, smiling face, feeling like the most blessed man on the planet.

"Hannah, I gotta tell you something."

Hannah nodded, her gleaming eyes streaming happy tears. "I have to tell you something, too, Lobo."

"Me first," he said, needing to say what he had to say, needing to tell this woman how much he loved her and that he wanted to spend the rest of his life together as husband and wife—and as parents to Tilly. "Hannah, I should've told you this a long time ago. I—"

But before he could tell her how he felt and propose marriage, hoofbeats came pounding up behind him, and a deep voice bellowed his name.

Lobo released Hannah and spun, drawing his Colts to face the Chantilly brothers.

It was not, however, the bounty hunters behind him.

Brock Boone vaulted from his stallion and marched straight at Lobo, scowling with rage and jabbing a finger at him. "That's my woman!"

Lobo holstered his weapons and braced himself, suddenly boiling with anger himself. "She's not your woman."

"She is," Brock said, drawing closer. "She just doesn't know it yet. Hannah Miles, I love you! I love you, and I want to marry you!"

Lobo shook his head, growling. First the doll, now this. Was Brock Boone's sole purpose in life disrupting Lobo's biggest moments?

"Get out of here, Boone," Lobo snarled.

But Brock Boone kept marching straight at him. The big man pulled off his jacket and unbuckled his gun belt, let everything drop to the ground, and pushed up his sleeves. "Put up your hands, Lobo, and we'll settle this like men!"

Hannah tried to stop them, but there could be no stopping what had to happen now.

Boone had invaded Lobo's territory and wanted to steal his pack.

Lobo would sooner die.

He removed his gun belt and handed it to Tilly, who smiled at him, her blue eyes shining with all the confidence in the world. "Beat him up, Lobo."

"Let's go!" Boone shouted.

Growling, Lobo turned and balled up his fists and stepped eagerly forward.

CHAPTER 55

A s Lobo was still rolling toward home, Laverne Chantilly exhaled a cloud of sweet smoke and pushed through the door of the Jasper Flats' marshal's office.

The marshal looked up from his desk with a startled expression.

The man's name was Tubbs, Laverne knew, just as he knew the other man, the one with the black beard and the deputy's star on his buckskins, was named Shaw. He knew these things because he had started, as he always did, by questioning people in saloons.

Yes, Lobo lived around here, they'd told him.

No, he hadn't come back. At least, no one had seen him.

The marshal? Man by the name of Tubbs. A friend of Lobo's, as a matter of fact.

Was that why the marshal looked so uneasy? Because Lobo was his friend? Did Tubbs recognize Laverne and Chester and guess why they were here?

Perhaps.

Whatever the case, Laverne was curious but not concerned. He knew Lobo was running just ahead of them and knew that they would soon catch up to him and all that money, and there was nothing this backwater marshal could do to change that.

"Afternoon," Tubbs said. "Help you fellas?"

"Where's Lobo?" Laverne asked.

"Lobo?"

"That's right. I know he's a friend of yours. Just like I know he has a lady friend south of here. Woman by the name of Miles. Have you seen him?"

"You fellas bounty hunters?" Tubbs asked.

"We're trying to help you uphold the law by hunting down wanted fugitives."

"And getting paid for it."

"That's right. You don't get paid for policing this town?"

"Well," Tubbs said, and made a show of moving around the papers atop his desk. "You boys are too late."

"How's that?"

"Lobo's dead."

"He's dead?"

"That's right. Just writing out the affidavit to this man here," Tubbs said, nodding toward Shaw. "He killed Lobo this morning on the road south of town. Isn't that right, Mr. Shaw?"

The deputy jumped a little with surprise. "Huh? Yeah, that's right, Marshal. Killed him today."

Laverne had seen poorer liars but not many.

"Sorry, boys," Marshal Tubbs said. "Looks like you're out of luck. Mr. Shaw already earned the bounty. Lobo's dead. You might as well head back to wherever you came from."

Laverne said nothing. He just stared at the marshal with dead eyes until Tubbs started to squirm.

"He's dead?" Laverne said.

"That's right," Tubbs said. "I'd stake my name on it."

"And your life?"

Tubbs blinked at him for a second. "Yes, and my life."

"In that case, I will see you shortly, Marshal," Laverne said, and walked out of the office with his brother in tow.

Out on the street, Chester finally spoke. "They're lying."

"Of course, they're lying," Laverne said. "Tubbs is friends with Lobo."

"Well, looks like we're out of luck."

"How do you figure?"

"He wrote out the affidavit. The bounty's gone."

"That tin-star marshal won't send in that affidavit any more than he'll wire for the bounty. He's just trying to fool us. Besides, even if he stops us from getting the bounty, Lobo's probably still carrying most of the money he got for bagging Hatley."

Chester grinned and nodded. "All right. Let's go get him."

"Someone knows where this Hannah Miles lives. We'll go to the mercantile and ask there. Miss Miles likely has an account."

"What if the merchant won't talk?"

"Somebody will talk." Laverne slipped his hand in his coat pocket and came back out with a crumpled greenback. "We'll start with the delivery boy."

CHAPTER 56

A slight breeze, weak as a dying breath, sighed past, ruffling the dress of Hannah, who had finally stopped trying to make peace and stood there, watching the two men circle one another, ready to fight.

There were no insults, no boasts, no outbursts of profanity. Because both combatants were men of character who recognized these things as weakness pretending to be strength.

This was it.

They were going to fight until one of them quit or died or could no longer continue.

Lobo knew he was in for the fight of his life.

Boone was bigger than him, not taller or longer-limbed but broader with bigger bones, his whole body armored in muscle. And yet the powerful cattleman moved lightly on his feet, circling gracefully, ready to spring.

Lobo moved laterally, studying Boone, watching for any weakness—an exposed target or a dropping of the guard or one foot crossing behind the other, putting him at risk of losing balance. But Boone made none of these mistakes, which came as no surprise. Lobo had, after all, watched Boone take apart a hulking bar fighter in Jasper Flats.

How could Lobo beat a bigger, stronger man with deep fighting experience and no apparent weaknesses?

As if to punctuate this question, Boone finally lashed out, throwing a stiff jab at Lobo's face.

Lobo slipped the punch with ease and countered with a jab of his own, smacking Boone in the jaw.

It wasn't much of a punch, but it unleashed something in Boone, who surged forward, slashing at Lobo with hard lefts and rights, trying to take his head off.

Lobo blocked a few of the shots and slipped most of the others, but a few got through, snapping his head back and filling his skull with sparks.

He might have been in trouble if he hadn't punched between Boone's attacks. Lobo's right cross smashed into Boone's square jaw and sent him staggering.

Lobo was off-balance when his punch landed, so there wasn't time to follow up. He got his feet under him and shook out his arms, tasting blood.

Boone gave his right fist a little shake then pounced again, swinging with all his might.

This time, Lobo leaped away like a wolf—then shot back in with his own attack.

He smashed Boone's nose with a hard jab but immediately leaped away again, not daring to throw a follow-up combination that might leave him going toe to toe with the bigger man.

And as expected, Boone launched an immediate counterattack, a barrage of thunderous punches slicing the air where a more aggressive Lobo's head would have been if he'd stood there, swinging.

Lobo circled away to the right then switched directions when Boone came swarming after him again.

"Hit him, Lobo!" Crazy Mary cried from the wagon. "Knock his dimples off!"

Behind her, the pups barked.

Closer by, Tilly gave more valuable insight. "You're faster than him, Lobo! Use your speed!"

Smart girl, Lobo thought. Smart and strong and wonderful, a girl who would make any father proud, a girl he loved with all his heart.

In one of those strange moments that so frequently invade drawn-out fights, Lobo thought, *And she chose my doll, not Boone's. This wonderful child chose me over him. And so did Hannah.*

These thoughts steadied him, filling him with tough hope and renewed energy.

Boone gave his fist another little shake and rushed forward, unloading a blistering combination. It was a fearsome attack, fast and powerful—but he landed nothing.

Because Lobo had seen that little fist shake, and his body had reacted, leaping away just in time. He hadn't thought about Boone's attack or his own retreat, not exactly. He'd merely registered the bigger man's unconscious tell. Lobo's fighting instincts, honed over years of quarreling with wolves, had done the rest.

Lobo relaxed then, letting his mind drift, realizing that conscious thought would only slow him. The way to beat this big, experienced, hard-punching man wasn't going toe to toe or working out some convoluted fight plan.

He simply needed to fight like a wolf, moving, always moving, in and out, riding the rhythm of the fight, never over-committing, never allowing his opponent to deliver a full-force blow, trusting speed and patience, timing and lightning reflexes to win the fight.

Boone had no idea he was shaking his fist before each attack. But he was. And it cost him dearly.

The fight stretched on and on, Boone pressing the action, attacking again and again, never without the telltale shake of his fist.

A few times, the determined cattleman switched directions abruptly and swung desperate punches that cuffed Lobo's head, each time filling his skull with stars.

Boone had dynamite in both fists. That was for sure. With one clean punch, he could finish it.

But as the fight dragged on, the cattleman slowed, breathing harder and harder, and some of the steam came off his punches.

Lobo kept circling, still light on his feet, his muscles coursing with the energy he had been conserving. His face had, over the course of their long fight, taken a beating, he knew. One ear rang, and it was hard to breathe through his nose, which was almost certainly broken, but he still had his vision in both eyes, which was more than could be said for Boone, whose right eye had swollen shut after catching multiple jabs.

Boone's fist shook again.

Lobo was already moving when the cattleman charged, bellowing like a bull elk.

Lobo evaded the attack so easily that he could have countered with either hand. Instead, he simply left a foot in his wake, tripped the big man, and sent him sprawling into the dirt.

Crazy Mary and Tilly cheered.

Boone struggled to his feet, huffing and puffing, again reminding Lobo of a bull elk. This time, however, it was a specific bull elk, one he and the pack had hunted for hours on end across a beautiful spring day, chasing it with leaden patience, nipping its haunches and scattering away from its occasional counterattacks, wearing the huge beast down as time dragged on and on, until they finally drove the massive creature into a shadowy hollow at the base of a mountain, where winter still ruled and the snow had not yet melted.

The big elk broke through the icy crust and was soon floundering in chest-deep snow. Lobo broke through the snow, too, but the lighter wolves with their padded paws raced across the crust and went to work on the elk, who blundered forward, bellowing as the wolves did what wolves do and put an end to him.

There was no snow here and no pack to finish the job, but Boone was nonetheless floundering and, as the fight progressed, gasping for breath.

And yet Boone kept on battling, a man clearly used to winning. But after every telltale shake of the fist, his punches were slower and less powerful.

Lobo varied his counterattacks, sometimes tripping and exhausting Boone, other times hammering him in the ribs, stealing his breath and his will to fight, and sometimes blasting him in the face, confident enough now to start sitting down on his punches and catching Boone with cleaner and cleaner shots.

But still the man kept coming. Either because he truly loved Hannah or just couldn't bear the thought of losing.

Whatever the case, Lobo kept pounding him.

The cattleman didn't quit or start cursing the way some men did in defeat, their character coming apart with their chances.

So Boone earned Lobo's respect, but that changed nothing.

Lobo continued to move, continued to counterpunch, continued to study his opponent, and continued to take advantage of Boone's fist-shake tell and exhaustion with all the deadly focus of a seasoned alpha determined to feed his family.

Boone exhaled heavily, his whole body seeming to go momentarily slack like a deflated bellows. Then he stumbled doggedly forward, shaking that fist again.

Lobo sensed the turning point, sensed that the fighting spirit was finally leaving his determined opponent, and sensed, in the manner of the wolf, that now was the time to kill.

Or to show mercy.

"Let it go, Boone," Lobo said. "You're beaten."

Boone shook his head stubbornly and staggered forward, pawing the air with punches made awkward by exhaustion.

Lobo hammered Boone's big chin with another stiff jab, but this time, instead of dancing away from danger, Lobo let him have it. A wicked right hand followed the jab, knocking Boone backward and kicking off a savage attack.

Lobo unloaded with both hands, punching with full force, stepping forward with every blow, driving the big man backward as he landed lefts and rights with full extension and full power, making Boone's head jerk back and forth with every shot.

Boone swung his head wildly, ducking away, and roared forward again, swinging with all his might.

The wolf in Lobo wanted to leap away, but Lobo, tasting blood, hung tight. With Tilly's voice shouting encouragement a short distance away, he finally stood toe to toe with the rugged Texan, trading shots, taking punch after punch as he blasted Boone with hooks and uppercuts and slashing rights that would have killed a lesser man.

A tremendous punch caught Lobo right between the eyes, and for an instant, he went away, his consciousness winking out into total darkness. But when he came to a second later, he was still on his feet, still punching, still holding his ground.

He would not surrender. He would not go down. He would not let this intruder rob him of his territory, his pack, or his pride.

Because there is no such thing as a droopy-tailed alpha.

This was Lobo's life, all he had in the world, and he would rather die on his feet than quit.

Barking with fury, he drove forward with strength and determination, sinking his fists into Boone's midsection again and again, making the cattleman groan and hunch, bringing his big chin down and forward.

Lobo shifted his weight, twisting his whole body and putting every ounce of power into a devastating uppercut that socked squarely into the bigger man's jutting chin, snapped his head back sharply, and sent him sprawling onto the ground, finally unconscious, finally defeated.

CHAPTER 57

"Lobo!" Hannah said, rushing forward, and he managed not to fall when she pounded into him, wrapping him in an embrace, squeezing him and telling him how horrible it had been and asking him if he was all right.

"I'm all right," he said, and stopped her from kissing him long enough to wipe his lips. Then he gave her a chaste peck. "I know I'm a bloody mess. There'll be time enough for kissing later. I promise you that."

"You did it, Lobo!" Tilly said, coming in to hug him from the side. "I knew you would whip him!"

"Took you long enough," Crazy Mary joked from the wagon. "What were you doing, admiring your handiwork?"

"No, ma'am," Lobo said. "I was just trying to survive. Because it seems I suddenly have a lot to live for."

He was in bad shape. His head hurt, his ears rang, and it was getting harder and harder to see out of his swollen eyes. There was no breathing through his broken nose, and by the throbbing behind his swollen lips, he believed he might have cracked a tooth. He knew his face was masked in blood, but there was no way he was going to put off what he had to do long enough to wash up or put on clean clothes.

No, he had waited long enough. Far too long, in fact, or maybe he wouldn't even be standing here feeling half-dead on his feet at this moment.

He was too tired to get down on one knee, so he simply took Hannah's hands in his own, which he was pretty certain were broken, based on their stiffness and the pain shooting up both wrists all the way to the shoulder.

"Hannah Miles," he said, loud enough for everyone to hear.

She smiled expectantly up at him, likely knowing exactly what was coming. She was, after all, a very smart woman—and pragmatic enough to want him to go ahead and ask right now, regardless of his bloody face and broken hands.

Because Hannah was a farm girl who'd lived anything but a charmed life. She didn't want a clean face. She wanted what he wanted: the truth. And, he hoped, true love that would last a lifetime.

"Will you marry me?" he asked.

Hannah nodded and put the back of her hand to her smile, crying again. "I will, Lobo. Nothing in the whole world would make me happier."

He wiped his mouth again, and they kissed, laughing happily together until he crouched down and put his arms around a beaming Tilly.

Picking the orphan girl up off the ground hurt every inch of his battered body, but he wanted Tilly up there with them for this.

They stood together, the three of them, in a loving embrace. Lobo leaned his head forward, and the girls leaned their heads in, and he said, "Tilly Kershaw Frampton, since Hannah and I are getting married, would you make our happiness complete and become our adopted daughter?"

Tilly's eyes lit up. "Really? You really mean it? We're going to be a family?"

Lobo nodded. "If that's what you want. I sure would be proud to be your daddy."

He had never seen such a huge smile. Tilly's sparkling blue eyes turned toward Hannah. "Miss Hannah? Would you be my mama?"

"Child," Hannah said, "I love you with all my heart. Nothing in the whole world would make me happier than for the three of us to be a family."

Tilly squealed with delight, kissing them both and thanking them and telling them she couldn't wait to be their daughter.

"It appears," Brock Boone groaned, sitting up shakily on the ground, "that an apology is in order. Blinded by desire, I attempted to interfere between what I now see is indeed a loving family. I do apologize and hope you can find it in your hearts to forgive me."

Lobo nodded at the cattleman, whose face was also a bloody mess. "Apology accepted. I'd shake on it but I busted both my hands on your head. You got sand, Boone. I have to give you that."

Boone struggled to his feet and smiled crookedly then raised a hand to his clearly broken jaw. "And I have to say you can fight. That's the first time I've ever been beaten."

"And that's the hardest fight I ever had," Lobo said. "Let's not do that again."

Boone chuckled. "No, sir. Once was enough."

Lobo was happy Boone was taking his loss like a man. Happy but not surprised. Everything he had seen of the man told Lobo that Boone had strength and character. They had just fallen for the same woman. That was all.

And Lobo would whup any man in the world for Hannah.

"For what it's worth," Boone said, "I wish the three of you well. And Lobo, if you need someone to stand by you during the wedding ceremony, I would be honored."

Lobo was about to say that sounded good to him when Hannah said, "What's that smell?"

Lobo, who normally detected smells before anyone, couldn't smell anything with his broken nose.

"I smell it, too," Tilly said. "It's sweet."

"Sickly sweet," Hannah said.

"I know that smell," Crazy Mary said, sounding alarmed. "It's the bounty hunters."

CHAPTER 58

⚜

L obo started toward his guns, but he was too late.

"Stay right where you are," a cold voice said, and two men came around the house with their pistols trained on Lobo and Boone. "You touch them guns, you're dead."

The one who'd spoken must have been Laverne Chantilly, Lobo thought, based on the top hat and pipe.

Which meant the one in the fur cap must be his brother, Chester.

Lobo had heard all about the Chantilly brothers. They were the best of the best, the deadliest bounty hunters in the West, and now they had him just where they wanted him.

If he tried to grab his guns, they'd fill him full of holes.

Besides, he doubted his broken hands would even work right.

They had him dead to rights. There was no way to beat them, no way to escape.

"Let me step away from these folks," Lobo said, knowing he was about to die and not wanting anyone else to get hurt.

Laverne grinned and gestured with his barrel. "That's right. Step over there away from the ladies. You must be Lobo, then. Couldn't say for sure with all that blood on your face."

"Lobo?" Brock Boone said, sounding angry. "I don't know who you men are or what you're doing here, but this man is Michael Miles, brother of Hannah Miles, who owns the property upon which you are trespassing. He and I just fought over his sister."

"Pipe down, buddy," Laverne said, but Lobo could see doubt in the man's narrowed eyes.

"Pipe down?" Boone said. "Do you know who I am? I am cattleman Brock Boone, personal friends of the Colorado governor. If you men plan on murdering Mr. Miles, you had better murder me, as well, or I will make it my personal mission to see you both hanged."

The Chantilly brothers hesitated, looking back and forth between Lobo and Boone.

"Well," Laverne said, "we don't make a habit of killing folks without paper on them, but if you insist…"

"Put down your guns!" Hannah demanded.

Everyone turned in her direction and saw that she and Tilly were each pointing one of Lobo's revolvers at the bounty hunters.

Laverne Chantilly laughed. "You think we're scared of a woman and a child?"

"How about a scattergun, sonny?" Crazy Mary asked, and the Chantillys turned again to see the old woman on their other side, pointing Lobo's double-barreled coach gun at them. "This thing will bust my shoulder but not before I send you both straight to hades."

Now, the gunmen hesitated, knowing they were in trouble.

A second later, that trouble multiplied again, as hoofbeats sounded and two riders appeared, guns at the ready.

"Put down the weapons!" Marshal Tubbs shouted.

"You heard the man," Shaw said. "Put them down."

And then, as if God Himself were using this opportunity to show Lobo His divine favor, two more riders hurried into view.

Plug and Tuttle added their guns to the mix.

Cursing, the bounty hunters did as they were told.

Tubbs arrested them. Apparently, he'd told the Chantilly brothers that he'd already authorized the affidavit declaring the death of the man called Lobo.

This was a different man that they were threatening.

And as the moment broke apart and Hannah and Tilly were once again clinging to him, Lobo had to think that the marshal's claims weren't that far off the mark.

He wasn't a different man, exactly. Part of him would always remain the man raised by wolves. But he was more than that now. He was a new man. A man far more blessed than that hard-edged loner.

Looking around at Hannah and Tilly, Crazy Mary, Plug and Tuttle, Tubbs and Shaw, and yes, even Brock Boone, he was humbled by gratitude. What had he ever done to deserve such friends as these?

"That was risky, pointing guns at those killers," he told Hannah and Tilly.

"We had to stop them," Hannah said. "No matter the risk."

"Right!" Tilly chimed. "I would've plugged them with hot lead!"

Lobo laughed, holding them close. "I believe you would have, Tilly. I really do. And the same goes for you, Miss Miles. Which shouldn't surprise me, I guess. Because the strength of the wolf is the pack."

Hannah stared at him, her eyes full of love and deep understanding, things every man hopes to find in a woman. "And the strength of the pack," she said, putting voice to that understanding, "is the wolf."

#

THANK YOU FOR READING *LOBO 3*.

I had fun writing this series and hope you enjoyed spending time with Lobo, Hannah, and Tilly.

Next up is *The Provider*. Will Bentley wanted to forget his past and live a quiet life. Then someone kidnapped his sister.

You can see the cover, read the blurb, and order a copy on Amazon.

If you enjoyed *Lobo 3*, please be a friend and leave a review. When you leave even a short review, you just bought my family dinner, because Amazon will show the book to more people. I sure would appreciate your help.

If you enjoyed the book but don't have time to review, please consider leaving a 5-star rating. It's quick and simple and helps a lot.

I love Westerns and hope to bring you 8 or 10 a year. To hear about new releases and special sales, join my reader list.

Once more, thanks for reading. I hope our paths cross again.

Until then, don't approach a bull from the front, a horse from the rear, or a fool from any direction.

John

ABOUT THE AUTHOR

I was born six months before man landed on the moon and lucky enough to grow up in the country, where my family lived largely off the land.

When I wasn't fishing, exploring the woods, or weeding the garden, I devoured comic books like *Two-Gun Kid* and *The Rawhide Kid* before moving on to the exciting adventure stories of Jack London and Louis L'Amour.

Our black-and-white TV only got three channels, though you could lose one and pick up another if you went outside and messed with the antenna. On its grainy screen, we watched *Gunsmoke*, *Bonanza*, and movies starring John Wayne and Clint Eastwood.

Now a husband and father, I love traveling the West and reading history and fiction alike. My favorite authors are Louis L'Amour, Elmore Leonard, C.J. Petit, and R.O. Lane.

As a writer, I hope to entertain you with fun stories of the old West. My good guys are good, my bad guys are bad, and you'll always find a touch of romance to sweeten the grit.

If you'd like to keep in touch, join my newsletter HERE.

ALSO BY JOHN DEACON

John's Amazon author page has all of his books in various formats:
Kindle, paperback, hardcover, and audiobook.

A Man Called Justice (Silent Justice #1)

Justice Returns (Silent Justice #2)

Final Justice (Silent Justice #3)

Justice Rides Again (Silent Justice #4)

Destitution

Heck's Journey (Heck & Hope #1)

Heck's Valley (Heck & Hope #2)

Heck's Gold (Heck & Hope #3)

Heck's Gamble (Heck & Hope #4)

Heck's Stand (Heck & Hope #5)

Lobo (The Lobo Trilogy #1)

Lobo 2 (The Lobo Trilogy #2)

Lobo 3 (The Lobo Trilogy #3)

The Provider (The Provider Saga #1)

The Provider 2 (The Provider Saga #2)

Made in United States
Orlando, FL
15 January 2025

57323527R00186